"*As real as it is heartfelt. When 13-year-old Suze hears her mother's voice for the first time in ten years, she's torn between an oath she made to her sister and overwhelming curiosity.* A Month of Mondays *is a tender story of a girl's desire to heal her family.*"

—Suzanne Selfors, author of
the *Ever After High School* stories

A Month of
MONDAYS

Joëlle Anthony

Second Story Press

Library and Archives Canada Cataloguing in Publication

Anthony, Joëlle, author
A month of Mondays / by Joëlle Anthony.

Issued in print and electronic formats.
ISBN 978-1-77260-026-1 (paperback).
—ISBN 978-1-77260-027-8 (epub)

I. Title.

PS8601.N68M65 2017   jC813'.6   C2016-906970-2

C2016-906971-0

Cover by Qin Leng
Edited by Kathryn Cole
Design by Melissa Kaita

Printed and bound in Canada

*Second Story Press gratefully acknowledges the support of the
Ontario Arts Council and the Canada Council for the Arts for our
publishing program. We acknowledge the financial support of the
Government of Canada through the Canada Book Fund.*

Funded by the Government of Canada
Financé par le gouvernement du Canada

Canadä

Published by
SECOND STORY PRESS
20 Maud Street, Suite 401
Toronto, ON M5V 2M5
www.secondstorypress.ca

This one is for my mum.
Her encouragement in everything I do is infinite,
but especially with this book.

Chapter 1

I have three women who think they're my mom. My sister Tracie has mothered me since I was three, when ours left us. Aunt Jenny steps in when an authority figure is needed and she thinks my dad's being a slacker. Caroline, the one who gave birth to me? She sends the checks.

So you can imagine how put out I was when Principal Farbinger kept saying he was going to call my mother. You'd think he'd know by now that I live with my dad. After all, I've spent half of junior high in his office for one stupid thing after another. I have never seen my school record, but I'd bet money Caroline's name isn't anywhere on it. Not if Dad had anything to do with it.

I looked down at the khaki overcoat Farbinger had ordered me to put on over my costume. "It's too big," I said. "I'll trip and fall." I was hoping the idea of an accident would make him nervous enough to change his mind, but he just ordered me to sit down.

"You should've thought of the possible consequences when you chose your outfit this morning, Miss Tamaki," he said.

"It's Halloween," I reminded him.

He grunted, but didn't answer. This was totally gross. Farbinger had been a pain in my side since day one, grade six, but you'd think by grade seven he would've moved on to some other kid. I wrapped my arms tightly around my middle and glared at the floor. Did he seriously expect me to wear his trench coat for the entire day?

The material billowed around my feet, and the icy plastic of the chair seeped through the coat, making my legs cold. Maybe someday they'd bronze this chair for me and stick a plaque on it that said something like: *In memory of Suze Tamaki—for dress code violations, habitual tardiness, and all-around smart-alecky attitude.* Eventually I'd make it to high school, but my legend could live on here.

Resigned, I sighed, leaned back, and took a look around. Not much had changed since last week. Coffee rings still marked the top of Farbinger's metal desk, papers overflowed onto the bookshelves, and there was a thick layer of dust on the slate-gray blinds. His coat smelled sickening too. Like cigarettes. I figured part of his plan was to accuse me of smoking when I returned it and then suspend me.

It was so stupid that he was making me wear his stinking coat all day just because my pink shorts said *Sleeping Beauty* across the butt. It was Halloween. I didn't know the school rules about no writing on our butts counted today.

I'd come to school in what I wore to bed. My theory was that I could sleep in until the last possible minute, put my hair up in pigtails, and make a run for the bus. And it had worked. I even brought my pillow to school for naps during my boring classes (which is all of them).

"I'm surprised your mother let you out of the house in such…such…attire," he said, taking the all-too-familiar yellow detention slip out of his desk drawer.

I wanted to shout: *My dad! I live with my dad.* But why bother?

The bell rang, ending third period, and I hoped Farbinger'd hurry up, so I could talk to Jessica before English. I shook my long bangs into my eyes to hide my impatience. He'd definitely make sure I was late if he thought I was anxious to get going.

"Miss Tamaki, I'm afraid I have no choice but to give you a detention tomorrow afternoon. I want you to think about what is and what is not appropriate for school."

Like I hadn't heard that one before. *Just give me the slip and let me go*. As if he were doing something of incredible importance, like signing the Constitution of Canada, he filled in my name with a gold pen while I squirmed.

"This is precisely the reason we have a dress code here at Maywood Junior High," he told me.

Hurry up already!

After a million years, he handed me the form.

"I think I need a pass for English," I said.

"You still have two minutes." He shooed me out the door. "And Miss Tamaki? If I hear that you've taken that coat off during the day, it's an automatic suspension."

Tempting offer. I could stay in bed and read all day. I raced out into the almost-deserted halls, his coat flapping behind me like a sail. Naturally, my locker was all the way on the other side of the building. When I finally got there, I spun the combination and thumped the door a couple of times— that was the only way to get it open. It still took three tries. There was no way to make it now. Our English teacher was really big on us being in our seats when the bell rang, and so far I'd disappointed him at least six times. About to be seven.

The bell clanged in my ears as I came tearing around the corner by the gym. Unfortunately, Mr. Franklin and Morty, two of our school janitors, also happened to be coming around the corner—only from the opposite direction.

We were on a preordained custodial collision course.

Like a conspirator, the belt from Farbinger's coat snaked

itself around my ankles, tripping me. I crashed into Franklin's enormous belly and bounced off. Morty caught him under the arms and swayed ominously from Franklin's weight, but in the end, they stood their ground. Nobody bothered to catch me, though. My right knee smashed into the tiled floor and books shot out of my arms, like they'd been flung from a car window. I don't know if Franklin was angrier at me for crashing into him, or at Morty for having to save him. Either way, he was not a happy custodian.

"What's your name?" he yelled after me as I scooped up my books and dove through the door into the classroom.

Mr. Baker stopped in the middle of roll call, and everyone looked at me standing in the doorway. Laughter rippled across the room. I must've looked pretty comical—my pigtails coming loose and Farbinger's coat hanging all the way to the ground.

"Glad you could join us," Baker said.

"No problem." I limped my way through a maze of backpacks to my seat.

"From your coat," he said, "I take it you've gone literary on us, Suze. Let me guess…. You're dressed as Sherlock Holmes for Halloween."

"Nope," I grinned. "I'm a flasher."

Chapter 2

When the last bell rang, I was so hyped up on the candy corn Jessica had given me during art class that I practically bounced down the hall. I zipped around a corner and barely missed crashing into Yoda, the night janitor who always arrives right when they let us out of school. Today might have been Halloween, but this guy looked so much like the *Star Wars* character that kids had been calling him Yoda for forever.

"Hello, Sooooz Tamaki," he said. "Why you running in the halls?"

"Sorry, Yoda. Too much sugar, I guess."

Smiling, he shook his head, and I jumped over his push-broom, making him laugh. I found Amanda and Leigh in front of their lockers and skidded to a stop, throwing my arms around them football-huddle style.

"Hey," I said.

"Hi, Suze," Leigh said. "You're coming to my house, right?"

"Can't. I promised Jessica I'd go with her." She was stuck taking her little sisters trick-or-treating, and I'd said I'd go along.

"Y'all can both come."

"Leigh has MoonPies," Amanda said, unwrapping my arm from around her shoulder so she could dig through the bottom of her locker for her bike helmet.

"My nana sent them to me," Leigh told us.

MoonPies are these really gooey chocolatey-cookie-marshmallow things from the US. You might be able to get them here in Canada, but Leigh swears the ones from Tennessee are different and way better, so she makes her grandma mail them to her. When Leigh comes back to BC after spending the summers in the South, she always lugs home a whole case of MoonPies in her suitcase.

"Why didn't you bring me any?" I asked.

"I did," Leigh said, "but Amanda scarfed them all."

"I had four," Amanda said.

"Yeah?" Leigh laughed. "Fourteen, maybe."

"Okay, maybe five. Come with us, Suze," Amanda said. "We always spend Halloween together."

"I know, but I already told Jess I'd go with her."

Amanda and Leigh liked to think of us as the Three Musketeers, and mostly I do too, but sometimes I'm more like a third wheel. And sometimes I'm not even sure if I really like them. I mean, I do, but we had more in common when we were kids. Now we're into different stuff. I was really glad when Jessica transferred to our school this year. For the first time since Leigh moved here in grade four and stole Amanda from me, I actually had my own friend.

"I gotta go," I said. "Bring me some tomorrow."

"If Amanda doesn't eat them all," Leigh said.

I heard Leigh yell "Ow!" as I ran off down the hall. Amanda had probably slugged her.

❋ ❋ ❋

We all stood on Jess's porch while the twins pushed the doorbell and banged on the screen door. Jessica and I rolled our eyes at each other.

"Trick or treat," they screeched when their mother opened the door. Their four-year-old laughter echoed through the neighborhood. "We tricked you!" one of them yelled. I had no idea which one it was because I couldn't tell them apart, but Jessica seemed to have no trouble at all. Of course, she'd known them since birth.

"It's about time you got back," their mother said, taking baby Elise out of Jessica's arms.

"They were having fun," Jess said. Her mom tried to usher us into the house with the girls, but that wasn't going to happen.

"We're not staying," I said. I reached into the foyer and got my backpack from where I'd left it. "We're going to my place to hand out candy."

"How're you getting there?"

"Walking," we said together.

She wrinkled up her forehead at that one. "You know I don't like you out after dark."

"Yeah, but it's only five o'clock," Jess said. "And there are streetlights."

"Not to mention fifty million goblins, ghouls, witches, and parents hitting up all the houses between here and there," I assured her.

"Please, Mom?"

"My dad will give Jess a ride home," I told her.

"Well…all right. But be careful."

We made our escape before she could change her mind and waded through their muddy driveway back to the unpaved street. Jessica lives on a dead end, which is practically a bog this time of year. Her house is really, really old, even though all around it are newer houses. The mud sucked at my cold feet, and I hoped I wouldn't lose a shoe.

"My mother drives me crazy," Jess said. "You don't know how lucky you are."

"How so?"

There was this pause as she realized what she'd said, because we both knew she was thinking about how controlling her mother was and that I didn't have one.

"Well, your dad's pretty cool," she said.

"Nice save." I laughed so she wouldn't think I was mad or anything, and she looked relieved. Believe me, she might have thought her mom was a pain, but having Caroline split when I was three was no joy either. I hardly ever thought about her, though, and I wasn't about to start. "Check this out." I handed her the bulging pillowcase.

"Not a bad trade-off," she said, feeling the weight of the candy we'd scored.

That was the deal. We took the girls out and got to keep all of Elise's candy. She was only nine months old, so she had no idea she'd been ripped off. I picked my way around a pothole. My thrift store Keds already squished with water though, so I wasn't sure why I bothered. "I'm freezing my butt off," I said.

"Maybe you should've kept Farbinger's coat."

"Yeah, right."

Even in the dark, the streetlight reflected enough so that when she smiled, I could see Jess had glitter in her teeth. She had glitter everywhere, actually. I grabbed the bottom of her dress just as she was about to drag it through a puddle.

"Your costume's getting soggy."

"I hope it's not ruined. It took me forever to make."

I didn't say anything. It wasn't that I didn't like her costume. It was just really weird. Who dressed up like a fairy from a Shakespeare play? I knew she wanted to be an actress, but still…. She was wearing this weird chiffon dress thingie and had ratted her curly hair so it practically stuck straight out. Then she'd painted her face a bunch of pastel colors, and with all the sparkles, the makeup was totally excessive. Not to be mean, but I think I'd have liked it more if she was…well, cooler. It's hard to stay under the teachers' radars when she's around, because she's so smiley and friendly to them.

On the main road, shadowy groups of trick-or-treaters moved up and down the walkways. Flashlights played across lawns, and pumpkins glowed on the porches. It was pretty awesome, actually. Nothing like the boring apartment building where I live. Inside these homes were families who probably ate dinner together and stuff.

"You know," I said, after we'd gone a few blocks, "it's pretty hard to tell you're twelve years old with all that makeup on."

Jessica brightened immediately. "You think I look older?"

"I was thinking younger."

The light in her eyes went right out. "Oh."

I knew she was disappointed, but that was because she hadn't heard my master plan yet. "And I'm vertically challenged," I said.

"You're not that much shorter than me."

I waved the pillowcase in her face. "True, but you're missing the point."

"Huh?"

"We could totally pass for younger and get a ton of candy. No one's going to know. Your boobs hardly show with all that loose fabric."

I could see her blush even under the makeup, and I nudged her with my elbow and snickered. If I had Jess's figure, I definitely wouldn't try to hide it like she does, but whatever.

"If you don't think we'll get busted…" she said.

I resisted the temptation to laugh at her unintended pun. "What're they gonna do? Arrest us? Come on. Just slouch a little."

We only had the one pillowcase between us, but people threw in two of everything anyway. By the time we got within view of my hideous green apartment building, our loot weighed more than my cat.

We were only about a block away when the skies opened up, dumping rain, drenching us in a matter of seconds. "Aaaggghhhh! Run!" I yelled, and Jessica and I took off full speed ahead. The deluge stopped as quickly as it started, and, by the time we got to my building, it was barely a drizzle. My shorts clung to my hips and the knee-high socks I'd worn gripped my calves with icy fingers.

"Oh, my God," she said, panting. "I'm sooooo drenched."

"You look like you lost a paintball fight too," I said, gasping for breath.

"Well, I can see the flowers on your panties through those shorts."

"*What?*" I totally fell for it, looking down.

"Joking."

"So funny." We hurried toward the building. "Weird…"

"What?"

"My dad's car is here. He usually works until nine on Thursdays."

"Maybe he's sick," Jessica said.

"No way. He never gets sick." We stopped at the box to get the mail. I rifled through the circulars, looking for the brown envelope, but it wasn't there. "Double weird."

"Now what?"

"No support check from Caroline."

"Well, tomorrow's actually the first."

"We always get it by the end of the month. *Always*." She may be an absent mother, but she has a very reliable accountant. We went around to the back of the building to our second floor walk-up. "Be careful," I said to Jessica. "These stairs are super slippery."

I didn't have any free hands because of the candy and my backpack, so when something orange and wet came up the stairs from behind and shot between my feet, Jessica had to put her hand on my butt to keep me from tumbling backward right on top of her.

"Stupid cat. Watch out, Sammy!" I yelled after her.

It was my lucky day after all, though. The apartment door was unlocked, so we didn't have to stand in the rain while I dug out my key. Inside, water pooled around us on the cracked linoleum, and two voices filtered in from the living room. One was Dad's and the other was a woman's. I knew right off it wasn't my sister's, but I didn't have a clue whose it could be. I nudged Jessica to stop her from going any farther.

"My dad's never had a woman here before," I whispered. "Especially when he's supposed to be at work."

Jessica raised her eyebrows and I smirked.

"Well, here we are, Jessica! Home sweet home!" I yelled, practically at the top of my lungs.

We giggled just like her little sisters and stepped onto the living-room carpet. My dad's expression wiped the smile right off of my face. His mouth was contorted into a sort of sick, twisted grimace that looked like the time he'd dropped an anchor on his foot and had forced himself to bite back a bunch of choice swear words.

A small woman with short blond hair sat in our only nice chair. She stood up when she saw us. Her dark tan was either fake-n-bake or from a recent trip to Mexico. Diamond rings glittered on her hands, and her long, red, manicured fingernails reminded me of claws.

She was smiling, but she kept twisting those rings, like maybe if she spun them around enough she'd be magically transported to another world. I understood the desire. I had it about ten times a day, myself.

Something was familiar about her, but I couldn't place it. A heavy, musky perfume enveloped the little apartment, making it stuffy even though it was cold. I breathed in the scent, and it reminded me of something, of someone. It reminded me of—

"Suze, you remember Caroline, don't you?" Dad asked, his jaw clenched so tightly the words could barely get through his teeth.

Chapter 3

Caroline was here in our living room.

Seriously?

The woman's eyes travelled between Jessica and I, and it occurred to me she didn't know which one of us was her daughter. But then she locked her gaze on me and smiled. "Hello, Susan," she said, standing.

"Umm…hi."

She held her arms open like she wanted to hug me, and I couldn't help thinking *Yeah, right* even as some invisible force propelled me into them. Her embrace felt a lot like she looked, fake and brittle and sort of cold. She patted my back and then released me. So much for the way I'd always imagined our reunion when I was a kid—me flinging myself into my mother's arms, her holding me tightly, even if I was soaking wet, both of us never wanting to let go.

I stepped back and stood next to Jessica, and Caroline sat down, perching on the edge of her seat and wiping her damp hands on her skirt. No one said anything for a beat, and then Caroline asked me who my friend was, and I introduced Jess. Another minute of silence passed while we all looked everywhere but at each other, and then Dad said he had to get back to work because his lunch hour was almost over, but Caroline didn't move, and so he didn't either. I guess he didn't want to leave me alone with her.

"Caroline stopped by the store," Dad said. "She wanted to meet you and Tracie."

That seemed kind of weird. After all this time, why didn't she call ahead or something? Dad sat on our ratty couch, his uniform shirt bunched up around his waist because he'd untucked it from his khakis. His normally dark face was chalky and I tried to tell myself it was the gray October light and our cheap lamps making him appear ill. Honestly, he looked like he wanted to hurl. I kind of felt the same way. Of course, I *had* eaten a lot of Starbursts and Smarties, so maybe that was why the contents of my stomach were unsettled and swishing around.

Caroline fiddled with her rings again, and I couldn't help but notice how large the stones were. And how sparkly.

I'd never seen anything quite like them in person—only on the Home Shopping Network.

"Pretty, aren't they?" she asked, when she noticed me staring. She held her hands up so I could examine them closer. I felt stupid checking them out like some gawker, but I pretended to care and leaned in a little.

On her left hand she had two rings, one with a huge single diamond—what I thought was called a solitaire—and the other with a band with diamonds all the way around it. On her right hand was a ring with a humungous green stone surrounded by tiny diamonds, all shimmering, even in the low lamplight. They had to be real to shine like that.

"Yeah, nice," I said, because what else was I supposed to say? What I was thinking was: *This woman is loaded*.

A flash of annoyance pulsed inside me because there are store-brand corn flakes in our cupboard, and she was wearing a year's rent on her hands. Who was I kidding? Those rings could be five years of rent for all I knew. It's not like I was a jewel expert or anything. The diamond studs in her ears could probably pay for Tracie's university tuition. Hard to believe she was related to us. And why hadn't we benefitted from some of her good fortune?

Oh, God. Tracie. The thought of her sent a wave of nausea through me. I looked around, but I knew she couldn't be here because there was no way she'd be calmly standing around admiring Caroline's jewelry like I was. She's no traitor.

I shivered. Dad noticed, but thought it was because I was so wet. He tossed me his stadium blanket. "What happened to you two?"

"Rain. *Duh.*"

"Grab a towel from the washroom," he told Jessica. "You guys better make some hot chocolate or something."

Caroline stood and brushed invisible dirt off her tailored skirt. "I should probably go," she said. "I have a ferry to catch."

She was leaving town and—what? That was it? Would I ever see her again? Would it be another ten years? Did I even care? She wrapped an elegant-looking cape around her shoulders and pulled up the hood against the rain.

"So…you're going back to Vancouver?" I finally blurted out, when it appeared she was going to leave without saying anything else.

"Yes," she replied. "But I'll be back with the moving truck on Saturday. I was here to check on the house, and I was going to call once I was settled, but I just…" She smiled. "I couldn't wait, so I dropped by the store, and it was time for your dad's dinner break—"

"And I'm already late getting back. We should go," Dad cut in. "I'll walk you to your car."

"Right. Of course," she said. "I'm sorry."

Caroline is moving back to Victoria? "You're going to live here?"

"Well…not here, with all of you…."

"Yeah, I knew that." *What does she think I am? A moron?*

"But I'm moving back to Oak Bay," she said. "We'll finally have a chance to get to know each other." She swooped in for another fake hug, but I took a step back, and she stopped, her arms outstretched. "And I've wanted that for so long, Susan."

Really? 'Cause I've been here the whole time. I obviously wasn't that hard to find. You could've known me all along. Of course, I didn't say that. Instead, I clamped my jaw shut and forced myself to smile like: *That's fine. Whatever.* The last thing I wanted was her thinking I needed her. As if.

I shut the door behind Dad and Caroline and turned the deadbolt.

"Well, that was awkward," I said, as casually as I could manage.

"A little," Jessica agreed.

I'd been so busy staring at Caroline's jewelry that I'd forgotten to get a good look at her face. For some reason, we didn't have any pictures of her. When I was little I used to fantasize that someday I'd be walking down the street and see a woman who looked like me, and we'd both stop and stare and she'd say "Susan? Can that really be you? My darling!"

And then we'd hug for real. But now she was gone, and I hadn't even checked out her eyes to see what color they were. "I would've walked right by her in the grocery store."

Jess half-laughed. "It's so weird, because we were just talking about her."

"Totally freaky. Maybe you have magic powers. Being a fairy and all."

She smiled at my lame joke and followed me into the kitchen, where I made two mugs of hot chocolate.

While I didn't think about Caroline a lot, I did have a few imaginary scenes I sometimes ran like movies in my head before I fell asleep at night. But in them, I'd usually just won a Best New Artist Juno, and she was a reporter who was trying to get an exclusive, or I'd picked up the Nobel Peace Prize for my work with…well, troubled countries. I never once imagined seeing her for the first time as I walked into the room drenched to the bone, shivering, and wearing wet pajamas with a drowned fairy at my side.

"Do you think Caroline showing up is a *trick* or a *treat?*" I asked Jessica.

"You really haven't seen her in ten years?"

"Nope." I spotted the familiar brown envelope on the counter. "At least she brought the support check."

"You're very calm," Jessica said, sipping her cocoa.

I mopped up some I had spilled. "Yeah…."

"I would totally freak out."

I was hiding it well. Apparently Jessica couldn't see my heart banging around in my chest like a Mexican jumping bean. Somehow, I doubt a kid too stupid to carry an umbrella in October was the daughter Caroline had been expecting. Or wanting. We'd probably never see her again.

The buzzer went off. "Oh, God. Do you think she's back?"

"Trick-or-treaters," Jessica said. "I'll get the door, you find the candy."

"I forgot to buy any." I rummaged around the cupboards to see if Dad had remembered, but all I found was a bag of mini Cadbury bars with only three left. "Give them the gross stuff from our pillowcase."

"Okay."

I stood slumped against the kitchen counter. Jessica's voice floated down the hall to me: "Oh, aren't you cute?" she cooed to some kids.

This whole Caroline thing couldn't really be happening. I told myself that after dropping in like that, she'd probably decide it was a big mistake and disappear for another ten years. Part of me wanted it to be true—didn't want to see her again—but a tiny little ache in the corner of my heart hoped it wasn't.

"I have to change," I called out to Jess on the way to my bedroom. "I'll find something for you too. You must be frozen."

"That'd be great," she yelled back.

Something made me stop to watch her, standing in the doorway and giving out the candy. The dim landing light illuminated a couple of tiny witches and a Frankenstein with a grinning mother standing behind them, her umbrella protecting them from the rain. A pain stabbed me deep in my gut. Jealousy, I guess.

I turned my back on them and went into my room. *Happy Halloween. Thrilling.* I bet none of those little kids had gotten the heart-stopping fright I'd had. I pulled black sweats and a black pullover out of the old-fashioned wardrobe Dad had bought me (because Tracie hogs the only closet), and peeled off the soaked socks. My frozen feet were all wrinkly and dead-looking.

"Overall, not a very good costume," I said to Sammy, who was now curled up in a damp ball on my pillow. "I'll be lucky if all I get for it is a detention. I'm expecting pneumonia, actually."

One golden eye opened a slit, but she didn't move. Yuck. She'd gotten my pillowcase wet and muddy. I made a three-pointer into the laundry hamper with the shorts, and the muddy knee-highs sailed in right behind them. I threw the now-gray Keds over onto Tracie's pigsty side of the room to confuse her.

"Back to normal," Jessica said, when I went into the living room with another set of sweats and a towel.

"I guess."

She was certainly an optimist. Things could never be "normal" again with Caroline around. What was my mother playing at, anyway? It didn't matter to me if she'd moved back to Victoria from Vancouver. Unless it meant we'd have to have regular visits or something. That didn't seem very likely, based on her interest in our lives so far. She'd only been a ferry ride away and we hadn't seen her at all.

The buzzer sounded again. "I'll get it. You chill," Jessica said.

Chill? I knew I'd never be able to relax until Tracie came home and I found out if she remembered the contract we'd signed when Caroline left us. She might've forgotten about it, but I doubted it. That piece of red construction paper was seared onto my brain, and it wasn't likely to have slipped her mind either. She was going to freak over Caroline's sudden reappearance—and somehow, I knew I'd be the one to suffer the most.

Chapter 4

After he got back from work, Dad drove Jessica home, and I have to say, I was glad to see her go. I mean, she'd been cool about Caroline, not bringing it up again, but not talking about it was almost as awkward. The whole thing was too weird to think about.

I had a mountain of math to do, but instead, I collapsed onto my bed with a book I'd found on the bus. It was the second book in The Testing trilogy, which was a little confusing since I hadn't read the first one, but it didn't really matter, because the words were mostly swimming in front of my eyes, anyway.

After dropping off Jess, Dad had gone to Uncle Bill's

to tie fishing flies for next year's camping trip, so when the apartment door slammed, I knew it was my sister. My stomach tightened as I waited for Tracie to come into our room. Part of me hoped she knew about Caroline already, that Dad had sent her a text or even called her. Unlike me, she always has minutes on her phone. The other part of me was scared of how mad she'd be if she'd already heard.

The door to our bedroom banged open and she came in, tossing all her school stuff on top of the dirty clothes on her side of the room. "Hey Suzie-suze-suze!" she said. "Man, am I beat." She flopped onto her bed.

Obviously Dad hadn't manned up and told her about Caroline's reappearance. I wondered if I should—or was it better to play dumb? If I didn't say anything, though, she'd find out eventually. That wouldn't be good, either. "What's up?" she asked, and I realized I hadn't answered her greeting.

I kept the book in front of my face. "Nothing. Just reading."

"Did you get in trouble at school again?"

"No." Actually, I had, but Caroline's appearance had driven Farbinger's detention right out of my mind.

I slid my eyes over to see what she was doing. Tracie was sitting on the edge of her bed, staring at me. I pretended not to notice.

"Farbinger didn't bust you for wearing pajamas?"

"Uh-uh," I lied, my eyes glued to the page.

She crossed the space between her bed and mine and pounced on me, tossing my book aside. She straddled me and pinned my hands above my head. Leaning over me and laughing, she let her long straight hair tickle my face. "You look guilty. What gives?"

"Get off!"

"Not until you tell me."

I tried to shove her, but she's really strong from all the hockey she plays, and I couldn't budge her. "I didn't do anything…it wasn't me," I said, squirming. Should I tell her? "It was…well…"

She swung her head so her hair grazed my nose, making it tickle even worse—a favorite torture trick of hers.

"Stop it!"

"Spill it!"

"Fine, but you're not going to like it."

Why did I say that? Not a great way to start this conversation.

Her eyes narrowed, but she didn't let me go.

"It's about…Caroline," I said.

She let go of my wrists and sat up, crossing her arms. She was still straddling me, so I was pinned to my bed, which was another mistake. I should've negotiated my freedom first. Sometimes I'm too stupid for my own good.

"What about her?" Tracie asked, glaring.

No point in dragging it out now. I took a deep breath.

"She was here. Today. When I got home from school. With Dad."

Tracie jumped off of me like I'd burned her. "Here? In our apartment?" Her voice had gone all screechy, which scared me even more.

Might as well tell her what I knew. "She's moving back to Victoria." I waited a couple of heartbeats, and when she didn't say anything, I added, "She wants to see us."

Tracie made a sound like she was blowing out a lungful of disgust. She tossed her hair and snorted. "Like that's gonna happen."

I considered my options…let it go, or say what I wanted to say. On her side of the room Tracie moved some stuff around, so she'd have a place to sleep. I closed my eyes, screwing up my nerve. "I wouldn't mind," I said, going for broke. "I mean, you know…just to see what she's like."

Tracie spun around. "What she's like? What she's *like*? I'll tell you what she's like! She's a traitor and a liar and an a…and a…an abandoner!"

"Well, it's been a long time—"

"Not long enough!" When I didn't say anything, she came back to my side of the room and stood over me. "You do remember that we have a pact, don't you?"

This time I decided to play dumb. I'm really good at that. "A pact?"

"Yes, a pact to never talk to her again?"

Here we go. This is what I was hoping she'd forget. Maybe if I acted casual. I picked up my book like the conversation was boring me, and I had no idea what she was talking about.

"You don't remember, do you?" she accused. I focused on the words on some random page. "Suze?" Tracie said. "I know you can hear me."

"Of course, I can hear you."

"Well, do you remember or don't you?"

Telling Tracie about Caroline had been a big mistake. I decided coming clean wouldn't be any smarter, and to stick with the "innocent bystander" routine.

"Sorry. Don't have a clue. Just tell me, and get it over with already."

"We signed a pact saying we'd never speak to Caroline again," Tracie told me. "Ever. In our whole lives."

"We did?" I sounded pretty convincing, even to myself. Maybe I should be the actress instead of Jessica.

"Yes! We did!"

Like always, Tracie was so sure of herself, so certain she was right. But I'd seen Caroline, and, I couldn't help it, I wanted to know more about her. My sister was starting to make me mad, actually. I was kind of sick of her trying to rule my life. I closed my book and sat up. "You know, I was only three years old when Caroline took off. I don't think I could even write my name then."

"Not then," she said. "You know what I'm talking about. When I was twelve and you were seven."

"Whatever."

"We signed it, and I've got it around here somewhere. I'll prove it to you."

Man, I *knew* it. She kept everything. She jumped up and pulled boxes out from under her bed. Oh, great—as if her side of the room wasn't a big enough disaster area. She lugged out stuff that hadn't seen the light of day for years. I should've just admitted I knew, but it was too late for that now. While I pretended to read, she dug through the mess, moving us closer to the threat of our room being condemned. I secretly watched over the top of my page.

When she started heaving plastic storage containers out of her closet, I decided to give in, because it was bad enough I had to look at her mess without it bleeding over onto my side of the room. "Look, I believe you, okay?"

A pile of shoes fell off the shelf above her, tumbling down and whacking her on the head, and I laughed.

"Shut up," she said, flinging random sneakers onto my side of the room. Oh, man. The worst thing is, I knew she'd never bother to clean up all this junk and I'd have to do it eventually. I picked up a runner and threw it at her. I missed on purpose, but she was plenty mad anyway.

"Why'd you do that?" she screamed.

This wasn't how I'd hoped it'd go when I told her, but I

should've known. She loves to be in charge of me, and finding this stupid pact was just one more way she could run my life.

"Keep your smelly junk on your side," I told her, instead of what I was really thinking: *You aren't the boss of me.* I didn't want to sound like a five year old.

"You're so lame," she said, as the shoe whizzed by my head. *Return to sender.*

I jumped off the bed, ran for the door, and kicked her new purse across the duct tape dividing line as I went. She slammed the door after me. In the living room, I shoved Sammy to one end of the couch and curled up under Dad's stadium blanket. I love Tracie. She's a great older sister. The best, really. But even the closest sisters fight, and years of experience were not wasted this time. I'd made sure I had hold of my book when I vacated the premises.

I stuck my cold feet under Sammy's warm body and she began to purr. Suppose Tracie actually found the pact? Could she seriously mean to hold me to it? Now that I was out here in the quiet living room, I started thinking maybe Tracie was right after all. We'd lived this long without a mother. What did we need one for now when we were almost grown up?

I must've drifted off to sleep, because one minute I'm reading about a big double-cross in the story and the next, Dad's shaking my arm.

"Fighting with Tracie again?" he asked.

"I like the couch."

"Yeah, right. Better get to bed."

"What time is it?"

"Late."

I hate it when you ask someone the time, and they say "late" or "time to go" or whatever. If I wanted to know that, then I'd ask that. What I want to know is what time it is.

"What time is it?" I repeated.

"Eleven-thirty."

As I went off to my room, it occurred to me I should probably get Dad to sign my detention slip. But in the end, I decided to wait until morning. He wouldn't be so mad if he was mostly asleep when I asked.

In the hallway, I examined the crack under the door for light. Black. Good. I could hear Tracie's muffled snores penetrating the walls. She's a big snorer. Once, strictly for blackmail purposes, I made a recording of her using the voice memo app on my phone, but she wouldn't pay up because she thought it was Dad. Next time I'd try video.

There's nothing Tracie hates more than being woken up, and I was annoyed enough with her to interrupt her beauty sleep just to get back at her for treating me like crap. I switched on my desk lamp and aimed the light directly at her head. Then I slammed the doors on my wardrobe a couple of times, dropped my backpack on the floor, and tossed some of her shoes from my side right onto her bed. She didn't even turn over.

A second later our door opened, and Dad stuck his head in. "What's going on in here?" he whispered.

"Nothing."

"Well, be quiet. We don't need Mrs. Kullbom hitting her ceiling with a broom handle all night."

"Sorry."

Our downstairs neighbor believed in payback, if Tracie and I were too noisy for her. I flipped off the light and felt my way to the bed. When I pulled back the sheets I heard the faint crackle of paper. Lifting the corner of the curtain and holding the paper up to the window, the streetlamp cast just enough light on it for me to make it out.

On a faded piece of red construction paper, written in purple crayon, was the pact:

We promise to never talk to our mom agaen.
Tracie and Susan

Chapter 5

I always wake up really early on the weekends. Maybe it's from all those fishing trips I used to take with Dad and Uncle Bill when I was little. Whatever the reason, I was up on Saturday way before the rest of my family. It was freezing in our apartment because we have electric heat, so we have to keep it really low or Dad says Tracie and I will have to get jobs to pay for it. He's only half-kidding.

Since it was the first of the month, I'd gotten my allowance out of Caroline's support check, and so I took myself out for coffee and a muffin at the Double Shot, a café not far from our house. By the time I got there it'd started to rain, so I made the coffee and muffin last about two hours, while I sat in a comfy armchair in front of a fake fire. The rain was really coming down hard by noon, and the barista kept giving me dirty looks for hogging the best seat, so I bundled up and went to the public library.

I walked up and down the YA shelves looking for something good, trying not to drip on any books. In the end, I checked out the first book and the third book in The Testing trilogy. Maybe the one I found on the bus would make more sense if I started at the beginning.

By then I was starving, but I didn't want to spend any more money. I figured Tracie'd be out with her friends, so I went home and found the place totally empty, except for Sammy, who twisted around my ankles, purring, while I made a grilled cheese and ketchup sandwich.

I took it out to the living room and plopped down on the couch to read while I ate. I'd just pulled a blanket over my lap when the phone rang. I had it in my hand to answer when I saw the caller I.D.—an unfamiliar Vancouver number. I let our old-fashioned answering machine get it. (Dad was too cheap to pay for voicemail as long as it kept working.)

A minute later, Caroline's voice filled the little apartment. "Hello, there. This is a message for Susan and Tracie."

Suze.

"This is your mother calling."

Ha.

"Just wanted to say hello and let you know the movers are here and…well…I'm now officially living in Victoria again. I'd love to see you both. So…well…call me back."

After she hung up I picked at my sandwich, pulling it to pieces and feeding bits to Sammy, trying to decide what to do. I hadn't really seen Dad yesterday because he'd worked the closing shift, so I didn't have a clue what he thought about all this.

In the end, I read my book and tried not to think about Caroline. She called back four more times over the next two days, but Tracie was home every other time and she stood between me and the phone, daring me to answer it. She even took the handset to bed with her so I couldn't secretly call her back.

As if I would.

Well, maybe I would.

I mean…I was considering it….

I was so lost in the story that when I turned the page of *Graduation Day* I must've let out a little shudder, and possibly some sort of worried noise, which apparently gave me away. Baker turned from the board and shot me the "stern teacher" look. "Suze, we finished silent reading fifteen minutes ago."

"Yeah, okay. Sorry." I'd blown through the first two

books in the trilogy and was only twenty pages from the end of the last one. How could I stop now? I made a show of closing the book, but held my finger in my place and kept reading under my desk. I just wanted to finish the paragraph, at least. Shouldn't Baker be glad I was reading books voluntarily?

Apparently not. He cleared his throat, so I shut the book, sighing at the unfairness of it all, and opened *Strunk & White* instead. Grammar. So exciting. While Baker diagrammed a sentence on the board, I leaned over Mike's shoulder to see the page number and quickly flipped to it. I tucked my hair behind my ears and stared up front. Baker could force me to look like I was concentrating, but he had no control over my brain.

I'd been reading, not only because it was more exciting than verbs and adjectives, but also to keep my mind off of Caroline…and because Tracie's smugness was driving me crazy. She thought she was so smart, saving that stupid contract. When the phone rang at seven o'clock this morning, and the caller I.D. showed Caroline's number, she'd waved the agreement in my face for the last time. I grabbed it and tore it into tiny pieces. Of course, she'd screamed bloody murder until Dad came stumbling out of his room (on his day off), and then she'd stormed into the bathroom and locked me out until I was so late I had to run for the school bus without a shower.

Typical Monday already.

If this was what life with Caroline was going to be like, I'd be happy to live up to my end of the destroyed pact. I imagined Tracie sitting in study hall, taping it back together so she could frame it for me. I wouldn't be surprised to see it hanging over my bed when I got home.

When the bell rang for lunch I bolted out of my seat, but I wasn't quick enough. Baker was waiting for me at the door. "Suze, may I talk to you for a minute?"

I stopped, shuffled back to my seat, and dropped my backpack on the ground with a loud thump. I figured Baker was going to give me detention for reading instead of paying attention.

I figured wrong.

"Suze, I'm a little concerned about you," he said, once everyone had cleared out. "Is everything all right?"

"Sure."

"Okay. Good."

I got up.

"The thing is—"

I sat down.

"The thing is, I didn't hand back the exam on *Great Expectations*, because I wanted to talk to you first. I remember you finished the test in record time, except you didn't answer all the questions."

"Yeah…."

"You read it though, right?"

"Yep."

"Well, why didn't you answer the one about the endings?"

"I didn't get the last question," I mumbled.

"What didn't you get?"

"The thing about two endings didn't make sense."

"What do you mean?"

"I just didn't get it. I don't know what the question meant."

"Do you have your book with you?"

"Probably. I guess."

I dug through my backpack and produced the tattered remains. Because of budget cuts, we all had to buy our own copy of *Great Expectations*. Now he would know I'd bought a used copy I found at the Salvation Army, so I'd have more money for phone minutes. He took the book and thumbed through it. The spine was loose, and a chunk of pages fell out onto the floor. He picked them up and tried to tuck them back in, but the book had pretty much had it.

"You know we read the abridged edition in class, right?"

I shrugged.

"Abridged means it's a shortened version of the book. This is the whole thing."

I wasn't sure what he was getting at, but I nodded anyway.

"Dickens wrote two different endings for *Great Expectations*. The edition I asked you to buy was abridged, but it still included them both. This one only has the original."

How was I supposed to know there were two endings? "Well, it was a really old book," I said. "I didn't see why I should waste money on a new copy."

"Why didn't you say anything when we discussed it in class?"

Probably because I didn't care. Probably because I was thinking about lunch. Like now. "I don't know."

"Suze, you know that's never an acceptable answer in my class."

Why was he bugging me? Didn't he have enough to worry about without causing me grief? I sighed heavily to let him know what a pain he was being. "When you were talking about the two endings in class," I said, "I looked at my copy again and there was only one. I didn't ask because I thought maybe you were talking about the movie or something. Okay? Can I leave now?"

That was the longest speech I'd ever made to Baker, and he surprised me by saying I could go. I must've thrown him off or something. Apparently he didn't really mean it, though, because on my way out he stopped me again. "Suze?"

"What?" I was really getting tired of him.

"Why don't you take my copy, read the other ending, and I'll let you finish the test."

"Did I pass already?"

"Well, yes. But the essay question was twenty percent of your grade, so you got a C-minus without it."

"Good enough. I gotta go."

And I was out of there. And this time he let me leave in peace.

When I got downstairs to the dungeon, which the teachers call the cafeteria, my lunch group was already at our usual table: Leigh, Amanda, and Jessica. Also, Brendan was there. He's the guy Amanda's kind of going out with, but not really because she says she's not interested in boys yet. All they ever talk about is baseball, and he won't even hold her hand in the hall, so it's not like it's a great romance or anything, but everyone kind of thinks of them as "together." Luckily, he only sits with us on the days his friends go to Robot Club, because having him around makes lunch kind of weird. I mean, we can't talk about anything good with him there.

A sandwich, an apple, and two brownies sat in a neat little pile on the table in front of my usual chair. "Hey, thanks, I'm starved," I said, plopping down in my seat.

Yummy egg salad, straight from Amanda's kitchen. I can never get my act together enough to pack a lunch, even though Dad makes sure we have stuff in the fridge. Last year Amanda had finally gotten tired of me drooling over her food and started bringing me lunch every day. Sometimes she's an awesome friend.

"Where were you?" Leigh asked.

"Baker wanted to talk to me."

"What'd you do this time?"

"I keep telling you," I said, smirking, "he's got a big crush on me."

We all laughed, and I rolled my eyes and made kissy noises.

"Well, I hope he doesn't get a crush on *me*." Amanda said. "I can't stand him." We all knew she said that for Brendan's benefit, but he didn't seem to notice because he was stuffing his face.

Leigh sighed. "Oh, I think he's a tall drink of gorgeous."

"Gorgeous?" I pretended to choke on my brownie, which I was eating first, just in case. "You've got to be kidding."

"Long, tall, and handsome," she said, probably quoting some old country song. Leigh always used what she called southernisms, which she supposedly got from her "mama" and the summer visits back to Tennessee to see her "kinfolk." Sometimes I think she just makes up her own, though. Leigh's all right, but she's totally boy crazy, which can be annoying. She practically goes with a different guy every week. Not that she ever actually talks to them in person. They just text.

"I think he's okay," Brendan said.

"You think Baker's gorgeous too?" I asked him, making red creep up the back of his neck. Good. Maybe he'd join the Robot Club and leave us alone.

"I meant he's a good teacher," he said, stuffing the rest of his lunch in his backpack. He mumbled something about the library and got away from us fast. Amanda barely noticed. Like I said, no great romance there.

"Mr. Baker's really nice to me," Jessica said.

"You guys are crazy," I told them.

My English teacher obviously had a bigger crush on me than I thought, though, because during last period I got a note asking me to come to his classroom for about fifteen minutes after school. Normally I would have told him I had to catch the bus, but I knew Baker wasn't going to give up until he'd said what he wanted to say.

When I walked into his classroom he wasn't there, but Amanda was leaning against the windowsill, looking out at the drizzly sky. "What? He has a crush on you too?" I asked her.

She jumped, startled. "Oh, hey, Suze. What're you doing here?"

"I told you, he can't get enough of me."

"Yeah, right."

"He sent me a love letter asking me to stop by after school."

"Me too. I mean he sent a note, not a love letter." She blushed, making me question what she really thought of Baker.

"He loves us both," I said.

"Well, well, ladies. Nice to see you," he said, coming into the room. Amanda blushed harder, and I laughed, looking meaningfully at her as Baker strolled over to his desk. I flashed her an evil smirk and puckered up. I swear her face turned purple, she was so embarrassed. My suspicions were confirmed. Gross, he was really old! At least thirty.

"I'm glad you both could come," Baker said.

As if we had a choice.

"Sit down, sit down." He gestured at the hard plastic seats, like he'd invited us to the Empress Hotel for tea. Not that I've ever been to the fanciest hotel in Victoria for tea or anything else. Baker seemed a little too cheerful to me, and worry began to creep up my spine like mold on bathroom tile.

"I have a little project I thought the two of you might be interested in," he said.

Uh-oh. This can't be good.

Chapter 6

"Have a seat up here." Baker indicated the front. I'd never voluntarily sat there before, but I grabbed a chair anyway. "I know you're probably anxious to get out of here, so I'll be brief," he said.

Thank God for small favors.

"We start our speech unit tomorrow in class," he told us. "I'm breaking everyone into pairs, and each team is going to choose a subject to research. A couple of weeks before winter break you'll all present them to the class."

I stared at the ceiling while he talked to us. I noticed Amanda looked right at him the whole time. Maybe that's why she gets straight As.

"What's that have to do with us?" she asked.

"Well, there's an odd number of students in both the Honors English Class and in Suze's English class."

The stupid class was what he meant. The class where I was the only one who read the books, and the rest of the class found summaries on the Internet. The class where we'd talked about *Great Expectations* for so long I could've written the book myself. The class where everyone else slept, and I read my paperbacks.

Until the year before there wasn't an Honors Class, but Baker talked the school board into letting him try it, so then all the smart kids got to stick together and do more homework or whatever. It was supposed to get them ready for high school, but I was glad I wasn't in it. From what Amanda told me, it was a ton of work.

"I thought since you two know each other," Baker continued, "maybe you'd like to work together on your project."

I sat up straight, alarmed. Do school work with Amanda? Was he crazy? His plan made it pretty clear he wasn't in love with either of us. In fact, I thought he must hate me. Amanda wore this really skeptical look, and I couldn't believe it. She didn't want to get stuck with me? Well, the feeling was mutual. But apparently it wasn't up for discussion. Baker had already decided.

"Do we have to do the speech twice?" I asked.

"Good question, Suze," Baker said. "I hadn't considered that, but we'll figure something out."

"What's the subject?" Amanda wanted to know.

"That's entirely up to you. But it needs to be something important. It should be a topic you feel strongly about. One that will affect you students, either now or in the future."

I didn't say anything, because I was thinking the whole idea sucked, and Farbinger had banned that word from school. Probably because I used it too much last year.

"It sounds interesting," Amanda said.

Suck-up works for describing Amanda, but I probably couldn't get away with saying that either.

"I hope you two will find it very stimulating to work together," Baker told us. "There's such a wide variety of issues to choose from."

"Yeah…I've already got a few ideas," Amanda said.

Who was she kidding? Sheesh! Even Baker hadn't just fallen off the teaching truck. She was making me gag.

"Suze? What do you think?" he asked.

"I guess if I have to," I said. "Sounds like you've already decided."

Amanda shot me a bug-eyed look, like she couldn't believe I'd be rude to a teacher. I didn't care. This was so unbelievable I couldn't even bother to fake it. You'd think working with your friend would be cool, but Amanda's a freak about school. She's all straight As and school government and pep rallies. I like to do what needs to be done, lie low, and skip the whole school spirit thing. I knew working with her would end up being a huge production, and I couldn't figure out why Baker was making us do it.

After five more minutes, which felt like five hours because of Amanda gushing about how cool it would be, he finally let us go. But not before she'd invited me over to her house to discuss it. She did it right in front of Baker too, and I couldn't think of any good excuse, so I said okay.

By the time we got to the front doors of the school I was so angry I wanted to whack something with my backpack—maybe Baker. He really burned me up. What was he thinking? That I was a total moron? An idiot? A sucker? Just because I was getting a C in English didn't mean I was completely stupid. I knew what he was up to. He thought Amanda could teach me something. Whatever.

I stopped inside the heavy doors. "Just a sec." I set my bag down and pulled my gloves out of my pockets. The wind whistled through the cracks around us. "Are you sure this is a good idea?"

"What?" Amanda asked. "Working together?"

"Walking all the way to your house. It's freezing out there."

"It's only seven blocks."

"Seven cold blocks."

"Well, if you weren't wearing a miniskirt—"

"This isn't a miniskirt. It comes all the way down to my knees."

"In case you haven't noticed, it's winter."

"It's not like we live in the Arctic. It's just rain."

How she'd turned the conversation around from me saying it was too cold to walk to her house to making me defend the weather, I wasn't sure. She's good at things like that. But I knew why she was being so snarky. It was because she didn't want to work with me, but we're friends, so she didn't want to admit it. I pushed past her and opened the door.

Technically it was still *autumn*, anyway. Sometimes Amanda is so smug it makes me want to puke. Her clothes are always spotless, and I think she even presses her jeans. And she always looks beautiful. That is, of course, because she *is* beautiful—the exact opposite of me.

She's got thick golden hair while mine's wiry black, with bleached-out orange streaks thanks to me allowing Leigh to play hairdresser a couple of months ago. Like in the romance novels I read, Amanda's eyes are *pools of green*. Mine are dull brown. And let's not talk about her perfect skin or I really will hurl. Amanda's got these really long legs, too, and she could be a model. Seriously. She really could, because her mother runs a modeling agency. Instead, she wants to be a professional baseball player.

"So what'd you think of Baker's idea?" she yelled over the wind.

I told her it was fine, but that's all I said. So what if Baker thought I was totally stupid? A real idiot. What did I care? There was no way I'd admit that to Amanda, though, because she'd probably agree. She yelled something at me, like "I think it will be fun to work together," but the wind whipped her words away so I wasn't sure what she said.

It didn't matter, because I knew what she was thinking. If she couldn't work with Leigh, then I'd have to do. Just like I "do" every summer when Leigh goes off to Tennessee with her mother. Suze Tamaki. The good old understudy friend.

Unlike the busy road I live on, Amanda's neighborhood is something from an old movie or a Christmas card. Big trees, perfect front lawns, mailboxes painted to look like log cabins, or to match the house. A few of them even have those Little Free Libraries out in front with really nice books you can just take. I actually love her street a lot, and as we walked, the surroundings made me calm down a little. Maybe working with her would be okay. After all, I'd known her since kindergarten. We'd done other stuff together, and it hadn't killed us yet.

Amanda lived in the prettiest house on her street, white with green shutters, a red brick fireplace, and a stone walkway. Exactly like the kind of place I'm going to live in when I grow up. Unless I'm super rich and I can get a mansion. She flung the front door open and the warm air rushed out to greet us in a way it *never* does at my apartment.

"Here," she said, handing me a hanger.

Designer coats hung neatly in the closet arranged by color, and gumboots lined the floor. Our closet was loaded down with fishing gear and hockey sticks, and most of the time we couldn't even get the door closed.

She started to hand me the red plaid slippers, but I stopped her. "Those are Leigh's. Mine are purple."

"Oh, right."

I unzipped my boots and slipped on the pair of fleecy slippers Amanda's mom, Heather, had bought me last Christmas to wear at their house, since no one's allowed to wear shoes on their hardwood floors. Today, my frozen toes rejoiced and snuggled in.

"Mom! I'm home," Amanda yelled. "Suze is with me!"

Her mother came into the room with her cell pressed to her ear and waved at us, smiling. She sets her own hours at the agency so she can be here when Amanda gets home—probably to keep her from accidentally killing herself somehow with a baseball and bat. After school one day last year, Amanda was hitting the ball against the house, and it bounced back and wacked her in the face. When her mom and dad finally got home from work, they'd followed a trail of blood through the house to her bedroom, practically having heart attacks along the way. By then, Amanda's nose had stopped gushing, and she was watching TV with an ice pack, but they worry about leaving her alone now. Sometimes she's not as smart as she seems.

We walked into the city dump, otherwise known as Amanda's bedroom. "Good to see your room's up to par," I said.

She threw her backpack down on a pile of laundry. If you could call it a pile. Mostly it was just scattered all over the floor. Amanda's mess made Tracie look like an amateur. I spotted a bowl of soggy cornflakes on the dresser. Thank God my father put a stop to Tracie bringing food into our room. Of course, paying the exterminator a hundred bucks two months in a row had something to do with that.

I cleared space on the rumpled bed and sat down. Amanda grabbed a few pairs of panties off the floor, unburied the empty clothes hamper, and dropped them in. Her face was red. It could've been the cold outside, but I think she was blushing. She has a problem with that, so I try not to tease her about it.

"Can I call my dad?" I asked. "I'm almost out of minutes."

"Sure. The landline's around here somewhere."

I pressed the pager button on the phone's cradle, and the cordless handset beeped back at me. I found it under a pile of sports magazines and smelly T-shirts. Amanda went to get us a snack while I called, and Dad answered on the third ring. I was really glad it was him and not Tracie.

He seemed distracted, probably by something on TV, so I told him I was having dinner at Amanda's and left out the bit about doing homework. As long as I went to school, that was about as much energy as he could muster toward my education. He didn't really care about my projects. Then, as we were about to hang up, he stopped me.

"Oh, hey, Suze, Caroline called. Again." His icy tone crawled through my ear and wormed its way into my heart. "She'd like to see you and Tracie this weekend."

Fat chance if she thought Tracie was ever going to give in. But me? I wasn't so sure. I didn't say anything.

"Suze?"

Still nothing.

"Hey, no one's making you see her."

"Dad? Can we talk about this later?"

"Sure. See you in the morning."

God, doesn't he ever listen to me? "I'm not staying over. I'm just here for dinner."

"Oh, right. Well, I'll probably be at Bill's anyway. Night."

He hung up the phone. Fishing, beer, house league hockey, basketball, and pizza. My dad's whole life. Me and Tracie too, I guess. Yeah, I knew we counted for something, even if it wasn't always super apparent.

Amanda came back into the room carrying juice, vegetable sticks, and some sort of organic crackers that looked like birdseed. "Guess what?"

"I give up."

"They want to fire Yoda."

"What?" This definitely got my attention.

"And not just Yoda, either. Mr. Franklin and Morty too."

"Well, I can get with firing Franklin and Morty."

"Su-uze," she said in that two-syllable way she uses when she thinks I'm being unreasonable.

"Okay, okay. I'm joking. What'd they do to get fired?"

"Nothing," she said. "My mom just told me that the school board thinks they can save a bunch of money by eliminating all the custodians. And not only at the Junior High, but the whole district."

"So who's gonna clean the schools?" A vision flashed in front of me of what detention would be like in the future—no more lounging in a desk and reading—I'd be cleaning toilets and raking leaves.

"They're going to hire some company that would do it cheaper."

"But Yoda's been the janitor at Maywood for a million years. And he's not exactly…well, you know."

Amanda nodded.

Some kids thought Yoda spoke bad English because he was from Croatia and had never learned it properly, but my dad had gone to Maywood back in the dark ages, and Yoda had worked there even then. According to Dad, he had something wrong with his brain—some sort of learning disability. He could do his work, but rumors were that he would freak out if anyone asked him to vary his routine.

His shift used to begin at one o'clock, but they changed

it to three o'clock a long time ago. For ages he came in at the old time, even though they told him over and over he didn't have to. I actually heard it was because he knew what bus to take and he liked the driver. On top of all that, he was kind of old to be looking for a new job.

"What's he going to do if they fire him?" I asked.

"I don't know. Retire, I guess."

"That sucks."

"I know."

We sat there munching on the hard crackers for a while, and then I got one of my most brilliant ideas ever. "Amanda! I know what we can do for our English project."

"What?"

"Save the janitors' jobs!"

"Seriously?" she asked.

"Why not? Baker said it should be something that affects us now or in the future. This totally does."

"I guess."

"Come on, this is a great idea."

"I was thinking of something more...I don't know... maybe about sports?"

I forced myself not to roll my eyes because I knew I'd never win an argument that way. "Sports are good," I said in my most diplomatic tone, one I usually reserved for talking Dad into something, "but I could use my Super Power on a project like this."

Amanda looked up from the carrot stick she was gnawing on and smiled. "Yeah…that's true. You could."

Last year, when I got in trouble for beating up John Boreman because he'd stuffed some grade sixes in garbage cans, Amanda had told me I had to stop fighting other people's battles for them. And I'd told her I couldn't help it, standing up for the underdog was my Super Power. After that, she and Leigh had called me SuperUnderdog for the rest of the year. It had died out over the summer, though, and neither of us had mentioned it in a long time.

"SuperUnderdog lives again!" I said.

Amanda jumped up and grabbed my arm, holding it up in the air like a winning prizefighter. "Able to save small boys from trashcans."

"To spot Kick Me signs from fifty paces away and destroy them!"

"Able to fight the big fight so the little guy doesn't have to!"

"Yeah!" we both yelled.

"We can do this," I said.

"I'm in!" Amanda threw her arms around me and gave me a bear hug, squeezing the breath right out of me.

This was exactly what I needed right now to take my mind off Caroline. A cause. Someone else's fight. Between us, Amanda and I could prove why the school's custodians were so important. I was still mad at Baker for pairing us up like I was a dummy or something, but saving the janitors' jobs…I could help Yoda. And if Mr. Franklin and Morty got to keep their jobs too—well, you couldn't win 'em all.

"SuperUnderdog and her faithful sidekick…" I paused for a minute, trying to think of a good name for Amanda, and then I got it. "Her sidekick, OverAchiever, to the rescue!" I shouted, jumping up and pumping my fist.

"Hey?" Amanda said. "*OverAchiever?*"

"It's a good thing in this case."

She laughed. "Yeah, okay."

Maybe working with Amanda was going to be all right after all.

Chapter 7

On Saturday, I woke up at six-thirty as usual. I'd spent most of my allowance for the month already, and there wasn't a lot to do that early, so I was snuggled under the covers reading a fantasy novel. It was kind of a lame story, but sometimes you gotta make do.

My back was aching from the lumps in the mattress, but it was way too warm in bed to get up, because the heat wouldn't be on in the living room yet. We should've listened to Dad when we were kids, and he told us not to jump on our beds. They really hurt now.

Tracie was still out cold. She lay on her stomach, her long, silky black hair spread out all over the pillow, drool running down the side of her mouth. Wouldn't her friends love to see her now? My phone battery was dead, so I scanned the room for the old-fashioned film camera I bought last month with my birthday money from Caroline. Usually it's on a hook by my wardrobe, but it was gone. No doubt Dad had borrowed it to take a picture of a fish or something and forgot to put it back. If he hadn't lost it overboard, already.

Before I could decide if it was worth climbing out of my toasty bed to look for it, the landline rang in the living room. Caroline hadn't called in a few days, so Tracie had stopped taking the handset to bed with her. Answering it was up to me. Dad had undoubtedly left to go fishing already, and my sister doesn't take calls before noon.

I knew who it was. Aunt Jenny. She believes in getting up at the crack of dawn and she never pays attention to what time it is when she phones. Her day starts then, so everyone else's should too. Luckily, I'm always up on Saturdays when she calls. I kind of wanted to ignore it because I was so warm in bed, but I figured I better answer, because I'd seen what we had in the cupboards, and, unless I wanted to go grocery shopping, we needed an invitation for dinner. She's a great cook, and always sends leftovers home with us too.

It had already rung four times when I found the handset in the kitchen behind the bread. "Hello?" I hopped up and down on the icy floor in my bare feet. The air was so frosty I could practically see my breath. That's the problem with electric heat. It's major expensive and you can't afford to have it on when you really need it most.

"Susan? This is your mother. How are you?"

Oh, man. Since it had been a few days since she'd called, I had thought I was home free. Apparently she was back at it again. Now what was I going to say? Maybe I could start speaking a foreign language. I took French at school, but everything I knew had flown right out of my head. I knew a little from the Japanese channel on cable. Would she fall for that?

"Hello? Susan? Are you there?"

No speak English. No Speak English.

The trouble was, I didn't really speak Japanese either. With Tamaki for a last name, people expected me to know it, which is actually kind of racist. I mean, Dad's family's been here since the *nineteen-thirties*. Besides, I'm only half-Japanese anyway, because Caroline's white. Dad and Uncle Bill are so Canadian, they always joke that they even say *sushi* with a Canadian accent. As in, "Do you want to get some sushi, eh?"

"Susan," Caroline said. "Look, I know you're there. I can hear you breathing."

No, you can't.

I held the phone away from my mouth. *It's probably my heart pounding.* I wondered how she knew it was me and not my sister. Maybe Tracie had already hung up on her a few thousand times. Why didn't I hang up?

"Susan, I'm sorry if I'm making you uncomfortable. I really want to talk with you and Tracie."

Ha. That's a good one. I could wake Tracie up so she could kill me now and put me out of my misery.

"I'm sorry. I shouldn't have called," she said, when I still refused to speak. "Maybe you can phone me when you feel more like talking. Your dad's got the number."

Whatever.

"Okay, Susan. I'm going to hang up now. Tell Tracie I called. And I'm sorry it worked out this way."

Me too.

"Susan?"

"What?"

Oh, man. I said it out loud. Now she knew for sure I'd been listening.

"I hope to hear from you soon."

The phone clicked in my ear.

Dad's door opened and he shuffled out, wrapped in his black robe and the slippers I'd gotten him three Christmases ago. His big toe poked out through the end of the left one. I made a mental note to get him a new pair this year.

"Don't tell me that was your mother calling."

"No. It was Caroline."

"Touché," he said.

I stomped back down the hall to our room and jumped into bed, hiding under the warm covers. My feet were cherry Popsicles—bright red and frozen solid.

"Was it for me?" mumbled Tracie.

"Shut up."

She rolled over and went back to sleep.

After a while I was too cranky to lie there, and I could smell coffee, so I put on my thick wool socks and wrapped my flannel robe tightly around me against the chill. In the kitchen I poured myself a cup of coffee, slopped in some milk, and dumped a ton of sugar into it. The only way I like it. I'm mostly in it for the caffeine. I slurped my drink while I waited for a waffle to toast.

"Not fishing today?" I asked Dad.

"No fish anymore," he mumbled from the couch.

"Never stopped you before."

He didn't bother to answer. The waffle popped up and I grabbed it, burning myself. What a great start to what promised to be a fantastic day. The tears welled up in my eyes, even though my finger didn't really hurt. What was wrong with me? I never cry.

When Leigh ruined my hair—giving me big orange streaks instead of the cool blue ones she'd promised—I didn't cry. And when the guy I kind of liked, Spencer, asked me to the Fall Fling and then wouldn't dance with me because of my weird hair, no one could tell I cared because I'd laughed it off. Crying was not my thing.

So why was I wimping out now over a stupid little burn?

"Dad?"

"Hmmm?"

He rustled behind the sports page a little but didn't glance up. He looked kind of sad sitting on the couch, black hair sticking out, his old stadium blanket wrapped around him, coffee in one hand, and the newspaper spread everywhere. It made me feel lonely for him.

"What do you think Caroline wants?" I asked.

"God only knows."

There was that frozen tone again that felt like ice water in my stomach. "Do you think she'll stick around this time?"

"Ask me something I can answer. Like what time the tide comes in."

I shoved his feet out of the way and plopped down next to him. "Do you think I should see her?"

"I told you, Suze, I don't care. I don't even know Caroline anymore. I haven't talked to her in ten years. I wouldn't have recognized her on the street."

"You mean the blond hair?"

"Well, yeah. Especially that. But the jewelry and the fingernails and the makeup. She never wore any of that."

"I hope you're not trying to talk us into seeing Caroline," Tracie shouted from behind us. I jumped about a mile and lukewarm coffee splashed into my lap. I hadn't even heard her get up.

"When's the last time I told either of you what to do?" Dad asked, his voice sounding world-weary.

"Maybe you'd like a date with her?" Tracie suggested, coming around the couch to face us. "Huh? Doesn't sound so good, does it?" Dad picked up the Sports section again. "I didn't think so," she practically snarled. "You're such a hypocrite."

Tracie stormed off, slamming the washroom door behind her.

"Why don't you mind your own business?" I yelled after her. "He never said we should see her."

"Just leave her alone," Dad told me.

"If you get a chair," I said, "I'll lock her in there."

Dad scowled into his paper, but I could tell he wasn't really listening to me. Maybe he was thinking about Caroline. Would he really date her? God! I never even thought of that. I tried to imagine us a happy little family. Caroline would come in and redecorate, get rid of all our old comfortable furniture. Maybe she'd even make us move. I'd have to go to a different school. I'd be the new girl and everyone would stare at me.

The coffee sloshed around in my stomach, trying to work its way back up. I handed the peanut butter-coated waffle to Dad, who took it absently and munched it down in three bites. The ringing of the phone broke the silence and the queasiness in my gut increased.

I jumped up and raced across the room to the kitchen, grabbing the handset before Tracie could come out of the washroom, and clicked talk.

"What!" I said.

"Suze?" Caroline asked.

Instead of answering, I screamed into the phone, "Why can't you just leave us alone already?" and smashed my finger on the End Call button.

And then I realized the woman had said "Suze."

Caroline always called me Susan.

Dang.

It had been Aunt Jenny on the phone.

I was in trouble now.

Chapter 8

Apologies for rude behavior don't fly with Aunt Jenny. Nope.
You have to work off your crime, which is how I found myself
raking leaves instead of cruising the mall that afternoon. I'd
had two choices. I could make Amanda mad by telling her I
couldn't meet up to do our survey about janitors, or I could
really aggravate AJ and refuse her request that I get my unre-
fined, unmannered butt over to her house and help with the
yard work. Guess who scares me more?

Aunt Jenny is soft and round, which might make some
people think she's one of those sweet motherly women who
love children. I've known her too long to be fooled. It's not
that she's a kid-hater or anything. AJ is a BS-hater though,

and as far as she's concerned, most kids are out to snow adults. She's probably basing a lot of her experience on me.

Dad had to work until five, Uncle Bill was watching golf on the big screen in the basement, the kitchen was full of good smells from AJ's cooking, and as usual, Tracie got off by volunteering at some hockey camp for underprivileged kids. She'd show up in time for dinner, though. You could bet on it.

After twenty-three blisters and about ten piles of leaves, AJ came outside and handed me a cup of steaming apple cider and a slice of fresh, warm bread slathered with butter. She lowered her round bottom heavily onto the porch steps and I collapsed next to her.

"Wanna tell me why you were so rude this morning?" she asked.

"I thought you were Caroline."

"And that's how you talk to your mother?"

"She's not my mother." I chewed on the bread. Butter rushed my taste buds, coating them with deliciousness. "It was Tracie," I said, after a while. I had to phrase this carefully because if AJ thought I was blaming someone else for my behavior, I'd be in even more trouble. "She was freaking me out, saying Dad and Caroline should get back together."

AJ's face showed her surprise. "She wasn't serious."

I told AJ the whole story, and when I was done she stood up, brushed off her butt, and started to go into the house. "I wouldn't worry about that little scenario," she said.

"Hey, AJ?"

She waited.

"Did you like my mother?"

"I think you should make your own decisions about Caroline," she said, and her voice was as icy as Dad's.

"Why does everyone hate her so much?" I asked.

"Who said we hate her?" She had her hand on the screen door.

"AJ, wait," I jumped up. "Look, I can tell she must've done something I don't remember, because you guys are all acting so weird. What'd she do?"

AJ took in a long, slow breath, and let it out just as slowly. "She walked away without any explanation." AJ went inside, letting the screen door slam behind her.

That was it? That's why everyone was so mad? Jeez. I was beginning to think Caroline had killed someone. She'd probably meant to explain. How many times have I meant to explain why I did something stupid, but then the moment slipped by? Too many to count.

I went back out to the yard and picked up the instrument of torture, dragging it around behind me, not really raking because my hands hurt. My heart kind of did too. What Caroline had done totally sucked, but now she was back. Maybe she'd changed. I kind of understood where my family was coming from, but why did they have to be so rigid?

I dug around in my pocket until I found the scrap of paper that I'd secretly written Caroline's number on. I'd used all my minutes on my phone and didn't have any money for more, so I'd have to be sneaky. Carefully, quietly, stealthily, I cracked open the heavy back door. The warmth and the wonderful smells of hot bread and vegetable soup filled my nostrils as I crept into the kitchen to use the phone.

I dialed the number.

Ring.

Ring.

"Hello?"

"Caroline?" I said. "It's me, Suze."

"Oh, Susan. I'm so glad you finally called."

"Yeah…." Wait! Was that AJ coming? I looked around for a place to hide. There was the laundry room, but she might be going in there. I chose the broom closet. It wasn't a mess like ours, but it was pretty full, and the only way to close the door was if I crammed myself into the mop bucket. I stepped into it and shut the door as quietly as I could, standing there in the dark. It wasn't until the water seeped through my tennis shoes that I realized the pail had about four inches in the bottom of it. Crap.

"Susan?" Caroline's voice came through the telephone. "Are you still there?" She'd been talking the whole time, but I hadn't heard anything she'd said.

"Yeah," I whispered. "I'm here."

"Everything okay?" AJ's slippers slapped against the hardwood as she walked past. I didn't dare answer. "Susan?" Caroline asked again. "What's going on?"

The footsteps faded. "What? Uh…nothing. Everything's fine."

"Okay, well…great."

"So…"

"I was thinking…would you and Tracie like to have dinner with me next Friday?"

"Dinner?"

"Yes. Around seven?"

"Uh…okay." Was I crazy? I guess so. "But just me. Tracie's…busy."

"All right. I'll pick you up."

"Okay."

We said good-bye and hung up, but I stood there completely frozen. My heart raced, practically humming. Sweat dripped under my arms. I'd agreed to dinner with Caroline. I couldn't decide if it was the bravest thing I'd ever done, or the stupidest.

I was so absorbed by my thoughts that when the door suddenly opened and the closet was flooded with light, I jumped, letting out a little scream. AJ yelped and clutched her chest. Once we'd both recovered a little, I stepped out of the bucket, dripping water everywhere.

"What the—"

"Sorry. Sorry," I said. I grabbed the mop and tried to clean up the mess.

AJ stared at me, her hands on her hips. "Suze? What were you doing in there?"

"Nothing," I said, not looking at her. "I just…I was making a phone call."

"To whom?"

"To…to…a boy."

She narrowed her eyes. "Does he have a name?"

"Uh…." I said the first one I could think of. "Brendan. I know him from school." Hopefully Amanda would never bring her boyfriend around. Or mention him to AJ.

"You want to try the truth?" AJ asked.

I don't know how she knew, but under her dark stare I totally caved. "Okay. Fine. I was talking to Caroline. She's taking me to dinner."

AJ's eyes narrowed so much I wasn't sure she could even see me anymore. "When? Tonight?"

"No. Next Friday."

She studied me for a moment longer, and then her face relaxed and she brushed her hands together. "Huh. Well, you better clean up this mess. And then it's time for lunch."

That was it? I'd told her I was going out to dinner with Caroline and that's all she had to say about it? There was no way she'd just let it go at that. And then panic surged through me. Tracie!

"Uh…AJ?" I called after her.

"What?"

"Could you…could you not tell Tracie?"

She rubbed her hand over her left eye like I was giving her a pain. "And why not?"

"Because she'll kill me?"

She nodded. "Fair enough." And then she walked off.

I leaned against the wall, shaky. What had I done?

✱ ✱ ✱

By the time Dad and Tracie showed up for dinner and we'd all sat down around AJ and Uncle Bill's dining-room table, I was sick to my stomach. AJ had made my favorite—salmon with blackberry-garlic sauce, scalloped potatoes, asparagus, and salad—but I took only a few spoonfuls of each dish. If anyone noticed, they didn't say anything. I was pretty sure if I put even one bite into my mouth, I might lose the lunch I'd forced down earlier under AJ's steady gaze. By now I was pretty sure just the *idea* of going to dinner with Caroline would kill me before Friday. And that's assuming Tracie didn't find out and do the deed herself first.

Everyone talked and laughed and ate so much they didn't notice me sitting there like a lump, pushing my food around on my plate. Tracie told them all about the hockey clinic she'd volunteered at, and Dad and Uncle Bill added stories about when they'd done the same thing in high school.

Everything was going fine, and except for some sidelong glances from AJ, I don't think anyone was paying attention to me and my lack of appetite. My stomach was churning, but I still managed to get down most of my food after all. We'd just about finished when Uncle Bill cleared his throat and looked around the table at everyone.

"So…I hear Caroline's back in town."

We all froze, like we'd been hit with one of those stunning spells in Harry Potter. And then AJ jumped up. "Time for dessert," she said. "Suze? Help me, please."

I scrambled out of my seat and started grabbing dishes randomly. If they were going to talk about Caroline, I wanted to be safely in the kitchen and out of the way.

"What?" Uncle Bill said, looking around at us. "Isn't she? We're not allowed to talk about her?"

AJ gave him a look, and he shut up. I grabbed a few more plates than it was safe to carry and followed AJ to the kitchen. When we came back with the apple crumble, Tracie was glaring at Uncle Bill. I wasn't sure what we'd missed, but I was glad we had.

"No," she said. "We're not going to see her."

"Is that the 'royal we', or are you speaking for Suze, too?" he asked. I wondered what he knew about my phone call earlier. I should've made AJ promise not to tell *anyone*.

"We signed a pact," Tracie told Uncle Bill, smugness all over her face. "Besides, Suze doesn't want to see her either."

"Is that true?" Uncle Bill asked me.

"Uh—"

"Can we drop this?" Dad asked.

"Yeah, I'm losing my appetite," Tracie said.

"If you don't want to see her," Uncle Bill said to Tracie, "that's fine. But Suze should be able to make up her own mind."

"Bill," Dad said. "They're my girls. I'll deal with it. Drop it, already."

"I just don't want to see Tracie bullying Suze the way you did me," Uncle Bill replied.

"I never bullied you," Dad told him, his voice raised. "It was the other way around."

For a second I thought they might start yelling, but then Uncle Bill laughed. "Oh, yeah, right! What about the time you—"

I stopped listening. I couldn't help wondering why Uncle Bill stood up for me like that. Usually he was pretty laid back; didn't get into family squabbles unless they were sports related. The rest of the night passed in a blur—more stories about when they were kids, everyone watching the hockey scores on the big screen downstairs, banter and teasing, the usual. As we were putting on our coats to go, Uncle Bill pulled me aside and gave me a hug.

"Don't let them push you around," he said in my ear. "Caroline messed up, but deep down she loves you."

I stood there, stunned, until Tracie said, "Earth to Suze. We're going."

I followed them out to the car in a daze. I was so freaked out by Uncle Bill's words, not to mention the huge hug. I could count the number of times he'd hugged me in the last year. Ever since I got boobs, both he and Dad kept me at a distance like I'd contaminate them with girl cooties or something. My whole life Tracie and the adults had told me what to do. So why was it so important to my uncle that I got to make my own choice about this? What did he know about Caroline that no one else was telling me?

Chapter 9

Whoever first said that Mondays suck really knew what they were talking about. My fried hair stuck out more than usual today, my sweatshirt was wrinkled because I'd forgotten to take it out of the dryer, and Tracie had been her usual charming self and eaten the last of the cereal. To add to the suckiness, Baker was waiting for me when I walked through the door, and *tall cup of gorgeous* were still not the words I would've chosen to describe him. My life was starting to feel like an entire month of Mondays.

He motioned me up to his desk. "Suze, come here a minute."

Now what? Was he going to drive me crazy all year?

Probably the stupid project again. I stood in front of him, making sure my hair was in my face so I didn't have to meet his eye.

"Good news. I've arranged with Madame Duke for you to switch your English and French classes around. Starting today you go to French this period and come to English seventh."

"Huh?" He couldn't possibly be serious.

"I thought it would be easier if you and Amanda had English together. Now get going before I have to write you a hall pass."

"I can't go to seventh-period English. That's the Honors Class," I reminded him. What an idiot. He couldn't even keep his own schedule straight.

"Sure you can. Now go. It's all arranged." He shuffled papers on his desk. I peeped through my hair curtain, not moving, but he didn't notice.

I tried once more. "Mr. Baker?"

He acted surprised, but I could tell he was totally faking it. "You still here, Suze?" His eyes were fastened on something really exciting in his grade book and he didn't even look up.

"Can't Amanda switch her classes instead?"

"No, it doesn't work for her. Now go, and I'll see you this afternoon."

It didn't work for me either, but that appeared to be too bad. There was nothing to do except go to French. Nobody cared what I thought. Not one person asked if I wanted to switch French and English. I bet they would've asked Amanda before they moved her schedule around. But she's special because she's a smartie. Who am I anyway? Nobody, that's who.

I took the long way to the French wing and even considered skipping, until I saw Farbinger bearing down on me. I ducked into the classroom as the bell shrilled and stood there with everyone gawking, until my teacher noticed me in the doorway.

"Bonjour, Suzanne," Madame Duke said. "Asseyez-vous à côté de Brendan."

I sat, because what else could I do?

"Hey," he said.

"Hiya."

"Class, s'il vous plaît, ouvrez vos livres à la page vingt-quatre."

I didn't have my book because I hadn't planned to be here, so I shared with Brendan. My mind zoomed ahead to the afternoon and Honors English. The thought of all those brainy kids together in one class made me shake. They weren't exactly a clique, but they all knew each other. I might as well tattoo *outsider* across my forehead.

The brains all look the same too. Not physically, but smart or something. You can pick them out in the hall, even if you're new like Jessica. This is her first year at Maywood, but I'd put money on it that she could name the brains already.

The thing that really annoyed me was that after Christmas I'd have to go back to my regular English class. Then everyone would think I couldn't cut it, even though I wasn't supposed to cut it. That wasn't the plan, right? To move me up? I didn't think so. After all, Baker had made it very clear exactly how dumb he thought I was by sticking me with Amanda in the first place—so she could help me.

"How come you're in French this period?" Brendan asked when class was over.

"Baker's making me go to seventh-period English for some stupid reason."

"Honors, huh? Cool."

It was starting already. "It's just so Amanda and I can work on our project together."

"Oh. The janitor thing?"

"Yeah, but don't let her hear you call them janitors," I told him. "They're *custodians*."

"Oh, right. Well, see you later."

"See you."

Naturally I assumed Brendan meant he'd see me in a few minutes for lunch, because there was Robot Club today. However, when I got to the table, my pile of food was there, but his seat was empty. Amanda sat pouting in her chair. "What's with you?" I asked, dropping my backpack and unwrapping the sandwich.

She didn't answer.

"Brendan's eating lunch with his English partner," Leigh explained. "And Amanda's jealous."

"I'm not jealous," Amanda said.

"Well, annoyed?" Leigh suggested.

"Who's his partner?" I asked. I figured it must be Danielle Mayers, the only girl in grade seven as pretty as Amanda.

"Brian Jacobson," Leigh said.

I laughed. "Let me get this straight. You're sulking because he's eating with some loser guy?" Amanda glared at me and crumpled up her garbage. "You've got to loosen the leash," I said, teasing, "or he's gonna break free."

I was kidding, but I swear her green eyes darkened as she glowered at me. I guess it was because I always tease her about Brendan following her around like a puppy. But he totally does. I mean, name another grade-seven guy who eats lunch with a girl and her friends. You can't. There aren't any. She threw her crumpled paper bag at me, but she didn't simply toss it, she pitched it straight at my head. Hard.

The thing was, I was having a rotten day too. A lot worse than Amanda had probably ever had in her life. That paper bag whacking me above my right eyebrow pushed me over the edge, just like the lemmings we'd read about in science class. I knew I had to get out of there fast, or I'd take her down with me. I was sick of life. Baker was driving me crazy. And most of all, I was not going to sit there and let Amanda throw garbage at me. I grabbed my food and backpack.

"Hey, Suze?" Amanda said. "You mean break free like your true love Spencer did at the Fall Fling?"

"Oh, grow up," I said. "I didn't even like him."

"Yeah, right. Ooooh, Spencer's so tall. And hot. Did I mention hot?" she said in what I guess was supposed to be my voice.

"Shut up."

"Uh, yeah, you mentioned hot. About a million times," she said, answering her own stupid question.

"Amanda, I'm warning you."

She sneered up at me from her seat. "What're you gonna do? Beat me up? Throw me in a locker?" She laughed. "I'd like to see you try."

Instead of punching her like I wanted to, I crushed my chips and dumped them over her perfect little head. I knew it would make her madder. At first she sat there, surprised, I guess. Then she stood up, towering over me and picked a chip out her thick hair. She threw it on the ground and stomped on it.

I mean, I had to laugh, didn't I? Anyone would've cracked up at that. She looked so totally ridiculous. So dramatic. Her face was stricken, like I'd squashed a kitten or flattened a helpless kindergarten baby. I guess she didn't like being laughed at any more than I liked being reminded of Spencer.

"You're going to be so sorry," she threatened me.

"What's your problem?" I demanded. "You're the one who insulted me."

"Well, you started it," she yelled.

She grabbed her milk carton and unloaded it all down the front of my black sweatshirt.

"You witch!" I said. Except the word I actually said started with another letter. I was so ready for a fight. I grabbed Jessica's pop and splashed it all over Amanda's white tennis shoes. For a tomboy, she sure could scream like a girl.

She tried to grab me in a headlock, but after living with Tracie for years, I was too quick and ducked out of the way. She chased after me, weaving between the tables, yelling. By this time, it seemed almost funny to me, and as I swerved out of her grasp once more, I was actually laughing.

Unfortunately, that's when I tripped over some stupid kid's school bag, and she tackled me while I was on the ground. After that, it wasn't so funny. But it only took about two seconds before we were being dragged up to Farbinger's office—I didn't even get in any good hair-pulling, which I know she hates.

Of course, I'd be the one in trouble. Amazingly Perfect Amanda would get off scot-free. Farbinger was really going to let me have it this time.

Chapter 10

Detention. On a Monday. Farbinger didn't even pull the usual "take this slip home and have your mom sign it" first. After keeping us waiting forever, he sent us to detention hall for last period. Same-day detention was reserved for people who really annoyed him, and surprisingly, I wasn't usually one of those kids.

I didn't have to be a brain surgeon to figure out this was going to be a long week. My only consolation was Amanda had won the pleasure of my company. For once I wasn't stuck taking the blame alone. Put *that* on your school record, Miss Perfect.

I'd forgotten my novel at home, and so I settled into

the desk behind a curtain of hair for a forty-five minute nap. Two minutes later Baker walked into the room, whispered something to the detention monitor, and they nodded together.

He crossed over to us. "Ladies. Come with me, please. Bring your stuff."

Good thing he kept his voice low, because the other three loser dudes in the last row were already taking siestas at their desks, and, trust me, you don't want to wake those guys up. We followed him out of the room. I hoped Baker wasn't going to try to be the peacemaker. Obviously he knew we'd had a fight, because Amanda and I had both missed English. Farbinger had kept us waiting for all of fifth, sixth, and seventh period before he'd bothered to banish us. Missing class was the best part of my day.

We trailed Baker down the hall, not sure where he was taking us, but then he stopped outside the library, and I got a clue. "I hear you two are having some troubles," he said.

I clamped my mouth shut. We had the right to remain silent.

"Does this have anything to do with your project?"

Yeah. Sure. The whole world revolves around your class. If this guy was trying to push my buttons, he was hitting all of them. I rubbed the toe of my boot against a groove in the tile floor.

"No," Amanda finally answered him.

"So if that's not the problem," he said, "then it's probably none of my business."

"Right," Amanda and I said together.

That was kind of funny—we sounded like Jessica's twin sisters. I glanced at her through my bangs. Her tennis shoes were stained and stuck to the tile floor when she walked, and the smell of sour milk on my sweatshirt was nauseating. I guess we were even. I sort of grinned at her. I didn't want to apologize first, especially in front of Baker, but the whole thing was pretty ridiculous.

She half-smiled back. "So how come you pulled us out of detention?" I asked Baker.

"Principal Farbinger said you two could use this time at the library to work on your project. If you think you can refrain from throwing food."

"We're fresh out," I told him, and he laughed.

Being excused from detention to go to the library was a first for me. Special treatment was probably a perk of being one of the elite students. *Great! I could get used to these sorts of advantages.*

When the last bell rang for the day, Amanda told me she was in the middle of something important and we needed to stay longer. I didn't want to, but I wasn't that hot on the idea of going home either, in case Caroline called or something. An hour and a half later Amanda looked up from the stack of school-board minutes the librarian had printed out for her.

"You know, you're supposed to be searching the web for stuff about custodians. Not clothes."

"This is a pop-up window," I said. "It opened on its own."

"Well, close it and get back to the custodian thing."

"Yes, Mother."

"Look, Suze, if you're not going to play ball, then we can't be on the same team."

My stomach tightened. "You don't want to be my partner anyway," I said. "You've made that clear from day one. But you know what? We're stuck together, so it would be great if you could treat me like I have some intelligence."

"Whatever."

"The whole janitor—"

"*Custodian.*"

"The whole *custodian* thing was my idea, remember?"

"Yeah, okay, okay. Can we just get back to work?"

"Fine."

I typed a new search into Google. This time it pulled up a page about how a janitor had spotted a kid in his school who didn't belong there and it turned out to be a drug dealer. That gave me an awesome idea.

"Look at this," I said.

Amanda leaned over my shoulder and read the screen. "Score! That's great."

"Yeah," I said. "But what I was thinking was maybe we could do a few tests of our own."

"What do you mean?"

"You know, sneak into other schools and see if we get caught."

"I don't think that's the kind of research Baker had in mind."

"So?" I said. "I want to get an A on this."

"The best you can get on any project in an Honors English is a B," she told me. "Unless you do something extra."

"That's what I'm talking about. Visiting other schools."

"Not something that gets us suspended."

"What, then?"

"Well," she said, "something like Leigh and Mitch. They figured kids would learn to read better if they practiced reading to dogs, so they borrowed a few mutts and are taking them to the elementary school for the grade ones to read to. And they're tracking their progress on charts and stuff."

I laughed. "You want to read our report to a bunch of dogs?"

I was joking, but Amanda tilted her chair back and looked me in the eye the way my cat, Sammy, does when she's challenging me. "Nope. Not dogs," she said. "I think we should give our presentation to the school board."

Something clamped itself around my heart. "You *are* joking, right? There's no way I'm getting up in front of those stiffs."

"Why not?"

Because I would die of a heart attack? "I'm not doing that," I said. "No way."

"Listen, Suze, I was talking it over with my mom, and she thinks this is a great idea." I *knew* it wasn't Amanda's idea. Figures Heather came up with it—she's really into activism and stuff like that. "I have to get an A," Amanda said. "That means we have to do something really stellar. The school trustees make the most sense, because they're the ones who want to get rid of the custodians."

Our second fight of the day bloomed between us.

"Adults hate me," I pointed out. "Especially ones in charge. Trust me, we won't get an A. We'll probably flunk."

"Suze—"

"Excuse me, ladies." Mrs. Woods jingled her keys at us. "But I'm closing the library now."

"You know we have to do it," Amanda said in a sing-songy voice.

Didn't she understand there was no way I could get up in front of a bunch of adults and do our project? It was too much to ask. I signed off the Internet and gathered up my stuff. "Let's talk about it later."

"You might as well give in."

"Look what time it is," I said. "I can't believe we stayed so late."

"You're in Honors now. You have to do that sometimes."

"Yeah, I guess."

I still didn't like the idea of staying at school any longer than I had to, and I made a beeline for the hallway. I didn't have to be told twice to go home.

"Maybe you can come over this weekend and do some more research," Amanda suggested.

"Sure. But not Friday. I'm going to dinner with Caroline."

"Caroline?"

"My mother." The words leapt over my tongue and spilled out before I could stop them.

"Your *mother?*" Amanda's voice echoed down the empty hallway, making me cringe. Instantly I regretted telling her. Why did I say anything? As soon as she was alone, Amanda would text Leigh. Then Brendan. Maybe even Jessica. By Friday it'd be front-page news: MOTHER RETURNS AFTER TEN-YEAR ABSENCE TO TAKE GIRL OUT TO DINNER. SISTER SUES FOR BREACH OF CONTRACT.

"So what's up with that?" Amanda asked. "Since when are you seeing your mom?"

I shrugged as casually as I could. Obviously she hadn't heard anything about it before now, so it was good to know Jessica hadn't told the world about Caroline. At least I knew I could trust her for sure. That's a big plus. You never know with new friends.

"She moved back to Victoria," I said, digging my gloves

out of my bag. "It's no big deal. We're just going out to dinner."

I tried to sound cool, but talking about it made my internal organs do loopty-loops. My heart fluttered against my ribs, or whatever there is in there to bump into.

Maybe Dad, AJ, and Tracie had their reasons for hating Caroline, but I like to think that not only do I fight for the underdog, but I also give people second chances. Besides, my curiosity was killing me. She might be really nice, regardless of what happened when I was a kid. And no matter how Tracie felt, I'd always wanted to get to know my mom. Whether it was a good idea or not, I'd be finding out in approximately four days and two and a half hours.

Chapter 11

I stared in the mirror, horrified. "Oh, Sammy, I look so bad."

My cat purred and rubbed against my leg, assuring me I was totally gorgeous. God, I loved her. Too bad she was a big, fat, hairy liar.

I tweaked my bangs one way and then the other. I was going for the messy-casual look, but what I got was the you-let-Leigh-screw-with-your-hair-and-now-you're-going-to-pay look (to quote Tracie). There were about two inches of grow-out, so my roots were all black, and even wrapped in a bun, I couldn't hide the orange. Who wants to wear a bun anyway? I ripped out the elastic band and let my hair fall down around my shoulders. *Screw it.*

I tucked my bra strap under my favorite black sweater and pulled on the front of it where it'd shrunk in the wash. A button popped off and rolled behind the toilet.

Great. I didn't have time to fix it, so I'd have to change. "I can't go to dinner with my mothe—with Caroline looking like this," I told Sammy.

She purred louder. At least she wasn't judging me for seeing Caroline. She was the only one, though. I'd managed to keep it from Tracie, but I'd had to tell Dad. I couldn't go out with Caroline without him knowing. He wasn't exactly ecstatic, but he'd told me I should do what I had to do. And what I had to do was find out more about Caroline before making a snap decision. Who knows? Maybe she'd turn out to be a great mother.

The little nagging voice that kept saying *A great mother wouldn't have abandoned you,* refused to be silenced, but I was getting good at drowning it out by thinking about how I'd rub it in Tracie's face when Caroline came through for me. In my room the clock blinked seven forty-five. I subtracted an hour for Standard Time, since I hadn't bothered to change it yet. Fifteen more minutes. Please, God, let Tracie and her friends do their usual Friday night pizza thing after hockey practice. My heart was beating at capacity already because of Caroline. It would fail for sure if I had to deal with Tracie.

I pulled things randomly out of my wardrobe and tossed them on the bed. Black sweaters, black T-shirts, black skirts, dresses, and pants. Everything black. Last summer, I'd decided it would be way easier to do laundry if all my clothes were the same color, so I'd hit the thrift stores and bought every cute black thing I could afford.

Since my choices were limited, and I wouldn't be caught dead in any of Tracie's clothes (mostly because she'd kill me), I pulled on my second favorite sweater. A lambswool number I'd gotten for three bucks at the Salvation Army, with only one tiny moth hole on the sleeve. A total score. To kill time, I folded the things I'd pulled out and placed them back in the wardrobe.

When I came out to the kitchen, the clock on the microwave read 7:01. Caroline was late. I poured myself a pop, flicked on the TV, and collapsed on the couch. My brain was mental mush already. Making plans so far in advance was a big mistake. Just keeping my big mouth shut around Tracie had been hard enough, but now I had to face Caroline and take bites of food and swallow them and not gag in front of her after a whole week of anticipation and anxiety.

On the TV, a balding plumber named Mick said, "I'll take Shakespeare for one hundred."

"This fairy queen spurned her lover for a changeling child in the woods of—"

"TITANIA!" I shouted before the host even finished reading.

"Who is Ariel?" Mick guessed.

"No, I'm sorry."

"Titania, you idiot," I told Mick.

"Who is Titania?" Janet from Calgary asked.

"Correct."

Usually I'm really lousy at quiz shows, but Titania was the fairy that Jessica had dressed up as for Halloween. Sammy jumped off my lap and ran away, unimpressed. I plucked her orange-and-white hairs off my sweater. Jess would probably have to tutor me when we got to our Shakespeare unit, because all that fancy language might as well be Swahili as far as I was concerned.

English class had been really weird all week. Baker had told me he'd transferred me to seventh period to work on my project with Amanda, but we had done regular class stuff every day. We hadn't had any time to work on our project at all. And he'd been treating me as if I were just like everyone else in the class. He'd even asked me a few questions.

I had to admit, Honors English was a lot more interesting than the regular class. For one thing, it moved right along. There was no time for reading under my desk. It was cool, too, because everyone said smart things instead of smart-alecky things. For once I wasn't the only one reading the assignments either. It was like a discussion period in there instead of the Spanish Inquisition. I was kind of getting into it. Too bad I'd have to go back to Lame-o English after Christmas.

By the time round two of the quiz show came on, I'd forgotten all about Caroline. Well, maybe not forgotten, but I was really having fun with the show because I'd actually gotten a science question right too. Maybe school wasn't such a waste of time after all. It looked like it might lead to big money. The phone rang, and I stretched across the couch to get the extension, not taking my eyes off the screen.

" 'lo?"

"Suze? How come you're home?" Amanda asked.

"I live here. Why are you calling if you don't expect me to be here?"

"I was going to leave a message for you to call me after you got back from dinner. I wanted to find out how it went with your mom."

Great idea. Tracie could've heard that message, and my life wouldn't be worth the paper my birth certificate was printed on. "Why didn't you text me instead?" I asked.

"I can't find my cell phone."

It was probably lost in her disaster area of a room. "Well, nothing's happened yet." *Dang!* I missed hearing the final question. "I'll call you later."

Amanda ignored the fact I wanted to hang up. "I thought you were going at seven."

Yeah, so did I, but I wasn't about to give her the satisfaction.

"Seven, seven-thirty. Something like that. In fact, I

think I hear someone coming up the stairs now. Don't wait up."

I clicked off the phone before she could say anything else. I'd invented the part about someone on the stairs, but it turned out to be true. I crept up to the door to peek through the peephole, but before I could, there was a thump, a rattle, and a jangle of keys. My brain did a quick calculation. Friday night. Dad works till ten. That meant one thing. *Crud.*

I vaulted the back of the couch like an Olympic gymnast and grabbed the remote. Tracie followed two steps behind me, lugging her school stuff and carrying a pizza box. My stomach growled as the aroma of grease and cheese wafted through the air. But I would die of starvation and leave my bones to wolves before I'd ask her for a piece after the torturous week she'd put me through.

"Hey, Suze," she said.

Well. That was a first. She actually spoke to me like I was her sister again, and not some evil traitor. I hid my surprise in hopes of pizza.

"Hi."

"You eat?" she asked.

Double surprise. I bit back a what-do-you-care auto answer. That wouldn't get me anywhere, and I was hungry enough to eat the box. "Not yet," I said.

"Here." She handed it to me. "It's macaroni and cheese pizza."

"My fave." I smiled, and she grinned back. When I was really little, Dad had asked me what kind of pizza I wanted and I'd answered macaroni and cheese. It was a family joke. I hadn't heard Tracie make a family joke since before Halloween. "Thanks."

I opened the box and slid out a lukewarm slice. As Jessica would say in her flowery faux-Shakespeare, the stench of pepperoni flooded my nostrils. I was so hungry I was weak, but not enough to eat meat. I plucked the pieces off and tossed them to Sammy, who'd returned when she smelled food and she scarfed them down, licking her tiny lips.

It was almost eight o'clock. I never waited this long for dinner. Plus I'd been so nervous all day I hadn't even eaten my lunch. The first slice was gone in about ten seconds, and as I inhaled a second piece, I hoped Caroline didn't take me to too fancy a restaurant. If she ever showed up. It was really weird that she hadn't called. Maybe I should've tried her, but I couldn't do that now…not with Tracie here.

"Do you remember that kid, Whitey Fresno?" Tracie asked, plopping down beside me. "He's in grade nine now."

"Sure, everyone knows Whitey. Class clown."

Tracie guzzled my pop and I was about to yell at her until I remembered the pizza and stopped myself. "Yeah, well now he's the class streaker," she said.

"What?"

"No joke. Today, during gym, we were playing basketball.

The guys were using half the court and we had the other, and out of God-knows-where, here comes Whitey running through the gym screaming like a maniac, totally naked."

"No way!"

"I'm not kidding. Everyone stood there totally frozen. Finally, as he was about to escape, Coach tackled him. The custodian, Mr. Fredrickson, helped drag him into the guy's locker room."

"The custodian?"

"Yeah. I knew you'd like that part."

"Excellent." Caroline and her dinner faded from memory as my brain mulled over how we could make this part of our presentation. "Anyone get any photos?"

"Everyone's phones were in their lockers."

"Too bad. That would've added a lot to our speech."

Tracie and I cracked up.

By eight-thirty I'd given up on Caroline. Besides, I wasn't sure I wanted her to show up now anyway. Aside from the fact I was seriously annoyed that she hadn't even bothered to call, this was the first night Tracie and I'd had a civil conversation in so long I couldn't even remember the last time. I knew Caroline would totally spoil it. When the phone rang, I shoved Tracie out of the way to get to it first.

"Hello?"

"Susan? It's Caroline."

"Where are you?" I demanded.

"I'm still in the office, but I'm leaving now. Are you ready?"

I glanced over at Tracie trying to see if she was paying attention. "You still want to?"

"I can be there in twenty minutes, if I hit the green lights."

A surge of anger pulsed through me. It's not like I thought she was dead in a ditch or anything, but she could've called before now. How could I tell Caroline what I thought of her and her stupid plans with Tracie listening in? Not only was my sister sitting right there, but there was no way I was ditching her for Caroline now. I wondered if it'd look suspicious if I took the phone into my room. Probably.

"How come you didn't call sooner?" I asked.

"Hmmm?" *Click. Click. Click.* She was obviously typing.

"I've been waiting since seven," I told her, trying to be cryptic, and also let her know I was annoyed.

The clicking stopped. "Didn't Sarah call you?"

"Who?"

"Sarah? My assistant." Caroline sounded genuinely confused.

"No one called."

"Oh, Susan, I'm so sorry," she said. "My meeting ran late, and then I was stuck in traffic, and I had something I had to finish here at the office once I got back. I really apologize. I tried your cell, but you didn't answer, so I asked Sarah to call you at home. That was around…six-thirty?"

I glanced over at the phone's base and saw the light flashing. "I must've been in the shower." I was going to have to get rid of that message before Tracie heard it, or else I'd be dead.

"Oh, I'm *so sorry*," Caroline said again. "I feel awful. Let me make it up to you…we missed our reservation, but you can choose anywhere you want to—"

"I think it's too late."

Tracie mouthed something at me that looked like "Say no." She probably thought I was talking to Amanda.

Caroline sighed. "I know I messed up, but I find it hard to believe it's too late for a fourteen-year-old to go out on a Friday night."

"Thirteen," I said.

"Pardon?"

"Thirteen. Not fourteen. I gotta go."

I hung up without waiting for her answer. After all, if it weren't for Tracie, I would've passed out from hunger by now. As soon as Tracie was in the kitchen, I erased the message and switched the ringer off on the phone. I was beginning to have an inkling of why Caroline was getting such an icy reception from the rest of my family.

Chapter 12

Tracie went off to shower. I sat there flipping channels, not really seeing what was on the TV, trying to figure out how I felt about Caroline ditching me like that. I knew I should be more understanding, that it was just a series of missed calls and grown-up work stuff, but the anger kept building until I had to pound a few raggedy throw pillows against the wall to keep from calling her back and telling her off.

And then something that really freaked me out happened. A fast-food commercial came on, showing a family eating out together, and I realized that the second Dad got home, he'd want to know about dinner with Caroline. I'd begged him not to tell Tracie before, and he'd agreed, but he hadn't been happy keeping my secret. What if he asked me how it went right in front of her?

I heard the hair dryer click off and I shoved Sammy out of my lap and jumped up. Bed. Now! And not to read, either. I'd have to pretend to be asleep. I took one step, tripped over Sammy, and fell flat on my face. I'd barely gotten to my feet when Tracie came out of the washroom.

"You look really tense," she said before I could make my escape. Her long, straight hair hung almost to her waist, shiny and healthy, exactly the opposite of my rat's nest. A pang of envy raced through me. If I could leave mine alone, it would look that awesome, too.

"No. I'm not tense," I said way too loudly. "I'm fine. Just tired." I moved toward the hallway. "Going to bed."

"At nine o'clock?"

"Yeah. Yep. It's been a long week."

Tracie narrowed her eyes. Apparently I was acting a little too…I don't know…weird?

Nervous.

"Really?" she asked, examining me to the point where I squirmed. "What do you mean a long week? How come? What happened?"

"Ummm…" Let's see. There were so many things to choose from. Without even mentioning Caroline, there was the fight with Amanda, Monday's detention, the project, and Baker being a pain in my butt, all stressful topics. I latched onto the one thing that would distract Tracie. "Uh, well, I got moved up to Honors English."

Her face broke into a smile. "Awesome news, Suze! Congratulations! Come here. Sit. Tell." Tracie motioned me over to the couch.

I'd chosen well. Of course she'd want to hear all about that. Tracie loved anything to do with school. She's like Amanda that way. I really should have gone to bed, but Dad didn't get off until ten on Fridays, so I still had some time. I sat. I told. She hugged me and offered to help any way she could.

"Baker's so hot," she said.

"Ew. Not you too. Leigh has a major crush on him."

"He was a first-year teacher when I was there and we all loved him."

"Gross."

Tracie laughed. "Just wait. You'll fall for him before the year's over."

"Doubtful."

She studied me. "You still look stressed. Get up."

"Why?"

"Just do it."

I stood up because when she gets that determined look in her eye it's easier than arguing. She shoved a bunch of junk mail off our dining room table, yanked the cushions off the couch, and spread them out.

"Lie down," she said. "On your stomach."

"Why?"

"Because I'm going to give you a massage."

The last thing I wanted was Tracie's hands on my neck. What if Caroline dropped by after all? "I'm good."

"Get up there. And take your sweater off."

"Can't we do this on the bed? It'd be softer."

"This is higher. It'll be easier for me."

I peeled off my sweater. "It's freezing in here." I climbed up onto the rickety table.

She threw Dad's stadium blanket at me. "Lie down."

"I hope when you have your own spa you're nicer to your customers."

"When you pay me, I'll be nicer."

Owning a day spa and salon was my sister's dream. She planned to get her hairdresser's license and then go to university and earn a degree in business, so she could open one by the time she was twenty-five. Before Leigh ruined my hair, Tracie always did it for me; now she wouldn't touch it. But sometimes she practiced manis and pedis on me and my friends. The massage thing was new and I wasn't sure how much I was going to like it. I lay down on the cushions anyway. They slid apart, and I hit my hip bone. "Ouch."

"Don't be a baby."

I had to kneel on the table while Tracie tried to straighten them underneath me.

"This is stupid," I said.

"You'll see. It'll be awesome."

She put some sort of smelly lotion on her hands...vanilla and maybe cinnamon? And then she started by rubbing my shoulders and I have to admit, it wasn't bad. Her hands were nice and warm against my skin too. I sighed. I began to feel a little melty under her strong fingers.

"See? Told you," she said. "Why're you so tense? It can't only be English."

I couldn't tell her I was worried about Dad coming home and asking about dinner. That wouldn't fly. "I'm not tense," I said instead.

"You are too."

"Am not," I said, like we were little kids.

"You lie."

Lie...of course! Why didn't I think of that? It's the one thing I'm really good at! I sighed, trying to set the right mood, one of resignation. "Okay, you're right," I said. "I'm a little stressed."

"Let me guess. Caroline?"

Bingo! "Well, yeah. The thing is...she talked me into going out to dinner with her tonight."

Tracie's hands tightened on my shoulders, making me flinch. "Uh...ow?" I said.

"Oh, sorry." She relaxed her grip a little, but not much.

"Don't be mad, okay? I was just curious." I rushed on

before she could dislocate my neck. "Anyway, I said I'd go with her, but in the end I decided you were right. I blew her off."

"Really?"

"Yeah," I said, warming to my lie. "She's a *poseur*. All fake and glittery and wanting to take us out to dinner, but in the end I realized I don't need her."

Tracie began to knead my shoulders again, this time a lot more gently. And as I said it, I thought maybe I was actually right about Caroline.

"I hate to say I told you so."

"No, you don't."

Tracie laughed. "Yeah, you're right. Hey, wait a minute," she said, seeming to remember something. Her hands squeezed me hard again. "Did she call here tonight? When we were watching TV?"

I tried to nod, but Tracie's grip on my neck was pretty tight. What had I actually said to Caroline and how closely had Tracie had been listening? "Yeah," I said. "That was her. She was begging me to go out, but I said no."

"Good for you."

This was turning out to be most excellent! Now when Dad came home, I could tell him the same thing, and no one would ever know Caroline stood me up. Tracie moved around the table and took one of my feet in her hands, stripped off my sock and started rubbing it. I almost purred like Sammy, it felt so good. "You know, Suze," she said. "I'm really proud of you. You stuck to our pact. I knew I could count on you."

That's the problem with lies. They seem harmless enough at first…but then your sister says something like she's proud of you, and then you feel like the total loser you are. But I couldn't back down now. Besides, this was better than having her hate me. The door rattled and I bolted up, the cushions flying out from under me. "Dad's home early, and I'm naked!"

I clutched at the blanket while Tracie got my sweater off the couch. "Chill, Suze. You've got your bra and a skirt on."

"Like I want Dad to see me in my bra."

"Why not?" she said, laughing. "You haven't got anything anyway."

I threw a couch cushion at her. "Shut up. You should talk." Tracie was only an A-cup herself.

"Better for playing hockey."

I was yanking my top over my head when Dad and Uncle Bill came in carrying pizza and a six-pack. They took a look at me sitting on the table and raised their eyebrows in unison.

"I don't want to know," Dad said. "But get down, Suze. That's where the pizza goes, not your butt."

"I was giving her a massage," Tracie explained.

"That doesn't make me feel better about seeing her on the table."

"You do massage now? Excellent," Uncle Bill said. "My neck's got this weird crick in it."

"I can fix that," Tracie told him.

God. My family is so weird. I'd climbed down and was about to escape to my room when Dad reached out, laid a hand on my shoulder and said under his breath. "So? How was it?"

Tracie didn't miss a thing, though, and she said, "She didn't go. She blew Caroline off."

"You did?" he said.

"How come?" Uncle Bill asked.

"I just…changed my mind."

"How'd she take it?" Dad asked.

"I don't think she cared."

That part was true. She didn't seem that bothered by my saying it was too late to go tonight. Dad glanced over at Uncle Bill, but I couldn't figure out what his look meant. Maybe *I told you so.*

"You know, if you didn't go because you're worried what we'll all think of you—" Uncle Bill started to say.

"That's not it," I said. "I just changed my mind."

"We have a pact," Tracie reminded us all.

"Yeah," I said.

"Want some pizza?" Dad asked, sounding like he wanted to change the subject.

"Nah, I think I'll go to bed."

I could feel everyone exchanging looks and I knew they were all about me, but I didn't care anymore. I'd gotten away with the lie, but it still sucked that I'd had to tell it to keep Tracie from killing me. I think I would rather have gone out with Caroline and then had a showdown with my sister. She looked pretty smug when she'd talked about the pact, like she'd won, and it made me want to come clean. But I didn't, because I'm pretty much a chicken.

I went off to brush my teeth, saying goodnight as I passed back through the living room. Dad and Uncle Bill were crowded on the couch with my sister between them, watching the hockey scores and eating pizza. They barely mumbled goodnight back. I couldn't help thinking, though, that they were my *real* family, so the lie had been worth it. Caroline was a stranger. A stranger who'd been back for a couple of weeks and had already hurt me. No one who really cared about me would do that. Not Uncle Bill, or AJ, or Dad…or even Tracie.

I climbed into bed, but I knew I wouldn't be able to sleep. I picked up one of Tracie's novels she'd left on my side of the room. It was called *Emma* by Jane Austen. I could hardly follow it, though, and after about six pages I was totally and hopelessly lost. I kept reading anyway, but mostly I pondered Caroline.

Now that I'd told everyone that I'd blown her off, I really couldn't see her, even if I wanted to. That was the worst thing about the lie—because in spite of everything that had happened tonight, the truth was, I still wanted to get to know my mother. If she called back, I knew I'd give her another chance. And I'd just made things a lot worse for myself by pretending to agree with Tracie.

I turned a few pages, but didn't really see the words. That seemed to be happening to me a lot these days.

"How come you're crying?" Tracie asked when she came in for bed.

"Am I?" I swiped at the hot tears streaming down my face. I hadn't even noticed them. "Sad book."

She gave me an odd look. "Suze?"

"Yeah?"

"*Emma* is a comedy."

Huh.

Ten minutes later her familiar snoring reverberated through the air, but instead of giving me that safe, comfortable feeling it usually did, it made me want to throw something hard at my sister. I stuffed the corner of my pillow into my mouth, bit down, and cried myself to sleep.

Chapter 13

As usual, I was out of minutes on my phone and all my friends knew it, so it wasn't until Sunday night that I dug it out of my backpack to listen to some tunes and saw that there was a message from Caroline. She'd left it right after I hung up on her Friday night.

"Hi, Susan," she said. "I was hoping you'd pick up if I tried your cell, but I guess you're probably mad at me, which is totally understandable. I just wanted to say I'm really sorry for the crossed wires. It's no excuse, but this job...well, it's a promotion, and it's really demanding. I'm trying to get settled, and there's so much to learn. Anyway, I *am* sorry, and maybe next time we can make plans for Saturday or Sunday, instead. That way work won't get in the way again. Please forgive me. I'd like another chance. I'll give you a call later in the week, okay?"

I stared at the phone in my hand, my finger hovering over delete or save. In the end, I kept it. I don't know why. But she sounded sorry, and I thought maybe someday I'd need proof for Tracie.

On Monday Amanda had bombarded me with the third degree, but I mumbled that dinner was fine, and we'd better worry about our project. That got her off on a custodian tangent. She's so easy to distract.

After thinking about it for a while, I did decide I'd give Caroline one more chance. Mostly because I was dying of curiosity. Where did she live? What did she do for a living? Did I look anything like her? I mean…if she didn't color her hair blond and wear so much makeup. Sure she was white, and I had Dad's Japanese blood, which gave me olive-toned skin, but we still might have the same ears or smile or handwriting. I once read this article in the paper about a kid who'd been adopted, and when he met his birth father, they had the same handwriting. That could be Caroline and me. I hadn't had a good enough opportunity to check her out, and I wanted to. But she was only getting another shot if she made the effort. No way was I going to call her.

In English, I thumbed through a well-worn copy of *Death of a Salesman*. Not a bad play at all. Depressing, but interesting. There weren't enough copies for all the classes, so Baker had given us two periods to read it, rather than letting us take it home. I'd actually finished it really fast and was thinking I was pretty cool. Some of the smarties in class were still reading the end while we discussed it. And people thought that reading romances was a waste of time. Ha! That's how I got to be a speed-reader—trying to get to the good parts.

"Now, let's move on," Baker said. He scrawled *Theme* across the blackboard.

Oh, no. Not theme. Whatever you do, don't ask me about theme. Ask me anything else. Ask me about the main guy, the Willy Loman dude. Ask me about plot. But don't ask me about theme. A person is supposed to be able to pick it out really easily, but I never could. I just didn't get it.

Baker ran his gaze over the class and saw me hiding behind my hair. "Suze?"

Figures.

"Umm…" What the heck was I doing in Honors English anyway? "Well." I spit out the first thing I could think of. "The theme of *Death of a Salesman* is that all individuals are important people, and society should value them for who they are."

"That's certainly a good example of theme," Baker said, "but I was looking for the definition of the word itself."

My face burned. Leaning forward, I let my hair cascade

around me. "I'm not sure," I mumbled, careful to avoid Baker's nemesis phrase *I don't know*.

"Suze," he said, "you gave an excellent example. I'm confident you can tell us the definition."

I flipped through the script, randomly searching for the answer, willing it to appear so I could read it off the page. But, of course, it didn't and I couldn't. All those smart beady eyes bored into me.

Finally, Baker decided it wasn't worth it and moved on. Thank God. "How about you, Brett?" he said. "Can you define theme?"

"Theme is a reoccurring, unifying subject or idea. It's the message of the play."

"Right. Leigh, how does Brett's definition prove Suze's statement true or false in regard to the play?"

I closed my ears to Leigh's answer. I couldn't believe I let myself get stuck in this class. Baker told me we were going to work on our projects. He didn't say anything about my having to participate in the class. The kids in Lame-o English got to watch the play on TV. I could've gotten some extra sleep in.

"Okay," Baker said over the bell, "we'll finish up this discussion tomorrow."

I grabbed my backpack.

"Suze?" he said, stopping me. "What's your next class?"

Oh, man. Was he never going to let up? "Art."

"Can you stay for a minute?"

"No. I'm working on a—"

"Give me thirty seconds, okay?"

I sank back into my seat. There was no use fighting it. As the classroom emptied, Baker walked over to the desk across from me and sat down on top of it. He was lucky it didn't tip over. I'd seen people fall flat on their butts doing that. I kind of wished he would. Maybe he'd break something and I could escape.

"So, how's it going?" he asked.

My defenses flew up. What was he up to now? Was he still worried about Amanda and me? Or was it because I wouldn't answer his question in class? "How's what going?"

"Honors English. What do you think of it?"

"I want out."

Baker took off his glasses and rubbed a little red mark on the bridge of his nose. Maybe, just maybe, without his glasses he was a tiny, little bit good-looking. But I still couldn't see gorgeous or hot. "Why?" he asked.

Because I was choking, that's why. Because I didn't have a clue. Because, because— "Because I don't belong in this class," I finally muttered.

"Suze, why do you think I chose you to work on your project with Amanda?"

"I don't know." *Oops.*

"You don't know?" I traced some kid's initials scratched deep into the desk and didn't answer. "Suze?"

"Well, you said it was because Amanda and I know each other."

"Did I?"

"Yeah."

"And you bought that?"

I looked up. "What do you mean?"

"Does that sound like me?" he asked, smiling. And then he chuckled. He actually chuckled. I didn't see what was so funny. That was what he'd said when he'd called us in to talk that day. He had no right to laugh at me.

"I don't know *why*," I said, being purposefully contrary.

"Try again."

I peeked through my wall of hair. Baker returned my gaze. I retreated. "Because I'm stupid, and you thought Amanda could help me?"

"You've got it half right."

"So you think I'm too stupid for even Amanda to help?"

He chuckled again. *Argh...* "That's not the part you got right," he said. "I don't think you're stupid at all. In fact, quite the opposite."

"Yeah, right."

"Really," he said. "The reason I partnered you two together is to challenge you to work up to your potential. I thought Amanda's high standards might encourage you."

"What makes you think I'm so smart? I'll be lucky to get a C in English."

Baker wiped his glasses with his tie. "Have you ever heard of kids doing poorly because they're not challenged?"

"No."

"Well, some kids are so completely bored they can't pay attention."

Like right now?

I wanted to get to Art. I needed to talk to Jessica. And our mural was not getting done while I was sitting here listening to Baker babble about how smart I supposedly was when everyone knew I wasn't.

"Let me ask you something, Suze," he said. "How long did it take you to read *Great Expectations*?"

"A couple of weeks, I guess." *Eleven days, actually.*

"And how long did we spend on it in class?"

"Forever."

"Exactly," he said. "That's my point. Most of the kids didn't even finish reading the book. And they had the abridged version. Most of them probably just rented the movie. Dickens is hard for some of them. Others are lazy. I think it's different for you."

"Different how?"

"You were bored because you'd finished the book weeks before we ever got to the test, right?"

"I guess."

"But you liked the book."

"It was all right."

"And you read the whole thing?"

"Except the second ending," I said, and smiled a little.

Baker smiled too. Okay, I'll admit it—when he smiled I could see a hint of hottie. But that was all. Just a hint.

"Right. Except the second ending," he said. "Anyway, what I'm trying to say is I think you belong in the Honors English class."

I shook my hair out of my face and looked at him. "Are you kidding me?"

"I'm completely serious. Now, you can't tell anyone this part," he said, "but the project with you and Amanda was a scheme on my part. I cooked it up so I would have an excuse to move you into Honors."

"What are you talking about?"

"The truth is," he said, "the administration would have looked at your record and told me I couldn't move you up. I sidestepped them this way."

"So you're saying after Christmas I don't have to go back to my regular English class?"

He grinned. "On one condition."

My heart thumped, pounded, crashed. I'm sure he could hear it. "What's that?"

"You have to get an A."

"On our project?"

"Yes. But not just on your project." He paused, wiping his lenses again. If he didn't stop cleaning them he'd wear a hole right through the glass. "You have to get an A in English for the semester."

The breath I'd apparently been holding leaked out. How could I do that? I was barely pulling a C at the moment. "But what if I don't want to stay in the Honors Class?"

"Well, then you can get whatever grade you like," he said. "But I think you do want to stay."

Maybe he was right. Maybe I did want to be in the class. And not only because I was afraid of what people might think if I went back to Lame-o English. Maybe I liked Honors. And maybe Baker's insanity was starting to rub off on me. One thing I did know for sure was no matter what, Yoda was going to come out of this with his job. I'd already worked harder on our presentation than anything I'd ever done for school, and I wasn't going to let him down. SuperUnderdog was on the job! And maybe with OverAchiever's help, I really could stick it out in Honors.

"So tell me what I have to do to get an A," I said.

"You can start by taking my copy of *Great Expectations* home and reading the other ending."

"And?"

"And write me an essay on the two endings."

"And?"

"And you'll have to keep up in class. No shirking when I ask you a question."

That wasn't all, and we both knew it. "And?" I asked, my heart racing.

"You and Amanda will have to do something worthy of an A for your project. An outside presentation. Something above average. Something like, oh, I don't know…giving your presentation to the school board?"

I *knew* it! Amanda had told him. She'd enlisted his help to try and get me to do something I couldn't do. I looked him in the eye, and he beamed. Why was he so nice to me? Why did he care how I did in English? Who was I? Nobody. Why should he lose sleep over me?

"I'll have to think about it," I said.

"Excellent choice," he told me.

With my backpack slung over one shoulder I stood up and headed for the hallway. At the door I turned to Baker. "You got the book with you?"

He pulled *Great Expectations* out of his back pocket and lobbed it across the room. I made a one-handed catch. "No less than three pages," he said. "Why one ending works better than the other."

"We'll see," I said, and made my escape.

Chapter 14

The bell rang, and two girls from grade six scurried out of the washroom. I tousled my hair with my hands, fixed my lip gloss, and studied my fingernails. I had all kinds of time. The way I figured it, I'd need to wait at least fifteen minutes or it would just look like I was late. It had to be obvious I was skipping. It was all in the name of Honors English. Not that Farbinger would see it that way, but hopefully he wasn't the one who would catch me.

Amanda was such a chicken. She claimed she wanted to make the extra effort, but where was she? Sitting in her algebra class while I took all the risks. Last night, I'd spent half an hour on the phone trying to convince her the only way to really test the custodians was to skip class and see if they noticed students in the halls who shouldn't be there. But she wouldn't do it. She didn't want to break any rules. Now that we'd decided to save Yoda's and the other jobs, getting in trouble was a chance SuperUnderdog was just going to have to take. With or without her chicken sidekick, OverAchiever! After about ten minutes I began to wish I'd chosen a better hiding place. For one thing, it was freezing in the washroom. For another, it didn't smell too good.

I tried reading *The Night Gardener* while I waited. Our latest English assignment was a free choice from the grade 7 summer reading list that we hadn't already read, and this book was seriously freaky in a good way, but it was hard to turn the pages with icicles for fingers. After a million years or so I decided I'd stuck it out long enough. Poking my head into the hallway, I scoped the scene before I committed myself. Coast was clear. I ran down the hall to two groups of lockers perfect for hiding between. More waiting. Ten minutes later, a familiar whistle warned me my plan was about to take off.

I peered around the lockers and there was Yoda, early to work as usual, carrying a bucket. When he was practically in front of me I dropped my book. He stopped whistling and looked around, confused. Then he saw me.

"Hi, Sooooz Tamaki." He picked up the novel and handed it back with hands pink and puffy from years of cleaning chemicals.

"Hey, Yoda."

"What you doing out of class?"

"Nothing."

"You skipping?"

I smirked.

"No skipping, Sooooz Tamaki. You go to class now so you be smart like sister, Tracie Tamaki."

Great. Bring Tracie into it. "All right, Yoda. I'm going."

I pretended like I was heading to class, but when I got to the side door I ducked outside. We'd been blessed with one of those rare dry days in November, and I'd seen Mr. Franklin and Morty outside earlier cleaning gutters and thought they might still be out there. Walking around the school grounds gave me a whole bunch of new problems, though. All the classrooms on the south side looked out on the schoolyard, so if I crossed the grass everyone inside would see me.

I glued myself to the wall while I strategized. Before I could make a decision, Mr. Franklin and Morty came out the same door I'd just slipped through. I couldn't have looked more guilty if I'd tried.

"What're you doing out here?" Mr. Franklin asked.

"Uhh…"

"Smoking?" He sniffed the air, scanning the ground for butts.

"No. I wasn't smoking. How dumb do you think I am?"

"Skipping, then? What's your name?" Franklin said. I made a mental note that he didn't know my name.

"Suze, right?" Morty asked. "Oh, she's all right. She's that floor hockey star's sister. You know, Tracie Tamaki. The one who always made sure the gear got put away after practice."

Jeez. I didn't know Tracie was so popular with the janitors. Especially since she hadn't gone to my school in years. I should've been dropping her name all along.

"You're her sister?" Franklin asked.

"That's what my dad says."

"Huh. Well, get to class."

"I'm going. I'm going."

As I walked away I overheard Franklin say to Morty that I sure was surly. Cool. I'd always sort of liked that word to describe me. Surly Suze. It had a nice ring to it.

I couldn't *actually* skip too much or I really would get in trouble, so over the next few days I pretended to be queasy in six different classes and took extra-long washroom breaks, instead. As soon as whatever teacher I could con into giving me a pass would let me out, I'd wander around, pretending to be skipping to see if anyone would notice.

Three times I got caught by Yoda, twice by Morty,

and once by Franklin. He was going to drag me down to Farbinger's office, but lucky for me we were outside again and a big gust of wind caught his toupee and tugged at it. He could feel it flapping around and saw me trying to keep a straight face.

"*Get to class!*" he screamed at me, clutching his head, and I ran off practically doubled over with laughter.

By Thursday night I was feeling convinced that A) the custodians notice when kids skip, and B) I was pressing my luck if I tried it again. That's when I got the brilliant idea of going to the high school. I waited until Dad was watching his fishing show on cable. When he was good and into it I approached him.

"Hey, Dad? I need a note to go on a field trip."

"You write it, I'll sign it." As predicted.

"Oh, sure. Okay." I pulled a blank piece of paper and a pen out from behind my back and handed it to him. "Sign this now and I'll write it before I go to bed."

He didn't even look up. He signed the blank piece of paper like he'd done so many times before. I used to feel guilty about tricking him like this but not anymore. I figured if he was slacker enough to sign a blank piece of paper, well, that was his problem. He should pay more attention to his kids.

At my desk, in my best handwriting, I wrote myself a note. *Please excuse Susan from first through fourth period. She had a dentist appointment.* I added Dad's work number so they could call him, because I knew they wouldn't.

On Friday morning I left before Tracie got up and went to the doughnut shop near the high school for breakfast. My plan was to roam the halls, both between classes and during, to see if any of the custodians noticed. If I saw Tracie or any of her friends, I'd tell them I'd prearranged it for my English project. They'd probably believe me. For a second I worried I was becoming a liar, but then I remembered I had to get an A or go back to Lame-o English. Plus, I needed to save Yoda's job.

The plan had seemed pretty easy in my bedroom the night before, but as I walked into the high school I was obviously smaller than everyone else and also alone, which really made a kid stand out. And not in a good way. Unfamiliar faces crowded around me, laughing, yelling, pushing. Amanda should've been here with me. It wouldn't have looked so suspicious. Especially since she's so tall.

I hadn't actually mentioned it to her in case she turned me in, but I knew she wouldn't have come anyway. After a while it seemed pretty clear no custodian was going to notice anyone in that crowd, so I found a washroom and hid out until homeroom began.

First bell rang and an eerie silence filled the school. I thought about aborting my plan and heading back to Maywood. But no! I had done this for a reason. SuperUnderdog was up to the challenge. I was not going to be conquered. I stood up straight, pulled my shoulders back and marched out of the washroom and *oof!*

I ran smack into Farbinger!

"What are you doing here?" we both demanded.

"You, young lady, are in a whole lot of trouble."

Farbinger made me sit in the high-school office under the evil eye of the receptionist while he had a meeting. One glance from her, and I didn't even bother pulling my book out of my bag to read. I was afraid the troll would eat it.

After about an hour, Farbinger came back and marched me to his car.

Dead silence on the drive back to the junior high.

Chapter 15

Farbinger called my dad at work. Since it wasn't technically an emergency, I had to sit there in the office until Dad could take his break and come to get me. About four o'clock, he dropped me off in front of our building.

"Sorry," I said again.

His face was stony. "We'll talk about it later."

When I walked into the apartment, the landline was ringing. "So how much trouble are you in?" Amanda asked when I answered it.

I shifted the phone to my other ear because my earrings were poking me. "How do you know I'm in trouble?"

"You weren't in class. And Leigh's sister saw you in the

office at the high school and sent her a text. It only took me about two seconds to figure out what you were doing. So? Did you get expelled this time?"

"Suspended," I said.

"For how long?"

"Two days. Monday and Tuesday."

"Did you tell Mr. Farbinger it was research?"

"He didn't ask."

"What do you mean?"

"He didn't ask," I said again. "Farbinger assumed I was up to no good, so I let him assume."

"Suze, why would you do that?"

"Because."

"Because why?"

Why *had* I sat there silently while he told me what a rotten kid I was? Because I didn't care what he thought. If Amanda had been caught doing everything I'd done this week, someone would've expected an innocent explanation from her, but not from me. I was always guilty without a trial.

"So what are you going to do?" Amanda asked.

"About what?"

I was totally sure I was home alone, so when a hand reached out from behind me and spun me around, I screamed bloody murder. *"AHHHHHHH! HELP!"*

Tracie grabbed the phone and pushed the End Call

button, disconnecting Amanda. By then, my heart had totally stopped. After a second it made a feeble attempt to start pumping again.

"*Oh, my God!* Where did you come from? I didn't think anyone was home."

Her eyes narrowed more than I thought possible. "I want to talk to you."

If looks could kill, I'd be one of those cadavers that they experiment on at the university (because my dad wouldn't be able to afford to bury me on his hourly wage). "How come you're not at hockey practice?" My rapid heartbeat made my voice shaky.

"It was cancelled today," she said, glaring at me. "And because it was, you're dead."

By now I was starting to feel a little bit more like myself, as in, I could breathe normally, and my heart had slowed down to its regular speed. "Why? What's your problem?" I tossed my hair like I didn't care and tried to get around her, but she blocked my way. That's when I noticed the giant red basket filled with food and wrapped in cellophane sitting on the couch.

"What's that?" I asked, curious.

"Oh, let's see…" she said, her voice dripping sarcasm all over the floor. She pulled a card off of it, and read aloud, "Susan, just a little something to say I'm sorry I had to work last Friday and messed up our dinner plans, but happy you agreed to give me another chance. I'll pick you up at seven on Saturday night. Invite Tracie, too. Love, Caroline."

Oh, crud, crud, crud, crud, crud.

"You talked to her again?" Tracie demanded in this really evil, low voice she reserves for when she's about to beat me up.

"You read my card?" I said, trying to divert her from throwing a punch. "That's private!"

"I thought *you* cancelled dinner last week. I thought *you* were the one who blew Caroline off. Doesn't look that way to me."

There was no denying it. I put my hands on my hips. "Okay, fine. She had to work late, but I'm still the one who called it off when—"

"Obviously you only did it because I was sitting right there!"

Dang. She had me. The best thing to do was to get out while I could. I grabbed my gift basket, which was surprisingly heavy, off the couch and lugged it off to our room. The phone rang. Amanda. Too bad. I wasn't in the mood to talk to anyone. I heard the machine pick up. One of the many problems with sharing a room with Tracie is I can never get away from her. She followed right on my heels.

"You *said* the pact was a good idea," she said. "You signed it. Remember?"

"No, I don't remember. I was a little kid."

131

"You do, too. I know it."

I pulled my books out of my backpack, one at a time, concentrating on stacking them perfectly on my desk, so I wouldn't have to look at her.

"I can't believe last weekend you stood there and lied to me and Dad and Uncle Bill like that. You told us to our faces you were done with her."

I thumbed through my notebook, pulling out old notes and putting them in my recycling bin.

Tracie made a fist and knocked on my head. "Don't you get it? I'm trying to help you. Caroline's only going to mess you up, and then you'll be like me and you won't trust anyone to stick around."

Did Tracie really not trust people? That was just stupid.

"*Hello?* Is anyone home? Suze? Are you listening to me?" she yelled directly into my ear.

It hurt, but I didn't even flinch. Instead, I tested my pens on a scratch pad, throwing away the dry ones. Tracie grabbed the little jar out of my hand and flung it across the room. I pushed past her and picked the container up off the floor. Meticulously I collected all the pens I could find.

"Suze, she *left* us."

I sat down on the bed and unzipped my boots.

"She didn't ask for custody. Or even weekend visits!"

Taking off my black jeans, I folded them neatly. It was four o'clock in the afternoon, but I didn't care. I climbed into bed and pulled the comforter over my head. Tracie yanked on the covers. I balled myself up and held on with all my might.

"Come out of there, you little brat. I'm talking to you."

She tugged. I held on. "Leave me alone," I said. "Just go away."

She tried grabbing down by my feet. I kicked at her as hard as I could through the covers. "Ouch!" she screamed. "I think you broke my finger."

"Good. Get away from me or I'll break them all!"

Tracie was practically snorting with anger now. She grabbed hold of me around the middle and tried to pull me off the bed. Blankets and all. The whole time she yelled the word *traitor* over and over and over.

"If you hate me so much, then go away!" I screamed back at her.

I tried to grab the sides of my mattress, while holding on to the covers, but I could feel myself sliding. With a loud thump I hit the floor like a landed fish. As I fell there was this huge ripping sound. The fabric gave way. My poor comforter—the only thing I owned that wasn't black. I peeked out from underneath it. Tracie stood over me, her hair loose from its ponytail, her face flushed, a large strip of pale green fabric in her hand. A piece of my comforter.

When I saw her standing there like that I snapped. I reached under my bed, located a hardback book and hurled it straight at her head. She saw it coming and ducked out of the way. I threw the covers off and put my face right in hers. For a second I wasn't sure if I was going to scream, cry, or kill her. Or all of the above. I must've looked mad because she took a step back, something Tracie never does. She's the toughest person on her hockey team and girls all across the league are scared of her. When she stepped back like that I knew she was mine.

"I'm calling a PST," I shouted at her. "*Get out.* I want PST."

She stared at me long and hard, grabbed her coat and backed out of the room. I heard the apartment door slam behind her. I sunk down onto the bed deflated, shaky.

It worked. I couldn't believe it. She actually left.

Shivering, I pulled my torn comforter around me and squeezed my eyes shut. I think I was in shock or something, because a minute ago I was sweating but now I was so, so, so cold. Maybe someone needed to slap me like on TV. What was weird about the whole thing was that from somewhere deep in my childhood, my reflexes had yelled out about the PST. I didn't even know I remembered that.

Private Susan Time.

Dad had come up with the idea when we were in grade school. The rule was if the fighting, or the sadness, or the frustration or whatever got so bad we desperately needed to be alone, we could call private time. If we did, then everyone else had to leave the room for one hour. Dad had never called one. But he had his own bedroom, so he could hole up there whenever he wanted. I think I'd only ever called PST the time my kitten died.

And the time Caroline showed up at Christmas.

It wasn't exactly true I hadn't seen her in ten years. She had stopped by the Christmas when I was seven. She'd breezed into the apartment with two huge foil-wrapped boxes. One gold. One red. One for me. One for Tracie. Tracie had run off to our room, but I'd torn into mine eagerly. When I got the box open, there was the most beautiful dress I'd ever seen. Sky blue with little white flowers, lace—yards of it. But it was for a little girl, a girl a lot younger than seven.

Caroline didn't even notice. After she'd left Dad and Tracie were sad, but I was fine. Except for my dress being too small, which was a bummer, I didn't really care about Caroline coming or going. She was a stranger by then. Tracie tried to explain that because she was my mom she should've known what size I was, but I still didn't get why it mattered. At least, not until I was older.

Tracie had called a PTT after Caroline left and spent her time writing the famous pact that she made me sign. I'd called PST then too, because back then I pretty much wanted to be just like my sister. Times had certainly changed.

As I pulled my torn comforter tighter, I wondered if it was just a coincidence I'd called another PST right after

Caroline reappeared. I forced my mind to go blank. I'm not sure how long I sat like that, but at some point a pounding on the front door snapped me back to reality.

I grabbed my jeans off the floor and pulled them on, then crept out to the hallway. The knocking got louder and more intense. Whoever was there rang the doorbell a couple of times in between knocks. Had Tracie forgotten her keys? Too bad. The witch could stay locked out until Dad got home. I smiled to myself until a man's voice yelled through the door, making me jump.

"Police! Open up!"

Chapter 16

Two RCMP officers stood on the porch, looming over me.

"I swear it was just my sister," I said, answering their question about what had happened for the third time. "She startled me and I screamed into the phone."

"Why didn't you pick up when your friend called back?" asked the male officer.

"I was fighting with my sister," I explained, hoping he had siblings and would understand. "She wouldn't let me near the phone."

Okay...that was only half true. But she probably wouldn't have let me answer it even if I'd tried. I was going to kill Amanda for calling the cops.

The female officer had her back to me, checking out the parking lot, while he fired more questions at me. "Where is your sister now?" he asked.

"Out. I don't know exactly."

I noticed the officer's name engraved on his badge. *Trampas.* "You alone here?" he asked.

"Yep."

"Mind if we take a look around?"

My mouth went on autopilot. "Do you have a warrant?"

He smiled. "Is there a reason why I need one?"

"I guess not," I said, moving out of the way. "I just thought I was supposed to ask you for one."

He grinned wider. "Not necessary in this case, unless you won't let me inside."

"Oh."

The officers stepped into the apartment, cautious, peering around corners. It was weird, like a movie or something. I looked around for the TV crew. Wouldn't that be cool to be on that show *Cops*? I'd really love it if they dragged Tracie away in cuffs yelling "It wasn't me. I didn't do nothing."

"I'm Jane Marley," said the other officer, shaking my hand. "What's your name?"

"Suze. Susan Tamaki."

"Nice to meet you," she said. "We're just going to make sure everything's okay, all right?"

I nodded.

"You wanna show us around, Suze?" Officer Trampas asked.

"Okay."

I was glad there was a woman here. I would've been uncomfortable letting a couple of men into the house, even if they were from the RCMP. They'd said Amanda called, but it didn't mean she really had. They knew her name, though. And she was a busybody, so I believed them. I showed them around the entire apartment. They even checked out the closets, the shower and under the beds.

"What are you looking for?" I asked them.

Officer Trampas said, "Someone you're afraid of could be hiding and you might be too scared to tell us. We want to make sure everything's copacetic."

"Oh." I wondered what *copacetic* meant. Probably fine or something. I'd look it up later.

"How old are you?" Officer Marley asked.

"Thirteen."

"Are you usually home alone?"

"Not always."

What was she getting at? I was old enough to stay home on my own. Until I started junior high I'd gone to AJ's after school, but last year, everyone had decided I could stay here until Tracie got home from hockey, and AJ had gone back to working full-time.

"Where's your mother?" asked Trampas.

"I don't know."

He stopped looking under the couch. "What do you mean you don't know?"

"I live with my dad."

"Oh. Right. Where's your dad?"

"Work. Sabin's Sporting Goods."

"Well, Susan," Officer Marley said, "everything seems to be in order here."

"If you've told us everything," Trampas added.

I was starting to panic a little. What did they want from me? Where was Tracie, anyway? Why didn't she come home and explain? Then I heard the front door bang open. Whew—now she could back up my story.

"Suze?" Dad called from the entry hall. "Are you okay?"

I sighed. *Great. Just great.* "Yeah, Dad. In here."

"Amanda called me at work," he said, hurrying into the living room. He grabbed me in a bear hug. "Did something happen? Why is the RCMP here?"

Oh, God. I was going to kill her. "I'm fine. Everything's fine."

"Will someone please tell me what's going on?" Dad asked, looking at the officers.

"Your daughter was talking on the phone to her friend when she screamed, yelled 'help,' and then hung up. The friend got worried when she called back and no one answered, so she dialed 911," Marley explained.

"Why'd you scream?" Dad asked me. I could tell he already had an inkling.

My whole life is so embarrassing. "Tracie. She startled me."

The look Dad gave me was totally different from what I expected. I thought for sure I'd be in huge trouble, but it was worse than that. Instead of mad, Dad looked exhausted. And disappointed. Definitely disappointed.

"Well, I think everything's under control," he told the police. "I'll take it from here. Thank you for checking on her."

He walked the officers to the door and I slipped away to my room. This was great, really fantastic. If Dad was disappointed in me now, just wait until Tracie told him I was going out to dinner with Caroline tomorrow night. Yeah. This was going to be some weekend.

Dad had to go back to work and he didn't get off until ten, so he gave me five minutes to grab my stuff and then drove me over to AJ's, where he dumped me off for the night.

"I'll see you tomorrow," he said.

Is this where I should tell him I'm going out with Caroline?

"Dad, I'm really sor—"

"I need to get going."

"Yeah, okay. Sorry," I said, climbing out of the car.

He'd called AJ while I was packing my bag, and she was waiting on the porch like she thought I might run away or something. I guess she didn't know there wasn't anywhere in the whole world I'd rather be than with her and Uncle Bill at that moment. The farther away from Tracie I was, the better.

I expected AJ to be really grumpy, but instead she made my second-favorite dish, veggie lasagna and garlic bread, and was super friendly. This didn't actually relax me, though. Instead I was wary, waiting for her to lose it or lecture me, or something. And then it occurred to me maybe she wasn't aware of my suspension, or the fight with Tracie, and the RCMP's little visit. I didn't know what Dad told her when he called, so I wasn't really sure. When I finally decided to bring it up, though, I knew she'd heard because she shook her head.

"Haven't you had enough drama for one week, Suze? Do we have to discuss it at the dinner table?"

"Uh, no. Definitely not," I said.

"Because seriously, I've had plenty of turmoil at my job."

She went on to tell us all about a co-worker who got in trouble for selling homemade tamales in the lunchroom and how management didn't want her bugging the rest of the employees, except everyone *wanted* to buy her food because it was so good. Now there was a big battle going on between management and the employees, and the union might even get involved.

I'd pretty much stopped listening by that point. It didn't seem that exciting compared to my own life. But I was glad AJ was talking. Especially since, for once, I wasn't the one she was upset about.

After we cleared the table, AJ asked me if I wanted to take a bath in her private bathroom. Uncle Bill had to use the one in the basement because he was a slob. I jumped at the chance because she's got this beautiful claw foot tub. We only have a shower in our apartment and AJ's got big fluffy towels and bubble bath too.

"Yeah. Can I?"

"You may," she said, correcting my grammar. Usually I ignored her when she did that, but now that I was in Honors, I should probably try to talk better, so I made a mental note of it. "May I?"

"Yes, you may," she said, smiling.

"Thanks."

It wasn't until I'd gotten the temperature perfect, and I was soaking deep in rose-scented water that I realized I forgot to lock the door. The reason I knew that is because AJ walked right in.

"Hey, I'm in here," I reminded her.

"I know. I want to talk to you."

"How about after my bath?" I asked.

"How about now."

Only it wasn't a question. Too bad I didn't realize

until too late that the offer of a bath was actually her way of trapping me so we could talk. I bet Tracie never would've fallen for it.

"I hear you've rescheduled dinner with Caroline for tomorrow night."

"Tracie's got such a big mouth."

"It wasn't your sister. Caroline called your dad. He has custody, you know. She has to clear those kinds of plans with him first."

"Oh."

"So…there are some things you need to know about her."

"Finally," I said. "No one tells me anything."

AJ had been pacing ever since she came into the bathroom and she didn't stop now. "First of all, and I'm not saying this to turn you against her, but she can't be trusted."

"What do you mean? Like she's a compulsive liar?"

"Not exactly." She ran her hand through her hair. "Not at all, really. But she says she'll do one thing, and then she doesn't always come through."

"Like be our mom?"

"Exactly. I just don't want you to get your hopes up."

"In what way?"

"Keep in mind this is only one dinner. That's all. She's not necessarily coming back into your life for good. Be cautious and—"

There was a light tap on the partially open door and

Uncle Bill stepped into the bathroom. "Jenny? What're you telling her?"

"Hey! I'm in the bath!" I reminded them both.

"We're having a little talk," AJ told him.

"Hello?" I said. "I'm not a little kid anymore. Can I have some privacy?"

Uncle Bill covered his eyes with his hands. "In a minute, Suze. Now, what were you and your aunt talking about?"

"Nothing," AJ said before I could answer.

Uncle Bill turned toward her voice, his hands still over his eyes. "You know, I wish you all would stop trying to turn Suze against Caroline before they've even had a chance to talk."

I was only half listening as I frantically tried to move what was left of the bubbles into strategic locations.

"No one's trying to turn Suze against Caroline. She's done a pretty good job of it herself, if you ask me."

"No one did ask you, Jenny."

"If you're just going to talk to each other, could you do that somewhere else?" I asked.

Uncle Bill, still covering his eyes, turned toward me. "Suze. You should go out with your mom and decide for yourself what kind of a relationship you want with her."

"*If* you want a relationship," AJ added.

"Great advice," I said. "But I'm in the bath here. Could we talk about this later? *Please?*"

"In a minute, Suze. I want to make sure—"

"Bill, I'm not trying to poison Suze's mind," AJ said. "But she needs to be careful."

"Okay!" I practically screeched at them. "If I promise to be careful and have an open mind, will you both get out of here?"

Uncle Bill felt his way along the counter and sat down on the fuzzy toilet seat cover. *Great. Make yourself comfortable.*

"Listen, Suze…" he said. I sunk as low as I could under the water, one hand across my chest and the other trying to cover my girl parts. Why couldn't anyone in this family remember I was thirteen, not seven? "I want you to know that in spite of what the rest of this family thinks of Caroline, she does love you—"

"I never said she didn't," AJ said.

"And," Uncle Bill continued, "she knows she made some mistakes. She'd like a chance to fix things if she can."

AJ lunged forward and grabbed Uncle Bill's arm, as if suddenly realizing what I'd been saying all along. "Bill! You shouldn't be in here while Suze is in the bath!"

He snorted. "I've got my eyes covered. Besides, I've seen Suze naked her whole life."

"Well, she's a teenager now! Get out." She hoisted him up by his arm and led him toward the door.

"I'm going. I'm going. But Suze—give Caroline a chance, okay? She really needs it at this time of her life."

With that bit of wisdom, AJ shoved him out the door and closed it behind her. As they walked away, I heard her say, "Yeah, well, the girls could've used her over the last ten years, but it didn't suit her schedule, did it?"

Her schedule? I sunk down into the tepid water. From now on I was going to stick to showers in washrooms with locked doors.

If AJ or Uncle Bill thought that little conversation was enlightening in any way, they were wrong. I was more confused than ever. I did know one thing, though. If Caroline was half as crazy as the rest of my family, we'd get along fine.

Chapter 17

On Saturday night, Caroline and I were stuck in bumper-to-bumper traffic on Douglas Street, but her car had seat warmers and a great stereo, so I didn't mind too much. She'd picked me up at AJ's and all the so-called adults in my family—Dad, AJ, and Uncle Bill—had hidden behind the curtains to peer out, while I picked up my backpack, a borrowed sleeping bag, and Caroline's gift basket and ran down the steps to the driveway. After dinner, she was dropping me off at Amanda's for a sleepover.

Caroline had gotten out of her fancy car to come up and say hello, but when she saw me, she looked relieved that she didn't have to and got back into her car pretty fast. We drove without saying anything for a while.

As we waited for some people to cross at a red light, Caroline broke the awkward silence. "I'm sorry to bring you all the way across town," she said, "but downtown's the only part of the city I'm familiar with."

"Didn't you grow up in Victoria?" I asked.

Caroline gave me a sideways look as she drove the car forward slowly and then finally to a stop in front of a crowded parking lot. "Well, yes. But I meant the restaurants. A lot changes quickly in that business."

"Oh."

A young guy in a blue jacket came around and opened Caroline's door. She climbed out of the car, her short skirt creeping up. The guy took her place in the driver's seat and smiled at me.

"Hi," I said, smiling back at him.

"Ummm...hello." He sat there, staring at me in a politely vague sort of way. Caroline rapped on my window. I pushed the button, and it slid down.

"Get out, Susan. He wants to park the car."

"Oh, right. Sorry."

I climbed out. How dumb could I be? I knew he was the valet, but I thought I was supposed to ride along and wait for him to open my door. Why did my dad even let me out in public?

The restaurant was tiny, crowded, and smelled spicy. Couples snuggled at intimate tables, candlelight casting a warm glow in their eyes. The place reeked of money. I hoped Caroline had brought her gold card.

"I have a reservation," she told the guy behind the podium. "Caroline Walker."

Walker? Who was Walker? One thing I knew for sure about Caroline was that her maiden name was McIntyre. I knew because I had a Grandma and Grandpa McIntyre when I was little and they were her parents. They both died right before Caroline split, and no one in my family ever talks about them.

Also, I had done a lot of Google searches on both Caroline McIntyre and Caroline Tamaki, but so far I hadn't found anything. No wonder. She was obviously using an alias. I wondered if that was so Tracie and I couldn't find her if we tried. If so, it had worked.

"Right this way," said the host or maître d' or whatever you call those people in a fancy-schmancy place like that.

At the table, he pulled out Caroline's chair, and she sat down gracefully. I tried to slip into mine quickly to avoid mishap. Instead I bumped the table so hard the glasses clinked against each other, wax slopped over the candle and extinguished the flame, and two or three forks clattered to the stone floor. I dove under the table to pick them up and clobbered a waiter with my elbow. In my defense, he did appear out of nowhere. It was like one of those stupid old movies. Only we didn't suddenly fall in love. Would Caroline miss me if I stayed under the table?

"I'll get fresh silver," the waiter said, straightening up and relighting the candle.

Back in my chair, I opened my menu and stared at it blankly. "Who is Walker?" I asked from behind my curtain of bangs.

"I beg your pardon?"

"Why's your last name Walker?"

"Oh, that. Well, I was married since I saw you last."

For a second I thought she meant she'd gotten married since Halloween, and then I got it. "Since you took off, you mean?"

"Yes. I suppose I do."

"So, are you still married?"

"No." She kept her eyes fixed on the wine list. "Not exactly."

"You've been divorced twice?" I guess that was rude but it popped out. One divorce is serious enough, but two in ten years? That's huge.

"I'm a widow," she said.

Oh, God. I am so lame. "Sorry," I mumbled into my menu.

"You didn't know," she said into hers.

Great. Very smooth, Suze. Let's see...so far I'd insulted her knowledge of the city, sat in the car like a dork, clobbered the waiter, and stuck my foot in my mouth so far I could taste my knee. *Hmm...yeah...dinner with Caroline. What a good idea.*

"May I get you a drink?" the waiter asked, popping up again without warning and placing silverware in front of me. He moved quickly around the table and stood behind Caroline's chair. Didn't want to get too close to me, I guess. Smart man.

"Yes, I'll have a six ounce glass of the Beringer," Caroline said.

He turned to me.

"Uh…lemonade?"

He smiled. "I'll be right back with your drinks."

We sat there studying our menus until he returned, placing glasses in front of us, and asking if we were ready to order.

"We might need some more time," Caroline said, "but we can order our starters now. I'll have the steak tartare."

A starter? I scanned the menu frantically. The word *tartare* caught my eye in a list of items under *Beginnings*. "Umm…this one," I said, pointing to *Salade au chevre chaud.* "It doesn't have meat, right?"

"Correct," the waiter said.

I had no idea what the heck it was, but it had the word *salade* in it, which I was pretty sure meant it was a salad of some kind. I could've chosen something in English, like the olive platter, but I only like the green ones stuffed with cheese that come in a jar. Somehow, I doubted any olives they served here would be the same.

"I'll give you a few more minutes," the waiter said as he left.

A few minutes for what? I wondered.

Through my lashes, and a mask of bangs, I watched Caroline sip her water. She clicked her claws on the tabletop. Today they were a weird shade. Not orange exactly, but an autumn color. Sort of burnt pumpkin. Kind of gross, really.

"I'm having the braised rabbit," she said.

I wrinkled up my nose. How sick. Who would eat a poor little bunny rabbit?

She must've seen the look on my face. "Oh, I'm sorry. Are you a vegetarian?" she asked.

"No," I said. "I eat fish."

She looked puzzled. "Don't some vegetarians eat seafood?"

I shook my head. "Nope." She was still frowning, so I explained. "Vegetarians don't eat any animals. Vegans don't eat any animals or animal products, like honey. People who eat fish but call themselves vegetarians are just misguided."

I didn't explain that I knew this because Amanda had totally embarrassed me at the lunch table in grade five. I'd been calling myself a vegetarian and she proved me wrong in front of everyone, reading the definitions aloud from an app on her phone.

"Oh," Caroline said. "I see. Do you want me to change my steak tartare?"

I shook my head. "I don't care what you eat."

"What are you having?" she asked.

"That salad thing."

"That's just the starter. You have to pick an entrée."

An ontray? Oh, then I remembered from French class. *Entrée.* "Uh, right. Okay." *Why couldn't we have gone out for fast food?* I opened the menu just as the waiter came back to take our order. "You go first," I told Caroline.

She asked a couple of questions while I tried to figure out what to order. I think maybe she was stalling for me. The only thing that looked even remotely familiar was the seared tuna, so that's what I finally ordered. But before the waiter took my menu from me I noticed the price of my dinner. Forget the gold. Caroline would need a platinum card.

When we were alone, she said, "Tell me about school."

Great. My favorite subject. Should I start with my impending suspension? Or maybe she'd like to hear about my hot English teacher. That might interest her. Or I could tell her about my friend Amanda who freaks out and calls the cops for no reason. That would be an entertaining story.

"School is just school," I finally said. "It's really not that exciting."

"What grade are you in now?"

What planet is this woman from? How could she possibly be my mother and not know what grade I am in? Maybe she isn't really my mother after all. Maybe she's some weirdo out to kidnap me…. Who am I kidding? Why would anyone want to kidnap me? "Grade seven."

"Junior high. Kind of sucks, doesn't it."

I laughed, surprised. "Yeah, pretty much."

"High school will be better," she said. "It was the best time of my life."

"Really?"

"Well," she said, actually cracking what appeared to be her first real smile of the evening. "It was good and bad."

"It was the best of times," I said. "It was the worst of times."

"What?"

"Dickens. He wrote that."

She raised one of her perfectly drawn-on eyebrows. A trick she'd probably practiced a few thousand times in front of the mirror. That's how I learned to do it. I raised one eyebrow back at her. I couldn't believe I knew more about books than a grown-up. I hadn't actually read the book, but it was a question on some quiz show. The more TV I watched, the smarter I got.

Giant pause.

Not the good kind where everyone's comfortable. No. It was the kind of silence where all the conversations at the other tables seem really loud, even though you know they aren't. I drew invisible designs on the tablecloth with my index finger and Caroline sipped her wine.

When my salad finally came there were these weird whitish hockey-puck things on the plate, hot and apparently fried. It seemed to be some kind of cheese. Wispy curly green and purple leaves decorated the plate, and the chef had drizzled an oily red dressing over it all. I was pretty surprised, but I pretended like it was exactly what I'd expected. Luckily it wasn't too gross or anything.

Out of desperation to fill the silence while we ate, I made the mistake of mentioning Amanda and our project. I managed to keep my big mouth shut about Honors English, though. I was trying not to think about that too much, because it made me break out in a sweat.

"Your project sounds very interesting," Caroline said. "So you're going to do the presentation for the school board?"

"I guess." I nibbled on one of the cheesy pucks. It was kind of tangy and soft like cream cheese. Not bad.

"You don't know?" Caroline asked.

"Yeah, I *do* know." Now she was acting like Baker. "We *are* doing it," I said.

I'd had to give in to Amanda's insane idea because what were my choices, really? Do it and make a fool of myself, or not do it, have to go back to Lame-o English, and have Amanda flounce all over school telling everyone how I ruined her GPA. I didn't really give a flip about her grade, but listening to her rant was another thing altogether. Also, Yoda was counting on me—even if he didn't know it.

"Remind me closer to the date," Caroline said. "I'd like to come."

"You would? How come?"

"Well, I am a parent, and this affects us all. Besides, I've never seen you give a speech before."

Yeah, well, she'd never seen me do a lot of things before, and I doubt she'd lost much sleep over it. Why wasn't it important when I landed my first fish? Or how about the time I skated all the way around the ice without falling when I was six? Where was she when AJ was a pinch-hit-mom and taught me how to bake Christmas cookies, or when Tracie had to tell me the facts of life?

"Well, if you want to come," I finally said, mostly for something to say, "I guess that would be all right."

"Great. I'll call you," she said.

"Maybe I should text you."

"Why?"

I poked at the salad wisps. "The thing is…Tracie's really, really mad at me for talking to you," I said. "I just think it's better if you don't call."

"I understand."

For a second her face crumpled around the edges, and I think she understood all too well. Then the happy plastic expression she wore all the time replaced her disappointment like lightning, but it couldn't hide her eyes, and I could see what I'd told her had hurt. But Tracie was hurting, too. Even if Tracie was acting stubborn, I guess she had a right to be mad too.

And that gave me an idea. I hadn't wanted to do the school board thing before, and I still didn't, but…if Caroline was going to come to it, and Dad, Tracie, AJ, and Uncle Bill were there too…and they were all rooting for me…maybe they'd be so proud of me, especially once the school board voted to keep the janitors, maybe they'd…I don't know… sort of come together, or forgive each other. And if Tracie saw Caroline there, then she might realize our mom was serious about being here for us this time. Assuming she was.

I finished the *salade* and glanced around the restaurant so I didn't have to come up with something else to talk about. And that's when I saw her.

I couldn't believe it. *Seriously?* Anger raced through me and my face heated up. This was unbelievable. "I have to go to the washroom," I told Caroline.

"Okay."

I got up, my chair making a loud scraping sound against the stone floor, and wove my way through the tiny tables. As I passed the one in the back, tucked into the darkest corner, I hissed, "Washroom. Now!" and kept going.

By the time AJ opened the door to the tiny washroom I was standing there, my arms crossed and my teeth bared. "What are you doing here?" I demanded.

She actually had the nerve to shrug and try to play innocent. "I just felt like going out to eat."

"An hour ago you were making dinner!"

"That was for your dad and Uncle Bill. I wanted a little 'me' time."

"And what? You just happened to choose *this* restaurant?"

She shifted from foot to foot. Someone tried to push the door open. The room was pretty small and AJ isn't, so she had to step closer to me, and the woman scooted in around her and slipped into one of the two stalls.

"So you're just taking yourself out to dinner?" I whispered to AJ. "Not here spying on me?"

"Of course not!"

I stamped my foot like a two-year-old having a tantrum. "How stupid do you think I am?"

"All right. It's not a coincidence. But I wasn't spying on you. I just wanted to make sure you were all right."

"What'd you think she was going to do to me in a restaurant?"

AJ's pudgy face had turned a little pink, and she nodded. "You're right. It was stupid of me. I'll…I'll get my food to go."

I let out a noisy sigh of frustration. "Oh, just…eat it here. But don't talk to us. I don't want her to think I'm a baby and you had to come along."

"I won't even look over at you. I'll get the waiter to move me to a table in the bar. And Suze…I'm sorry."

Part of me wanted to thump AJ, but instead I grabbed her in a quick hug and then ducked around her and back out into the restaurant.

"Everything okay?" Caroline asked when I came back.

"What? Yeah, sure. Fine."

We sat there, kind of smiling, kind of not. So awkward.

Waiter to the rescue. He set my tuna down in front of me, and it was tiny. Three stalks of asparagus tented over it, tied with what looked like a green onion. Two new potatoes rolled to one side. When I cut into it, the tuna was raw and almost completely red in the middle. I ate the potatoes and the asparagus.

Caroline cut into the little stack of meaty bones on her plate while I watched through my shield of hair. It looked like chicken, but I knew she was a heartless woman chowing down on the Easter Bunny. What she didn't ask, and I wasn't about to explain anyway, because it was personal, is why I didn't eat meat.

When I was little, AJ told me that I should only eat things I was willing to kill myself. She told everyone that, but the rest of my family ignored her. I took it to heart, though. I was willing to catch a fish, and I knew how to gut it and even cook it, so I ate fish. But I couldn't really see myself butchering a cow or plucking a chicken, so I gave meat a miss.

"Don't you like your tuna?" Caroline asked when she noticed me not eating.

"Ummm…" I leaned across the table and whispered to her, "It's not cooked all the way."

"It's seared," she explained. "That means they flash cook the outside. That's how it's supposed to be."

"Oh."

Figures. Rich people liked their food raw. Oysters, salmon, even hamburger. That's what her steak tartare was. I saw it once on the Food Network.

For the rest of the night we exchanged small talk, but my mind was far away, trying to figure out the best way to get my family to sit together at the school-board meeting. I had a feeling that if I could save the janitors' jobs and make everyone I love proud of me, they'd realize it was worth trying to get along. And then I could have a fair shot at getting to know Caroline for real.

Chapter 18

I'd only agreed to go to dinner with Caroline if we weren't too late and she took me to Amanda's afterward, because we'd already planned a sleepover. AJ thought I should be grounded for being suspended, but I'd explained to them I'd been doing research and Dad let me off. Besides, this was the first sleepover we'd invited Jessica to, so I could hardly miss it.

When Caroline pulled up in front of Amanda's, I jumped out of the car and she popped the trunk so I could get my overnight stuff and the giant gift basket that I'd brought along to share. But then I stood there on the sidewalk with the door open, not sure how to say good-bye.

"Call me anytime," she said.

It seemed weird to just walk away. I stuck out my hand, but instead of taking it she fumbled around in her purse and gave me a card. "Here's my home address and cell. Work number, too. Call me there if that's more convenient."

"Okay."

"Susan?"

"Yeah?"

"Can I ask you something?"

"Sure."

"What happened to your hair?"

How rude! Did I comment on her faux blond? No! "Nothing happened to my hair," I said. "It grows this color."

"Really?"

Was she actually stupid or trying to be cool? "Why?" I asked.

"No reason. Except I thought you might like to visit my stylist before your big speech. My treat."

I allowed myself to imagine a salon as fancy as the restaurant we just ate at, but then I shook it off. "I'll let you know."

I slammed the car door and flew up the walkway without looking back. I don't know why it made me mad, her mentioning my hair like that. I guess because it seemed like she was throwing her money around to show off or something. If she wanted to help, she should have paid more child support, not taken me to fancy restaurants where I didn't know what fork to use.

I'd barely knocked when Amanda threw open the door and warm air rushed out as usual. "Hurry up," she said.

"I've got an amazing movie picked out," Leigh said. "It's got this real gorgeous actor from Atlanta. You haven't heard of him yet, but—" Amanda dragged her off to the family room.

As I shut the door behind me, I caught a glimpse of my hair in the entryway mirror. It did look pretty bad. Maybe I would take Caroline up on the offer to get it fixed after all. What did I have to lose?

I changed into my slippers, and I could hear laughter drifting through the house. Amanda's dad, Steve, came down the hallway and wrapped me in a warm hug. "How's my favorite reader?" he asked.

"Good," I said, hugging him back. He was solid like a tree trunk, all muscle. "How's my favorite sports journalist?"

He ruffled my hair and gave me a friendly noogie. "Awesome, as usual."

Steve loved me because I was the only one of Amanda's friends who read his book cover to cover. I don't even think her mom made it through the whole thing. It wasn't like I was a big fan of baseball, but when someone I knew ended up on the *New York Times* Best Sellers list, I kind of had to read his book, didn't I? He even signed a copy for me.

"Read anything good?" he asked me.

"Ummm...*Death of a Salesman?*"

"Heavy."

"Suze?" Amanda yelled from the family room. "Talk about books later. Leave her alone, Dad!"

"You're in demand," he said.

"Always."

Steve grabbed my sleeping bag and pillow, carrying it through the kitchen to the back of the house for me. "I've got some books you might like," he said. "Don't leave without them."

"Okay. Thanks."

Steve's friend at the *Victoria Times Colonist* wrote reviews of teen novels and he gave them to Steve for Amanda, but she only liked sports memoirs, so I got them. Fine with me. I'd found some really good stuff in the piles he'd handed over.

"About time," Leigh yelled when I came down the steps into the sunken family room. Steve dropped my stuff and made his exit. "We thought Amanda's dad had dragged you off to talk baseball or read books!"

"Hey, Suze," Jessica said. She looked a little nervous, and I was sorry I'd left her here for hours on her own. One thing she probably hadn't been expecting was how loud those two got at sleepovers. I hoped they'd at least tried to include her.

"Hi, Jess."

"Finally, you're here," Amanda said. "How long was

your dinner, anyway? Is there food in that basket?"

"Yeah," I said. "All kinds of cool stuff."

I hadn't actually unwrapped the cellophane yet, because...well, the whole idea of Caroline sending me a gift basket seemed kind of weird. I had checked it out through the wrapping, and it was full of things like smoked almonds and chocolate espresso beans.

"Let's make the bed," Leigh said, "and then we can break it open."

Amanda's couch is this huge sectional and if you arrange it with the two ottomans in the middle and all the couches surrounding them, you can turn it into a giant, and I mean *giant*, bed. We've been doing it for years.

"Like this," I told Jessica, showing her where to push the loveseat.

Once we'd spread our sleeping bags and pillows out on it, we ripped open the gift basket. "Where'd you get it?" Amanda asked, tearing into a bag of gourmet gummy bears.

I felt myself blushing for some weird reason. "Caroline sent it to me."

"Why?" Amanda asked.

"Yeah, why?" Leigh wanted to know.

I popped some smoked almonds into my mouth and chewed them slowly, not sure what to say. I hadn't told anyone except Jess that she'd stood me up last weekend, so I just shrugged. "I don't know. Just to be nice?"

"It looks like something you'd send a client," Leigh said. "Not that I'm complaining. These chocolate-covered blueberries are delish."

I was kind of glad to hear Leigh say that, because I thought it was a weird thing to send to your kid too. I mean, what was I? Forty years old? Or someone she worked with? I crunched on caramel corn and tried not to hold it against Caroline. It was the thought that counted, right?

Sort of.

I guess.

"Oh, my God!" Amanda said. "There's a bottle of wine in here."

"No way."

"Yes way." She held up a small dark bottle with a gold foil top.

"It must be fake," Jess said. "Sparkling grape juice or something."

We all crowded around Amanda to see better. "It's real," she said. "It's Prosecco. My parents had that on New Year's."

"It's our lucky night," Leigh said.

I rolled my eyes at her. None of us had ever had a drink, except maybe a sip of beer from our parents. "I still don't think it's real," I said.

"Only one way to find out. Let's get glasses." Leigh grabbed the bottle from Amanda and leapfrogged over the back of the couch. We ran after her, stumbling on the stairs, bumping into each other, laughing. Leigh had just managed to peel the foil off when Steve and Heather came into the kitchen.

"Whatcha got there?" Amanda's dad asked.

"Nothing," all four of us said at once.

He raised his eyebrows.

"Hand it over," Heather told Leigh, and she did. She held the bottle up to the light. "I can't see it without my glasses." She gave it to Steve, who read the label to her.

"Where'd you get this?" he asked.

"It was in Suze's gift basket," Amanda explained. "Her mom gave it to her."

"I don't think she knew there was alcohol in it," I said. "It was kind of buried under the snacks."

Steve popped the cork as if he'd done it a thousand times. He probably had. He and Heather belonged to a wine club and went to vineyards in the Okanagan for their holidays sometimes. "Perfect for two," he said, pouring it into a couple of crystal glasses.

"You girls stick to pop," Heather told us as they left, carrying my bottle.

"Well, at least we didn't get in trouble," Amanda said.

No, but only because Heather and Steve are cool.

We grabbed pop and went back to the family room to watch movies. I was glad it was dark, because my face burned with embarrassment. What was Caroline thinking?

* * *

"Are you awake?" I whispered to Jessica hours later.

"Barely," she said.

I told myself I should shut up and let her sleep, but she'd answered me, so I said, "Do you think the gift basket was weird?" For some reason, it was still on my mind even though all the snacks were history.

She propped herself up on her elbows. The light from the TV flickered across her face. I'd muted the sound once I was sure Amanda and Leigh were finally asleep, so it was totally quiet except for their deep breathing. "Weird how?" she asked.

"I don't know…I mean, isn't it a little strange to send your daughter a gift basket of food?"

Jess shrugged. "A little. Did she send it because of last weekend?"

"Yeah."

"So, she meant well."

"I guess."

"And it was kind of awesome," Jessica said, her eyes closing.

True.

I lay back on my pillow and stared up at the shadows on the ceiling. Yeah, maybe it was a weird gift to send your kid, but Jess was right. She meant well. And it was definitely yummy. Maybe when Caroline got to know me better, she'd send me baskets of books as apologies.

Or maybe, eventually, she wouldn't even have a reason to apologize.

Chapter 19

On Monday morning, Dad's voice crawled through a thick fog of sleep. "Suze, get up."

"Huh?"

"Get up."

I snuggled down under the covers. The mattress spring poked me in the shoulder and I shifted. "It's the middle of the night."

"It's five o'clock," he said, not going away. "Get up."

What was wrong with him? Why was he torturing me like this? One eye popped open and I spotted his shadowy figure hunched over my bed. "I got suspended, remember?"

"You're going fishing," he said, as if this news would excite me.

Fishing? Was he kidding me? Did he really have some half-baked idea about me spending my day off from school on the ocean? Well, he could forget it. I turned back over. He whipped the covers off and the cold air hit me like a wave cresting the side of the boat.

"Get up," he said. "Uncle Bill will be here in twenty minutes."

"Dad, I don't want to go fishing."

"Too bad. Twenty minutes." I clawed at the covers, but he disappeared with them into the night. Morning. Whatever. "Don't make me come back for you," he called.

I hunted around blindly for a blanket. If I could get warm I could go back to sleep and maybe they'd leave without me. No blanket to be found. *Dang.*

There was only one option.

"Shove over," I said to Tracie.

Apparently she didn't like the feeling of my frosty feet against her warm legs. "What are you doing?" she screeched.

"Dad took my covers."

"What? Get out of my bed. DAD!"

I'm not sure if he pulled me out or she kicked me off the mattress, but thirty seconds later I found myself in the kitchen with a cup of coffee in my hand and Dad standing over me. "Why can't I stay home?" I begged.

"You used to love fishing."

"Yeah, when I was a kid," I grumbled.

He ignored me. This was crazy. The last thing I wanted was to go out on some boat at the crack of dawn in freezing cold weather and fish for phantom salmon.

"I don't have a fishing license," I tried.

"Got you one at work on Saturday."

"My rain gear is way too small."

"Bill's bringing Jenny's stuff."

"Her coat will be huge on me."

"We'll roll up the sleeves."

"I've got my period."

"That was last week."

How did he know that? Boy, my trump card was shot down like a stationary target. Not that you couldn't fish with your period, but usually just talking about anything girlie caused Dad to back down in embarrassment.

Now what?

There was nothing to do but get ready to go fishing. Fine. I'd go on the stupid boat, but he couldn't make me fish. I would keel over and die before I'd have any fun. And if he told anyone I went, I'd deny it. There was no way I was going to get all smelly and fishy. Forget it.

Ten minutes later Dad's phone beeped. "Uncle Bill's in the parking lot."

"I can't believe you're making me do this."

"It'll be fun," he said, marching me to the door. "Have a good time."

"Wait! What? Aren't you coming?"

"Not today. I've got stuff to do." He shoved me out the door and shut it behind me.

"This is so unfair!"

Uncle Bill sat in his car in the parking lot, the motor running. "BC is idle-free," I reminded him as climbed in.

"I didn't think I'd have to wait so long."

He backed out and headed for Sooke where he kept his boat. We didn't talk the whole way. In fact, I think I might've fallen asleep, because the drive seemed really short. It was no time at all before I was standing next to the car, pulling AJ's massive raincoat over my life jacket because it was too bulky to go underneath it. I didn't bother with the pants since I had on gumboots and the coat hung down almost to the tops of them.

"I look stupid," I told Uncle Bill.

"Yep," he said.

"Thanks a lot."

"No problem."

I'd been going out on boats my whole life, and Uncle Bill put me to work stowing our stuff in the little cabin, while he set up the downrigger. When it was time to go, I leaned over the edge and pulled in the bumpers after we were clear of the dock. The water was choppy, and a stiff wind bit at the exposed skin on my face. It had started to drizzle too. Yep. This was tons of fun. I kind of wished Farbinger had given me in-house suspension. I'd be at school stuck in the office, but at least it'd be warm and dry.

Once we were out far enough to fish, Uncle Bill killed the engine and turned on the trolling motor so we'd move really slowly and drag our line out behind us. I watched as he put a ten-pound weight on the downrigger line. "You want to do it, Suze?" he asked.

I looked away. It's not like I was interested. "No, thanks." Dad could make me go on the boat, but I wasn't casting out a line. The thrill I used to get as a kid was long gone. Uncle Bill wrapped his line around his hand, twisting it five times, and then snapped it into the release clip. After he'd put the rod in the holder and tightened up the tension, he sat down to wait, the waves thumping against the side of the boat, sloshing my breakfast coffee around in my stomach.

"Couldn't you have told me whatever it is you want to say at the White Spot over blueberry pancakes?" I asked.

"Who says I have anything to say?"

"Why else would you trap me here?"

"I thought it'd be fun, actually."

I couldn't help shaking my head and laughing at that. *Fun? Seriously?*

"What?" he asked.

"When is everyone going to remember I'm not a little kid anymore?"

"Probably never if you keep getting in trouble at school."

We sat there in silence, while the rain methodically drenched everything around us. At least AJ's raingear was top quality, and I was dry underneath.

"We've been having lunch once a month. For a while now," Uncle Bill said, totally out of the blue.

"Who has?"

"Caroline and I."

"What?" I was so shocked that I literally rocked the boat as I turned to face him.

"I ran into her on my monthly business trip to Vancouver last June. We had lunch. And the next time I was there…well, we met again."

"Does AJ know?"

"She does now. But I didn't tell her at first, because I knew what she'd say."

"What would she have said?" I asked.

"Oh, probably something about how I was opening old wounds."

I stared at Uncle Bill through my soggy eyelashes, trying to process what he was saying. Had he cheated on AJ with Caroline? Did they have an affair back when I was little, and that's why she left? And now they were back at it? My stomach lurched with the motion of the boat and I thought I might throw up. "So you're the reason she's back?" I asked.

He frowned. "No. *You're* the reason she's back. You and Tracie. I just encouraged her to give it a try."

"So you're not having an affair?"

Uncle Bill had just taken a sip of coffee from his Thermos bottle, and he spit it out with a spluttering cough. "An affair with Caroline? Hell no! Why would you even think that?"

"Well, sorry, but that's how you made it sound. Old wounds and all that."

"I meant Caroline's and your dad's old wounds. And you girls. And AJ, too."

"What's AJ got to do with it?"

"She and Caroline were roommates at university. That's how we all met. I was dating Jenny, and she fixed up Caroline with your dad."

"Oh." I'd never known that. But I didn't really know anything. Still, I was glad there weren't any affairs in their past. That would've made it a whole lot harder to want to be around Caroline.

Something tugged on Uncle Bill's line, and he jumped up just as the release clip snapped and his rod bounced up and down. He grabbed it, but before he could start to reel it in, the line went slack. Whatever it was had gotten away.

"So why'd you have lunch?" I asked while he reset the downrigger.

"She wanted to hear about you girls."

"And you told her?" I really didn't like the idea of him talking about me to a complete stranger, even if she was technically my mother.

"I didn't tell her anything personal," he said. "Mostly I encouraged her to come back."

"So this is all your fault?" It came out angrier than I meant it to, and Uncle Bill's face sort of crumpled.

"Yeah. I guess it is."

We sat in silence some more, the wind whipping my hair out from under AJ's hood and the rain making it stick to my face. Finally, I asked him the same question I'd asked AJ and she hadn't really answered. "Why does everyone hate Caroline so much?"

He shrugged again. "I guess because she just walked away without an explanation. She hurt a lot of people—your dad, AJ, you girls…me."

"But now you think she's changed? Or regrets it or something?"

"I don't know how much she's changed, but I know she regrets not being around for you and Tracie."

I thought about that. All this time, I'd kind of figured I'd been the one who got cheated because I didn't have a mother around. But maybe Caroline actually missed her daughters. "What do you think I should do?" I asked Uncle Bill.

He sat down next to me and reached out, moving the sodden hair away from my eyes, and said, "I think you should give her a chance."

"Even if it tears me and Tracie apart?"

He closed his eyes like this was all too painful to talk about. "Can I change my answer?"

"To what?"

"To—I have no idea what you should do?"

I bumped him with my shoulder in frustration. "No," I said. "You can't. Because you're the grown-up, and I need help here."

"The thing about being the grown-up," he said, "is that it really sucks sometimes."

"Yeah? Well, welcome to my world."

Chapter 20

When I'd gotten up to go fishing, Dad had made me pack an overnight bag, along with my homework, to take back to AJ and Uncle Bill's. I wasn't sure why I couldn't be at home because it was his day off, so it's not like I could have gotten into trouble, but he'd said it wasn't up for discussion.

Uncle Bill did end up taking me to the White Spot for breakfast, but we didn't talk about anything important. Mostly he told me why the Canucks would definitely win the Stanley Cup this year, and I pretended to be interested. Between Dad and Tracie's fanaticism, I knew enough to make intelligent comments that satisfied Uncle Bill. But mostly I let my mind wander to school and what I might be missing in Honors.

Part of the deal with being suspended is you are expected to do the homework, but you get zeroes for any tests you miss. I really hoped Baker didn't give a pop quiz on *Death of a Salesman*.

"Earth to Suze," Uncle Bill said. He was standing next to our table, putting his jacket on, holding the bill.

I jumped up. "Oh, sorry."

"You ready to go?"

"Yep."

Uncle Bill dropped me off at his house on his way to work, and AJ met me at the door. I followed her directions to leave the raingear outside and take a shower before lunch without question. When you got an order from AJ you didn't wait around to see if she meant it. This time, I made sure I locked the bathroom door, so I didn't have any visitors.

AJ and I get along fine, and she's cool most of the time, but unlike every other adult I know she does have expectations for me. Not just in school either, but in life. When she warns me about my grades she's not messing around. She was just as serious when she taught me how to bake cookies. She made me learn how to make seventeen different kinds before she decided I was well enough educated in the art of cookie dough.

After I'd dried my hair and changed into sweats, I went downstairs, and AJ informed me that she'd taken two personal days off work because I'd messed up, and we weren't going to waste them. I couldn't figure out why she'd stayed home when Dad had Monday and Tuesday off this week, but when I tried to ask she cut me off.

"Your father has stuff to do."

I ended up spending the rest of my suspension doing homework while AJ hovered. The trade-off was that the food was great, and there was no big sister glaring at me for forty-eight hours, which I thought was more than adequate compensation.

"When you've finished labeling the furniture on that worksheet," AJ said, leaning over me and smothering my shoulder with her huge bosom, "I have another blank one for you that I got off the Internet."

Great. "Okay."

I wondered what Jessica was doing. I bet she wasn't labeling parts of houses *en français*, even though she had to take the same test as me on Wednesday. Boy, was I stupid when I admitted to AJ that we had a midterm in French. In a matter of seconds she had my textbook open, my notes spread out, and my butt in the chair. She even scanned the worksheets I'd already filled out and removed the answers so I could do them all over again for practice.

What I couldn't figure out was why she was so interested in homework. She'd always expected me to keep my grades up, but she'd never been so hands on. Was this because I got suspended? Had Tracie told her about Honors English, and now she thought she could smarten me up? Had my father lost his job and she was preparing me to enter the work force? She was acting like somebody's mother.

Ohhhhh...slow old Suze. Of course! I wasn't suddenly Miss Popularity for no reason. It was my mother...good ol' Caroline. She'd certainly stirred the pot with her creepy long fingernails, hadn't she? It was almost like AJ was pretending she was my real mother, and there wasn't any room for anyone else.

Very interesting.

My devious mind wondered how I could benefit most from this situation. I've heard of kids playing their divorced parents against each other, but, quite honestly, I've never really thought of my parents as divorced. I guess they must be if Caroline remarried, but to me there wasn't any tragic breakup, mudslinging, or one parent waving their purchasing power in the other one's face. There were four of us for a while, then there were three of us for a long time, and now there were four of us again. Kind of.

"Suze?" AJ called from the kitchen.

"Yeah?"

"How about a break?"

"Great. My favorite quiz show's on in a few."

"I was thinking you could help me make dinner," she said, popping her red, doughy face through the little archway over the breakfast counter.

I stood up and stretched. "Yeah, sure."

Another mother-daughter moment? I didn't think so. AJ'd had plenty of time over the last ten years to step into the role, but although I could count on her as one of the adults I could go to in a crisis, I didn't think of her as my surrogate mom.

In no time at all I had a frilly yellow apron tied over my jeans, which was not my idea, and a pile of vegetables to chop for the salad. "So, what's this I hear about Honors English?" AJ asked.

I knew it. Tracie the Traitor.

"Huh? What do you mean?" I asked, playing the innocent. It never actually works, but it's a reflex. What can I say?

She lasered me with the no-BS look. I shrugged it off and acted totally casual. "It's not a big deal. I'm doing a project with Amanda, and so I'm sitting in on the Honors Class with her."

AJ flung a pinch of salt at her saucepan and then, without telling me what to do or anything, which she knows I hate, she simply crossed over to me to adjust the carrot on the cutting board and reposition my knife hand. Slicing was easier now, but I hoped I didn't have to learn seventeen ways to chop carrots. "What's your topic?" she asked, moving back to her pan.

"Janitors. I mean, custodians." Amanda had a heart seizure every time I called them janitors. "The school district wants to get rid of them."

"Ohhh…" she said, stirring slower and slower while she tried to remember something. "I've heard of that. Oh, I know. Trina, across the street, she works for the Malahat School District, and they did that."

"Yeah, I know. We've been trying to dig up some info on how it's going for them, but no one will answer our emails."

AJ stirred cream into the fish chowder and added some fresh dill. "Maybe you could interview her."

"Really? Cool."

"You can do it after supper if she's free."

My heart jumped a beat and I almost cut off the tip of my finger, instead of the green part of the carrot. "I don't want to interview Trina on my own," I said. "I need Amanda."

"Mrs. Blevins to you, not Trina," she said. "And you don't need Amanda."

"I could text her," I said. "Her dad will bring her over."

"You can do it on your *own*," AJ said. "Besides, I don't think Trina would want to talk to a bunch of people."

"Amanda's not a bunch of people."

AJ nailed me with her laser look again.

"Okay."

"I'll call her after we eat," she said.

✦ ✦ ✦

Joëlle Anthony

Once the table was cleared, I washed the dishes while AJ dialed Mrs. Blevins. "Trina, hi. It's Jenny. I wanted to ask you a favor."

I turned on the faucet to rinse a plate, drowning out most of what AJ said, because I didn't want to face her wrath if she thought I was eavesdropping. But when I shut the water off to scour the soup pot, the conversation sounded too interesting to ignore, so I took my chances, scrubbing very, very quietly.

"I see," AJ said. "Okay. Well, of course, I understand. It could be confidential, though."

I stretched my eardrums. It didn't sound like Mrs. Blevins wanted to be interviewed.

"Uh-huh. Well, if you feel that strongly then I certainly understand. Of course. Hey, don't sweat it. I'll see you at Weight Watchers on Thursday. Okay. Bye."

AJ hung up the phone and came out to the kitchen to dry. I kept scrubbing the already clean pot in slow circles, waiting for whatever she had to say. You don't rush AJ.

"She's afraid to talk to you," she said after a minute.

"What do you mean?"

"She's worried it could get back to the school district."

"What could get back?"

"Let's just say the whole 'firing the custodians' thing isn't working out too well, and she doesn't think she should talk about it."

Now I was really interested. "Not working out how?"

"I think we better drop it, Suze."

"Really? How come?"

"She's not only afraid it could get back to them. She's afraid of losing her job."

"What?" I said. "From talking to some kid for a dumb school project? What happened to freedom of speech?"

"There's another thing called confidentiality in the workplace. And your project may have farther-reaching consequences than you imagine."

I rinsed the pan and handed it to AJ. "Maybe if we went over there together."

She tossed her towel down on the drain board and gave me the look again. "I said we should drop it."

I tried to match her stare, but even though I learned it from her, I'm still the student and she's the master. "Yeah, okay."

"Don't forget that paper on *Great Expectations*," she said over her shoulder on her way out.

Sheesh. AJ must've spied in my notebook and seen my homework list. I watched her push through the swinging door into the dining room, her hips barely making clearance, and I thought again of the seventeen kinds of cookies we'd made over that grade six Christmas break. I don't even really like cookies anymore, and for the first time I wondered if that might have been her plan. Maybe she *was* a kind of mother to me, and I'd just never known it. After all, it isn't like I've had much experience with them.

Chapter 21

I picked up a baseball jersey and threw it in the hamper. Amanda looked up from her sports magazine. "Not everything on the floor is dirty," she said.

"How am I supposed to tell?" I picked up some more clothes and stuffed them in with the jersey.

"Yeah, I guess you can't. Mom'll wash it all, anyway."

Must be nice to have someone do your laundry. I tried to imagine Caroline doing mine and laughed.

"What?" Amanda asked.

"Nothing." I pushed her feet out of the way so I could search under the bed. She sprawled out on the mattress and flipped the pages. While it was true I was cleaning her room, I wasn't doing it out of the goodness of my heart. I was strictly in it for the twenty bucks. And if she was smart, she'd tip me, too.

"Maybe we should work on our project while you clean," she said.

"It depends," I said. "I don't want you doing anything messy."

"I won't. I'll use the computer. Have you seen it?"

I looked around for her laptop. If it was on her desk, it would be a while before I could unearth it. Then I spotted a corner of it sticking out of her closet and handed it over. She opened it up, but the battery was dead. "Now I suppose you want the cord," I said.

"Yep."

"Why's it dead, anyway? Playing computer baseball?"

"Yeah, and you should see me pitch," she said, her eyes lighting up. "I'm so good at this game. You wanna play against me?"

"I think I'm cleaning your room."

"Oh, right. Okay…the cord?"

I found it plugged into the wall.

"I just want to play one inning," she said. "To get my brain moving."

She must've thought I didn't know anything about baseball, because that one inning lasted so long that by the time she was ready to work, I'd made a ton of progress on her room. "Look," I said. "You can actually see your desk."

"Cool."

Then we both heard footsteps, and Amanda jumped up, and I dove for her place on the bed. By the time Heather opened the door, I was kicked back with the laptop and Amanda was fumbling around with the neat piles I'd made on her desk like she'd organized them herself.

Heather stood framed in the doorway, smiling at us and looking regal. She was so beautiful, sometimes I couldn't help staring at her. She was what my dad would call a stunner. It was pretty easy to believe she was once a big-time model. In the living room, there was a framed photo of her on the cover of Italian Vogue from when she was sixteen. "It's good to see your floor, Amanda," she said.

"Yeah, well what choice did I have? There is no way you're getting in here to clean."

"And I'm very grateful," Heather said.

I muffled my laughter.

"Mom, are you just checking on me?" Amanda asked.

"Actually, I came to tell you that your dad and I are going out to dinner, and the two of you aren't invited because it's a romantic night out."

Amanda and I rolled our eyes at each other. Her parents were so in love, it was sick. And kind of cool. "Suze," Heather said, "I'm willing to suspend my no-sleepovers on school nights rule if you two need more time to work."

"Oh, no thanks. I've been at my aunt and uncle's since

Monday, and I went to school from there this morning, so I'm thinking I need to go home tonight. For more clothes and stuff." Honestly, I was kind of missing my own lumpy bed.

"Okay," she said. "We'll give you a ride when we get back. That'll still give you a few more hours together. And there's leftover chicken in the fridge."

"Suze doesn't eat meat," Amanda reminded her.

"Oh, right. Of course. Sorry, Suze." She pulled a couple of twenties out of her wallet. "You can order Chinese food instead. Or raid the freezer for pizza."

I really hoped Amanda would choose the Chinese food, because I could do with some spicy Szechuan vegetables.

"Definitely Chinese," she said, grinning at me. She knew me so well.

"Okay. Have a good time. And remember, Mrs. Wadkins is home next door if you need her." She turned to go and then looked back at me. "It must be nice to have a friend like Suze to keep you company while you clean."

She was barely through the door before Amanda started cracking up, so I jumped up and clamped my hand over her mouth. She threw me down on the bed, the two of us giggling uncontrollably. We both knew her mom would *not* be cool with Amanda paying me to clean her room. That was our secret. And one I was happy to keep, because I would finally be able to buy some minutes for my phone.

✦ ✦ ✦

An hour and a half later we weren't laughing anymore.

There were two things you had to keep in mind when dealing with Amanda. One, she knew everything, and two, she was always right. Needless to say, our friendship wasn't always smooth skating on fresh ice.

"The meeting's right around the corner, Suze," she told me for the tenth time.

"I know."

I really knew. It was all I could think about. When I wasn't thinking about Tracie, Caroline, Baker, AJ, and all the rest of my schoolwork. Grade seven was turning out to be a lot tougher than I'd ever imagined it would be.

Amanda sat there staring at me. I glared back, but this time she didn't give in. "Don't worry so much," I said. "I'm getting graded on it too, you know."

"Yeah, well, my grades are important to me."

"And mine aren't?"

"Everyone knows you're a coaster."

She'd said it under her breath, but I heard her. I tossed the empty Chinese food container into the trash bag.

"What's that supposed to mean?"

"What?" she asked.

"I heard what you said. What do you mean? You think I just coast through school?"

"If the shoe fits."

"At least I'm not an overachiever."

"Whatever."

We sat there for five solid minutes, biting our lips to keep from saying what we really thought. I wanted to call my dad and ask him to come get me, but then Heather would want to know why I went home early. I crossed my arms and let my hair fall into my face so she couldn't see she'd hurt my feelings. Who did she think she was? It was just one little speech in the fabulous life of Amanda Whitmore. It probably wouldn't even affect her grade that much.

I, on the other hand, had everything riding on it. If I wanted to make it in Honors English, I had to do a totally awesome job at the school board meeting. And Caroline was coming. And Dad was getting off work early so he could come, and AJ and Uncle Bill would be there, too. Plus Tracie. Amanda's parents had seen her give a million-and-one speeches. She had nothing to worry about.

"This is a lot more important to me than you think," I finally said.

"Yeah, right."

"It is. You think you know everything, but you don't know the half of it."

"Whatever."

I stayed hidden behind my curtain of hair and said, "If I do well on this presentation, then Baker says I can stay in Honors English."

"Really?"

I flipped my hair back and glared at her. "Yes, really. Why is that so hard to believe?" Hot tears sprang up. I opened my eyes wide like a cartoon character to keep them from falling. If I blinked I'd be toast.

Amanda's face softened a little. "It's not hard to believe," she said. "Really. I didn't mean to sound that way. I'm sorry, Suze." She scooched over on the bed next to me and put her arm around my shoulder. "I'm really nervous about this. You know how I get before speeches."

"Yeah. Well…"

It was true. No matter how many overachiever things she did, Amanda always freaked out a little beforehand. Or a lot. I didn't want to forgive her, but we had a lot of work to do.

"I swear," she said, squeezing me closer, "I'm sorry. I didn't mean to make you cry."

I shook off her arm. "I have dust in my eyes from this disgusting room," I said.

Amanda laughed. "Yeah, that's it."

She gave me a second to pull myself together, and then she was back to business. "We're actually in good shape," she said. We have all our photos picked for PowerPoint, we can cite three examples of custodians deterring drug activity, plus the guy who took a bullet for a kid—that was in the US, but I think it counts. And I'll crunch a bunch of numbers to prove how ineffective it is cost-wise to subcontract those jobs."

"And we have the survey you did at the mall, plus I have all the little speeches written out." I did—in my mind, if not on paper. "All I have to do is type them up at school."

"You can use my computer," she offered.

I shook my head. "Thanks, but no thanks. Yours has too many fancy features."

The school computers were old and easy to use. True, they sometimes crashed and made you lose everything, but I didn't have to worry about breaking them. You couldn't pay me to touch Amanda's brand-new laptop.

"You should at least know how to hook it up," she said for about the billionth time.

"I know how. I'm not a total idiot," I reminded her for the zillionth time.

Again, we found ourselves glaring at each other. I don't know why Amanda has to pressure me so much. Then again, maybe based on my past performance, she *should* be worried.

After all…I was.

Chapter 22

When Dad picked me up, he smelled funny. It took me a minute to realize it was the paint splotched all over his clothes—a light blue, like the morning sky.

"What happened to you?" I asked.

He smiled. "You'll see."

As soon as we opened the door of the apartment the stink was overwhelming. It was that fresh but chemical smell that you only get from paint. I walked into a different living room than I'd left two days ago.

It wasn't one of those truly stunning makeovers you see on TV, but it was definitely different. The white walls, which actually had more of a gray tinge to them, were now the pale blue that was all over Dad's clothes. The thrift store lamp had been replaced with one of those tall, skinny black floor lamps, and there was a pale yellow area rug in front of the couch, covering a section of the ugly brown wall-to-wall carpet. "Wow."

"What do you really think?" he asked.

"It's great. You did all this?"

"Yep."

"How come?"

He shrugged. "It needed it, don't you think?"

"Well, yeah." But the fact he'd done it was still weird. We'd lived here for as long as I could remember, and every time Tracie and I had begged him to let us paint our room he'd told us it was a waste of money, because it was a rental, and we'd have to paint it white again if we moved out.

I flopped onto the couch and was surprised to see new yellow pillows and a soft throw. "Hey," I said. "Where's your stadium blanket?"

"In my room. It's getting kinda ragged."

"True." I had a hard time imagining Dad curled up watching hockey under a fuzzy yellow blanket, but he looked happy, so I let it go.

"You like it?" he asked.

"Yeah. Sure. It's nice." He looked like he wanted more so I added, "The lamp's cool."

He nodded.

I couldn't put my finger on it, but he was acting weird and it made my stomach a little queasy. What was up? "Well, I think I better get to bed," I said. The anxious way he was looking at me was freaking me out.

"Yeah, it's pretty late."

I stood up, but didn't leave. "Was this why I had to stay over at AJ's? So it'd be a surprise?"

He nodded. "Yep."

I wondered why he didn't send Tracie to AJ's too, so it would be a surprise for her. Probably because it's harder for her to get to her school from our aunt and uncle's house. But then it hit me: it had to be my sister's idea in the first place. Maybe she wanted to be nice for once, since she'd been so mean lately. "Did Tracie help you?"

His smile disappeared. "Uh, no. It was just me."

"Well, it looks good, Dad. I love it."

His smile came back and I gave him a hug. He held me close, stroking my hair like he did when I was little. "I'm glad you're home. I missed you."

"I missed you, too." When he didn't let go of me, I said, "I'm going to bed now."

He dropped his arms. "Okay. Night."

I'd only taken about two steps into our room, when Tracie sat up on her bed and said, "Oh, the princess returns."

"What's your problem?" I asked.

She glared at me. "You."

I tossed my school bag under my desk and started undressing. "What'd I do now?"

"Don't play Little Miss Innocent, Suze. You've got everyone bending over backward to make sure you're happy, and I'm sick of it."

I shook my head. "Seriously, Trace. I have no idea what's up your butt."

"AJ and Uncle Bill whip you off for two days of luxury and good food—"

"I went fishing and did homework. Hardly—"

"And Dad, who's never given a crap about this place, is suddenly sprucing it up."

"What's that got to do with me?"

"As if you don't know."

I pulled on the T-shirt and shorts I sleep in and jumped into bed. The sheets were like ice. I'd forgotten to brush my teeth, but I was too tired to bother. I snuggled down under my torn comforter. "Tracie?" I said. "Just tell me what you're mad about so I can go to sleep."

"You really don't know?"

She stood over me, making me nervous. I didn't like to be in such a vulnerable position when she was mad, so I sat up. The paint fumes were giving me a headache already. Or maybe it was my sister. Sighing, I said, "I really, really, really don't know."

"Caroline called and invited you to stay over at her fancy house."

"What?" My heart pounded around in my chest like it wanted out. Staying over at Caroline's wasn't something I'd even considered. After our dinner fiasco, I wasn't sure I had the nerve to spend that much time with her. "When?"

"I don't know," she said with a sneer. "But you can't tell me Dad trying to fix up this place is a coincidence. The last thing he wants is for you to go over there and see how nice other people have it when our apartment is cold, damp, and ugly."

Based on her clothes and jewelry, Caroline probably did have a pretty nice place, but how would Tracie know that? As far as I could tell, she hadn't even seen her in person. "How do you know Caroline has such a nice place?"

"I remember," Tracie said.

"You remember what?"

"Nothing. Never mind." She flipped off the light.

"But—"

"And shut up. I'm going to sleep."

I lay there for a long time, wondering where Caroline lived and what her place was like. Was Dad really worried I would like it better and want to move in with her? It seemed a long shot that he'd painted the living room and bought some pillows just to win me over, but he'd never shown an interest in the place before, so…maybe Tracie was right. He'd seemed nervous when I came in too. And that hug. He'd held onto me for so long.

Dad hadn't said much about Caroline to me, but he'd obviously been talking to her, if she'd invited me to sleep over. And if Tracie was telling the truth, whatever she'd said had made him worried he might lose me. I got out of bed and went back to the living room where Dad was camped out in front of the TV. The fuzzy new throw was folded neatly on the arm of the couch and he was snuggled under his old gray stadium blanket, watching the sports news.

"Oh, hey," Suze," he said, putting the TV on mute. "Was it too loud?"

"No. I…I just wanted to say…" I debated mentioning Caroline and then decided not to. "I just…really love the new living room. It's great."

He smiled up at me. "I'm glad."

"So…thanks for doing it."

"No problem. Want to catch the scores with me?"

I started to say no. I really was exhausted, and it was only Wednesday. The weekend seemed forever away, even though I'd just had a two extra days off for my suspension. But in the end, I plopped down on the couch next to him, after all. It was worth it to be a little tired, and I cuddled up to Dad under his blanket. He turned the sound back on and we watched the highlights of the Canucks' win. No matter what Caroline's house looked like, this shabby little apartment I shared with my dad and sister would always be my home.

Chapter 23

On Monday afternoon I sat on the hard wooden bench outside Farbinger's office, but this time I wasn't in trouble. Madame Duke had asked me to meet her here after school. It could only mean one thing. They were moving me up to the next level of French. When Duke had handed back the tests I'd almost fainted. I'd gotten a hundred percent. A hundred percent! Me! Suze Tamaki! *A hundred percent!*

Merci, AJ! If I was smart enough to get a hundred percent, then I could be *parle*-ing with the other smarties. The door to the hallway opened, and Baker came inside.

"Hey, Mr. Baker," I said. "*Ça va?*"

"I'm fine, Suze. How are you?" He sounded so gloomy, not like the regular cheerful Baker.

"*Très* awesome," I answered, grinning.

"I thought maybe you'd like me to go the meeting with you," he said.

Huh? "This meeting? Why?"

"For moral support."

Moral support? What's he talking about? A knot tied itself in my stomach. Somehow I didn't think we were going to be discussing moving me up, after all.

Farbinger's door flew open and his pinhead attached to his scrawny little neck stuck out, twisting around like a turtle. "Come in, Miss Tamaki. Come right in."

I glanced nervously at Baker. Suddenly I was a criminal, who wanted her lawyer present. The only thing was, I hadn't committed any crimes—at least, none I hadn't already been caught for. "Baker—I mean, Mr. Baker—is coming in with me."

"Of course," said Farbinger. The two men exchanged one of those adult-to-adult looks that kids aren't supposed to notice, and the knot cinched itself tighter.

Farbinger's office always seemed tiny when it was just the two of us, but throw in tall, lanky Baker, and Duke, who was already sitting in there, and it was positively claustrophobic. Farbinger arranged himself in a big, luxurious leather chair behind his beat-up metal desk. They'd cut the school band this year. Maybe it was to buy his ergonomically correct lounger.

Baker grabbed some folding chairs from a closet I'd never noticed before, and we sat on the cold metal seats and waited. I was glad to have an ally, even though I didn't know why I needed one.

"You did very well on last week's French test," Farbinger said, not looking at me. He flipped through a photocopy of my test.

"*Oui,*" I said, smiling. Maybe this was going to be okay after all. "I got a hundred percent."

"You've never gotten a hundred percent before," he said, his tone skeptical. "On anything."

Any optimism I had over how this might go evaporated. "I've never studied before," I explained.

The tension thickened in the room, until we were looking at each other through an almost visible haze. Baker cleaned his glasses while Farbinger studied my test. Duke twisted a rubber band around a pencil, as if she was going for a record or something.

"You say you studied?" Farbinger asked me.

"Yeah. While I was suspended. At AJ's house."

"AJ?"

"My Aunt Jenny." I shook my hair into my face. Something was wrong. Something was really, really wrong, and I didn't want Farbinger to see how scared I was.

"Well, it certainly paid off," he said.

"Yeah." The blackness in my heart swallowed my voice.

Baker cleared his throat. Still no one said anything. Finally, I couldn't stand it anymore. "What's the problem here?"

Farbinger looked meaningfully at Duke. "Perhaps you should tell her, Madame."

"Well," she stammered, not looking at me, "it's such a dramatic improvement. We wanted to make sure that you were…that is…we were just curious…"

"We wanted to know how you did it." Farbinger said. He looked at me like I was a toad. One they were going to cut up in biology. Instantly, I got his meaning, and I didn't like it one bit.

"You think I cheated?" I demanded. "Is that what you're saying?" Everyone's gaze flew to different parts of the room. Even Baker didn't look directly at me. Duke's face got very red, and Farbinger studied my test some more. "Oh, that's fine!" I shouted. "You're all a bunch of hypocrites. You teachers tell us all day long if we want to get ahead, then we need to study. Finally I do, and this is what happens? You accuse me of cheating?"

"Now Suze, calm down," Baker said in a low voice. "No one's accusing you of cheating."

"Yes, they are," I said. "And do you know what? This sucks. This really sucks."

"I'll have none of that language in here, young lady," Farbinger said.

I turned on him. "Well, it does. And there's no other

word for it. For the first time in my life, someone actually believed in me." I jumped out of my seat, waving wildly at Baker. "So I started to think that maybe he's right. Maybe I can make something out of myself. I like French. I could probably do better in there too. And now you're all calling me a cheater. Thanks a lot. I really appreciate your support." I pushed the metal chair out of the way so I could get out the door.

"Just a minute, Miss Tamaki. I didn't excuse you."

I couldn't believe it. This was not happening to me. In ten days we had to go in front of the school board and give our presentation, and now I had to deal with this? I wanted to slam the door behind me so hard the windows shattered, but Farbinger was dying to expel me, and there was no friggin' way I was going to give him a reason to. Instead, I thumped my butt back in the chair and crossed my arms.

"Young lady," he said, "I should call your mother right now for that outburst. You're insubordinate, you fight with other students, you skipped class and left campus. Based on your behavior lately, why exactly should I believe you?"

I flipped my hair into my face and shut my mouth tight. I didn't have to answer his stupid questions. Besides, I didn't trust myself not to yell at him that I still, and always will, until I graduate and move out of the house, *live with my father!*

"Suze," Baker said. "I think you need to tell Mr. Farbinger the truth."

I turned my anger on him. "Oh, great. This is all your fault, and now you don't believe me either?"

"I do believe you," Baker said. "That's not what I meant. I think you need to tell Mr. Farbinger the real reason you were skipping class."

Only one other person besides my family knew why I'd played hooky. Amanda. Figures. What a big mouth. I was never telling her anything again. "Why? What difference would it make?" I asked.

"Just tell him," he said.

"If there's something you want to say," Farbinger told me, "now's the time."

"Fine," I said. "I was skipping class as research for my English project. I wanted to see how many times the janitors would catch me."

"You knew about that?" Farbinger asked Baker.

"Not until this morning."

"Well, that's still no excuse for hanging out at the high school."

"I was testing their custodians. *For my project.*"

For the first time since I'd laid eyes on the weasel, Farbinger was at a loss for words. "Well...well, you should've prearranged it with Mr. Baker first. And why didn't you tell me that's what you were up to when I had you in here for truancy?"

"You didn't ask," I said.

"Ask? Of course I asked."

"No, you didn't," I said. "You accused me of skipping class and going to the high school to see a boy. I don't even know any boys there."

"Well…" Farbinger was losing ground, and he knew it. He rooted around in his brain for something to pin on me, and remembered the test. "Regardless," he said, "that doesn't have anything to do with your French midterm. I think you should take it again right now."

"A perfect score doesn't constitute cheating," Baker said. "And there's no use in springing it on her again. No one could pass it under these circumstances." Baker patted my shoulder, and I pulled away from him in spite of the fact he was sticking up for me. "Suze's doing an excellent job in English. If she's inspired to do well in her other classes, then I think that's great."

Farbinger hemmed and hawed. "Perhaps I should call your Aunt Jenny and verify your story," he said.

"Sure, why not?" I told him in my surliest voice. "She'd love to see you again."

I saw a flash of panic cross Farbinger's face as he remembered meeting AJ. In grade six he'd left me sitting in his office for five hours because he'd forgotten I was there. He'd actually gone to a staff meeting at the high school. I was too scared to come out without permission (I was young and naïve then, instead of the hardened criminal I am now), so at four o'clock I'd finally used his phone to call AJ because I didn't want to get locked in the school overnight. Believe me, I knew he was not anxious to see her in here again after that. Especially if there was any chance I had been wrongly accused.

"Yes, well…probably no need to call your aunt," he finally said. "I suppose if Madame Duke's satisfied that there are no shenanigans going on, then we'll let it go for now."

She nodded her agreement. She had wrapped that rubber band so tight I was sure it was going to break and send the pencil spinning across the room like a propeller. I hoped if it did, the pencil would boomerang back and hit her in the face. The witch had accused me of cheating without saying a single word to me. She was definitely on my list of untrustworthy adults now.

"You may go, Miss Tamaki," Farbinger told me.

Before I left I stared hard at each of them, one at a time. Farbinger was already thinking about what he'd be having for dinner, Duke looked relieved, and Baker smiled at me.

I was still pissed.

I shoved my chair out of the way so I could get out of the office. Just before I slammed the door, I heard Baker telling Farbinger I was a good girl, and he wished it hadn't come to this. He also said he didn't think I'd ever cheat.

All was fine and dandy to them. But what about me? I'd studied for hours, sweated through dreams about getting lost in Montreal and not knowing the language, worried all morning before the test, only to get a hundred percent—my best score ever—and then been accused of cheating. And I'd been totally humiliated too.

I ran to my locker to get my coat. I had to get out of this stinking school before I threw up all over Yoda's shiny tile floor. I was pretty sure I was now scarred for life. I wondered if I could sue the school district for slander. AJ could testify that I studied, and Baker could be a character witness. Speaking of Baker, what if he hadn't shown up at the meeting? What would have happened to me then? I might not only have flunked, but could have been expelled. Next time it came to studying, I'd have to decide if it was really worth it. I'm sure Baker, Duke, and Farbinger would all sleep fine tonight, but what about me? What about *my* feelings?

Chapter 24

Jessica had waited for me in the library while I met with Farbinger. When I showed up, one look at my face told her not to ask what had happened. Now we sat together on the city bus, Jess reading, me staring out the window and scowling at the buildings as we crept past in traffic that barely moved.

At first, she'd been really nervous about taking the bus all the way across town because her mom and dad had never let her take public transportation alone. But I'd assured her that Tracie and I had been riding it by ourselves for years, and I knew exactly how to get to Oak Bay. We decided not to mention it to her parents, though. They might think she was too young to be on the bus without an adult, even though she wasn't.

After twenty minutes or so Jess seemed to realize I was right and relaxed. Now she was reading a play. Every once in a while she'd laugh, or I'd hear her whisper a line of dialogue like she was testing it out, but mostly she left me alone to sulk.

My brain said if they were going to call me a cheater then I should dump the whole janitor thing too, just in case. Forget the school board. Let the custodians fight their own battles. I could return to Lame-o English, get some reading in, and enjoy my average life. If I didn't do the presentation, Caroline wouldn't have to come and pretend she was interested in me either. And Dad could work his full shift without losing any pay. Amanda would get her A without me, regardless.

The problem was my heart. I tried to ignore the idea that people were counting on me, but like a splotch of red ink on a white shirt, it wouldn't go away. No matter what I told people, I did want to be in Honors English. And I liked how it felt getting a perfect score on the French test. At least until they called me a cheater.

Also, there was the whole Yoda thing. On my way to Farbinger's office, I'd seen him scrubbing graffiti off some lockers, and he was singing and smiling while he did it. He might be all right financially if they let him go, but what would he do every day? You got the feeling that the only reason he got up in the morning was because he loved his job. How could I let the school board take that away from him without a fight?

And if that wasn't enough, there was also this sort of stupid hope I could keep Caroline interested in me if I was more of a model daughter—one who got As and could do presentations without choking. If a school project would make her stick around, well…maybe it was worth it.

"Suze?" Jessica said.

"Hmmm?"

"Are we almost there?"

I'd been staring out the window but not really seeing anything, and now I looked around, getting my bearings. Oak trees overhung the streets, some with branches low enough to scrape the top of the bus. Cars lined every available inch of curb space, and scaffolding blocked the cracked sidewalk as workers painted a Victorian house with a fresh coat of paint. I took the card Caroline had given me out of my purse and checked the address. "Next stop," I said.

"Are we going to her office?" Jess asked.

"Nope. Her house."

She looked surprised. "Does she know we're coming?"

I rang the bell. "She's at work. Come on."

Once we were safely off the bus and I'd pulled Jessica to the sidewalk, I checked the street signs and figured out which way to go. It was one of those cold, windy, blue-sky, super-sunny, early December days. The slicing wind off the ocean bit our cheeks, turning them pink. I took a deep breath, expecting fresh air, and inhaled exhaust from an SUV, instead. *Blech*.

"Okay. Three blocks up this way," I said between coughing fits. I peered around some parked cars, and we dashed across the street.

"Suze?" Jessica said. "Why are we going to her house if she's at work?"

"Huh?" I scanned the house on my right for an address.

"Why are we going there?"

"Oh," I said. "Just to check it out."

I wanted to see what kind of money this woman had. Living in Oak Bay is pretty expensive, and I needed to know if Caroline lived in some dinky apartment or what. And all those diamonds. Were they real or cubic zirconia? It wasn't like I hoped to cash in on them or anything. But it was almost like I needed to know if Caroline was sincere or not, and if she actually had all the money she appeared to have, then that made her more real.

Jessica stopped walking. "You mean we're spying on her?"

"It's no big deal," I said, tugging on her arm. "I just want to get a look at the house. You know, see what it looks like. Find out if she's got a cat. That sort of thing."

"A cat?"

"Well, I could never get close to someone who doesn't love cats," I said.

Duh.

Jessica shook her head and laughed a deep belly laugh like she thought I was crazy. I'm glad she could let go so easily, because my stomach was tightening with every step. For one thing, the closer we got to Caroline's street, the bigger the houses were. And they weren't apartments either. BMWs and other fancy cars sat in the driveways. The large front lawns were immaculate, planted with exotic grasses and climbing flowers too, like these people either had gardeners, or lots of leisure time. Maybe I didn't want to know how rich Caroline was. Maybe it would be intimidating. Maybe it would make me mad. After all, what did she need a big house for?

"That's it." I pointed.

"Egad!" Jessica said.

My thoughts exactly. Well, maybe not exactly, Jessica does have a weird way with words. But *wow*.

A large porch wrapped around a three-story yellow Victorian. Deep purple and lavender shutters framed millions of ornate windows. Some of them were even round like a ship's porthole.

"Do you think she *owns* that house?" Jessica asked.

"Maybe she rents it," I said. "Either way, it's got to cost a fortune."

"So, what are we going to do now?"

"I want to get a closer look."

"How close?" she asked, giving me a squinty, suspicious look.

"I'm not going to break in," I said. "I want to see the backyard, and then we can go get a slice of pizza. I need to know if there's a cat."

"Why don't you ask her?"

"I just thought of it on the way over. But it's important."

"Are you serious?"

"Absolutely."

"You're really weird."

Maybe, but I knew from experience that cat people got along. Tracie might even like Caroline some day if she was feline-friendly. "Come on," I said. "Nobody will notice us." Jessica still looked worried, and I grabbed her arm again and dragged her along. "I'm just going to look in the backyard. Besides, I *am* her daughter. If anyone asks I could say that." But I hoped no one did, because the last thing I wanted was for Caroline to get wind of the fact that I was sneaking around her house, checking it out.

We passed under a vine-covered trellis into the back-yard. "Unbelievable," I said.

A little round summerhouse, painted to match the big house, sat smack in the middle of the grass. I had always wanted one of those. I let my imagination wander for a second…me reading out there in a wrought-iron lounge chair with a rose print cushion. I was immersed in a tale of romance, the summer winds whispering around me…no one named Tracie within shouting distance….

"That's pretty cool," Jessica said. "Okay. Can we go now?"

"Jess, you're acting like Amanda." I made chicken noises at her.

"I can't help it," she said, laughing.

"Just one minute. I'm gonna look in the kitchen window and then we're outta here, okay?"

"*Suze*," she said, sounding exactly like AJ.

"I'm not doing anything wrong. Relax."

I figured if Caroline did have a cat, it might be in the kitchen. Or at least there'd be a food dish or a litter box or something. Maybe a cat bed. I climbed up some narrow, rickety stairs to the back door, and I really did try to hurry because it looked like Jessica was about to keel over from heart failure. All the pink had drained from her face, and she was white, white, white. She was definitely losing Best Friend Forever points with me. We weren't even doing anything—yet.

"Suze," she said, "I don't think you should be up there."

"It's okay. I'm just looking. Calm down."

The steps led to a glass-paned door, but Caroline had hung some lacey curtains over the window so there was nothing to see. I leaned off the edge of the little stoop and peered in the window over what was probably the kitchen sink.

"Hey, I think I see something that looks like a cat dish," I said.

"Great. Let's go," Jessica whispered.

"I can't tell for sure, though." I stretched out as far as I could, holding onto the windowsill for support.

"You're crazy, Suze."

Standing on my tiptoes, I balanced on one leg, stretching, reaching. A bottle of dishwashing soap sat on the counter blocking my view. If only I could lean a tiny…bit…farther.

In a sudden flash my reflection disappeared and something black-and-white lunged at me from inside the house. I screamed, lost my balance, and crash-landed onto the rhododendron below. I flapped around uselessly, trying to untangle myself from the girl-eating bush, but like in that Harry Potter book, the more I struggled the faster I stuck.

The door opened. "Is someone out there?" asked Caroline's voice from above me.

"Help?" I said, grinning up at her in a way that I hoped looked sweet and innocent.

"Susan? Is that you?" She came down the stairs and yanked me hard out of the bush. And let's just say she didn't use any motherly tenderness when she pulled.

"Ow!"

"What are you doing here?" she said. "What's going on?"

"Nothing...I wasn't doing anything. I just..." I brushed myself off and scanned the yard for Jessica. Clearly, she'd bailed on me.

"Well?" Caroline asked.

"I was looking around," I explained, "and then something flew at me from inside the house, and I lost my balance."

"Do you generally go peeking into other people's windows?"

"No," I said, keeping my eyes on the ground. "Really. I don't. I swear." What could I say in my defense? And where the heck was Jessica? "I just...we were just..."

Caroline looked around the yard. "We?"

"Jessica's here somewhere."

"Well, perhaps you better go find her," Caroline suggested. "And then come in, and we'll have some tea and discuss it."

"Okay. Sure."

Caroline went back inside, and I limped around to the front of the house looking for Jessica. She was standing on the corner a block away, doubled over. When I caught up to her, the tears were spilling from her eyes.

"What's wrong?" I said. "Don't worry. Caroline's not mad. At least not at you. She wants us to come in for tea."

Jessica didn't say anything. Why was she crying? "Jess?" I asked, touching her shoulder.

She looked up at me, and that's when I saw she was laughing—uncontrollably hard, tears streaming down her face, one of those silent, hurt-your-gut kind of laughs. "Cat," she spluttered between giggles.

"What?" I asked, confused. "What's so funny?"

"It was a cat that jumped at you and made you fall," she gasped, breaking into another burst of giggles.

"A cat?" The black-and-white shadow suddenly made sense.

"Yeah. Caroline's attack-cat."

I stood there, shaking my head, laughing a little but nothing like Jessica. It *was* pretty funny, though—the whole cat thing—but still…she was really laughing hard. I wondered if she was maybe a little hysterical. Should I slap her? Before I could decide, a sharp, stinging sensation made me examine my leg. Oh, great. I'd torn a hole in my best tights. Blood oozed out of a scrape below my knee and I dabbed at it with my thumb, making it hurt worse.

When I looked up at Jess, the tears were still running down her cheeks and I knew I didn't want to go back to Caroline's. We were a mess. "You know what?" I said. "Let's get out of here." I grabbed her hand and led her back toward the shops and the best pizza place in town, *Escape From New York*.

"Wait," she said. "I thought we had to go in for tea."

"I hate tea," I said. "It tastes like hot water poured over gym socks."

"But what about Caroline?"

"I'll explain it to her later," I said. "She'll understand."

She'd have to. If anyone understood running away, it would be Caroline. I figured she owed me one.

Chapter 25

We were in the thick of doing our presentation for the Honors English Class, and I don't think I'd taken a single deep breath the whole time. My heart was pounding, and I had that hot, prickly feeling under my arms.

Amanda pushed a key on the computer and the next chart came up on the big screen. I was glad she was doing the tech stuff because all I was good at was surfing the Web. "If you'll look at this chart of the survey we took at Mission Elementary," I said, "one hundred percent of the kids knew the names of all the janitors in their school.

"Of those kids," I continued, "ninety-four percent were very sure their custodians knew their first names. Four percent thought the janitors might know their names. And the other two percent were confused by the question, so we let them go to lunch."

The class laughed. All right! A little laughter. *Don't think about the audience*, I reminded myself. *And breathe.*

"The results at Maywood Junior and Senior High were similar to the grade school results, except we got a lot more smart-ass—I mean smart-alecky comments." *Oh, that was great. Beautiful. Wonderful job, Suze.* I hoped Baker didn't flunk us. Amanda was gonna *kill* me for that later.

"You may be wondering," I said, "why it's important for the janitors to know the kids. I'll tell you why. Safety."

I explained about all the custodians who had caught street kids dealing drugs, and I gave examples of ones who had foiled abductions. "One custodian even took a bullet for a student in Texas. Luckily he lived to talk about it. And just a few weeks ago, at our very own high school, a streaker ran across the basketball court during gym class, and it was the janitor who helped drag him into the locker room."

Even though everyone had already heard about it, they . burst out laughing, which made me feel really great. This presentation was actually going okay. Maybe Honors English wasn't so hard, after all. When I finished, I sat down at our table while Amanda covered the budget. The way we figured it, a sub-contractor would save the school some money up front, but our custodians would be out of work. The school district would be responsible for unemployment for the younger workers and probably force retirement on the older ones.

"Plus," Amanda said, "when workers get lower wages, it weakens the economy, which isn't good for anyone because then the budgets keep getting cut."

We wrapped up our presentation with a slideshow of the custodians at Maywood doing what they do best. Sweeping, changing light bulbs, emptying garbage cans, raking leaves, helping a kid pick up his scattered books, and even plunging a toilet. We had added the music from that really ancient movie, *Chariots of Fire*, so it looked and sounded really pro.

We rocked!

***

"Why are you running?" I asked, chasing Amanda up the street.

"I'm not running. You're just short."

She had a point there, but it wasn't exactly the kind of point I like to hear. "What's your problem?"

She finally stopped. "Well, let me see…the visuals were out of order, and I don't know how that happened because it's on a computer. The music didn't match the slideshow the way I wanted it to, even though I was up half the night trying to make it work. The figures might not be accurate because apparently the stupid company they want to sub-contract with *does* do some minor maintenance after all, not just cleaning. You called them *janitors* instead of *custodians* four times. You said *smart-ass*. And I still don't think you should tell the story about Whitey streaking across the gym at the high school."

"Is that all?"

She speed-walked toward her house.

Okay. So I was being sarcastic. But we'd done an excellent presentation. Even Baker had told us we'd done a good job. I didn't know why Amanda had to get so bent out of shape over everything.

"No, Suze, that's not all," she yelled over her shoulder at me. "You need to learn how to work the computer. I can't be responsible for everything."

"Come on, Amanda. I know how to work a computer." I trotted after her. "But I don't want to wreck it. It's so expensive."

"That's just an excuse."

Maybe. Maybe not. If she was this particular about everything else, then the last thing I wanted to do was mess up her new laptop. Besides, why did we both need to know how it worked? Sometimes Amanda created things to worry about.

"Fine. I'll practice doing it," I said, finally catching up. "But you're still going to run it for the presentation."

If she wanted to waste our time, then whatever. I had bigger things on my mind. Like how Tracie was going to react when she found out Caroline was going to the school-board meeting.

Chapter 26

Dad dropped Jessica and me off at Caroline's on Saturday morning. He waited in the car to make sure we got inside okay, but he didn't get out or anything. On the porch, I pressed the bell just as Caroline opened her front door.

"Welcome," she said. "Come in."

She leaned forward like she was going to hug me, but I was already moving past her. I stopped and we did one of those fake hugs where you barely touch each other, and then I hurried inside.

"Hello, Jessica," Caroline said.

"Hi, Mrs. Walker."

"Call me Caroline."

"Umm…okay. Just don't tell my mom. She'd think it's rude."

Caroline laughed. I was too busy checking out her living room to really pay much attention. It had really high ceilings and that fancy white trim all the way around the room. The couch was red velvet, but it looked soft and squishy and like it'd be a great place to read a book.

"Come in, come in," Caroline said, even though we were already in. She shut the door behind her, and we all stood there wondering what to do next. "How about some tea?"

"Sure. Great," I said. I didn't want to be totally rude.

She headed for the kitchen. "If you want to take your stuff upstairs, you're sharing the first room on the right, on the second floor. Don't climb out any windows and disappear on me," she said, laughing.

"We won't," Jess said.

"I think she was joking," I told Jessica in an undertone on the way up some steep, creaky stairs. After we'd bailed on her the day I fell in the bushes, I'd used Jessica's phone to call from the pizza place Tracie and I had discovered on one of our adventures. I'd told Caroline we'd been in kind of a hurry and she'd sounded relieved to hear we weren't planning to come back after all.

On the second-floor landing, the sun played across the wooden planks and a musty but pleasant odor filled the air, kind of like the bookstore downtown, giving me a warm, comfortable feeling. Our room only had one bed in it, but it was huge. Not just wide, but high.

"Look at that," I said, pointing at some weird little steps on either side of the bed. "They made this for shorties like me. I hope I don't fall out."

"I wish I had a room like this," Jessica said. She threw herself across the mattress. "Oh, Romeo, Romeo, wherefore art thou Romeo?"

I examined the bed closer. The solid wood frame looked like it weighed a ton. "They must've built it in this room," I said. "How else would they get it up the stairs?"

"I'm kind of afraid to touch anything," Jessica said, looking around. "It's like a museum in here."

"It reminds me of Miss Havisham's without the dust and the old lady," I told her. Oh, great. Now I was as bad as Jess, comparing the room to literature like she did to plays. I hoped Honors English didn't turn me into a total geek.

Two antique chairs with flowered cushions sat in one corner. A delicate end table between them created what they call "an inviting seating area" on those home décor shows Tracie likes to watch. Next to a wardrobe so big mine would've fit inside it, sat a vanity with glass bottles and a huge bouquet of fresh flowers.

"I'm so glad you came with me," I said.

"It'll be fun. Plus I don't have to babysit all weekend."

"Bonus!"

Caroline had jumped at the idea of my inviting Jessica to come along, which made me think she must be nervous too.

"I guess we should go drink that tea," I said.

"Yeah." Jess didn't look any more excited about it than I felt.

"Race you!" I said, trying to cheer us up.

She surprised me by pushing me out of the way, but I grabbed her arm and pulled her back, cutting off her exit. By the time we made it downstairs, we were breathless from shoving each other and wrestling our way down. We fell into the living room, laughing.

Caroline was standing over a tea tray she'd set on a coffee table, staring at us. She tried to wipe the shock off her face by replacing it with a fake smile. "My," she said. "You two must love tea."

"We must," I said, and behind me I heard Jess trying to swallow her giggles. I think maybe we were both freaking out a little.

Caroline had just picked up the teapot when her phone chirped. She handed the pot to me. "Help yourself," she said, pulling the phone out of her pocket and looking at it. She immediately started texting someone.

I filled Caroline's cup, then I put about an inch in my cup and the same in Jessica's. I raised my eyebrow at her and nodded to it and she winked back at me. "Sip it," I mouthed, but Caroline was so into her phone, I doubt she would've heard me if I'd said it aloud.

Jess and I sat down on the fat velvet couch. It was so poofy, my feet barely touched the floor. We pretended to drink our tea while Caroline stared at her phone. It beeped again, she sent another text, and then a minute later, it rang.

"I have to take this," she said to us and hurried out of the room.

"Gee, this is fun," I said to Jessica.

She shrugged, always polite.

I nodded at the tray. "I thought you were supposed to have cookies with tea."

"Maybe she's getting them," Jess said.

"I'm not drinking this," I said. "It tastes like dishwater."

"How do you know what dishwater tastes like?"

"I have an older sister, remember? She's tortured me in ways you've never thought of."

Jessica laughed. "I'll have to remember that one."

We were still sitting there, not really saying anything, when Caroline returned. She'd put on a leather coat and was buttoning it up. "Susan? I'm sorry, but I have to run to the office for…an hour. Actually, maybe two."

"Now? On Saturday?"

"I'm really sorry," she said.

She fiddled with the buttons on her coat, like she was

upset or something. Of course, she was abandoning us after fifteen minutes, so she *should* feel bad.

"Okay," I said, because what else could I say?

"I'll…I'll try to hurry…. Make yourselves at home."

"Okay," I repeated.

She grabbed her purse from a hook in the foyer, and we heard the front door shut behind her with a loud thump.

"At least we don't have to drink the tea," Jessica said.

"I guess." I stood up. "Let's check out the house while she's gone."

"What if she comes back?"

"She said she'd be an hour or two. Besides, knowing her, she'll be gone for days."

Or years.

"You lead," Jessica said.

"Let's check out the second floor first," I said.

Jessica followed me back up the stairs and down a dim hallway. There were three other doors besides the guest room, and I ignored the dubious look she flung at me as I opened the first one. "Washroom," I said, peering in at the claw-foot tub and then moving on. The house smelled old and the hallways were narrow and creaky. Maybe it was haunted. I hoped we didn't find out.

I pushed on a door that was partly open and looked in.

"Wow. That's some office," Jessica said, leaning over my shoulder for a peek.

It had everything Caroline could possibly need to run a business—computer, printer, copier, phone, and enough office supplies for her to start her own store. I wondered why she had to go to her real office at all.

If that was her office supply store, her personal department store was right next door. The entire room had been transformed into a totally amazing walk-in closet. One whole wall was mirrored, and suits, jackets, pants, skirts, blouses, and eveningwear hung in rows, arranged by color. Above the racks, shoes and handbags lined the walls.

"My God," I said. "Do you think these are all her clothes?"

"They must be," Jessica said, taking it all in.

I fingered some of the fabrics. Expensive. I checked out the labels. Designer. We ended up goofing around in there for at least an hour.

"Check this out." I held up a gold sequin cocktail dress in front of Jessica.

"I could wear it when I win my first Tony Award," she said.

"Is that a Prada bag?" I asked, pointing.

"Don't touch it. It's probably alarmed."

After a while, a flame of anger burned in my gut, kind of like when I first saw her house, car, and diamonds. Everything I owned came from a thrift store. Why did she have so much, while we had nothing?

"Come on," I said, swallowing my anger. "Let's check out what's upstairs."

"I don't know, Suze," Jess said. "I bet that's Caroline's bedroom."

"So what? I'm not going to touch anything."

I ventured toward the stairs while Jessica waited at the bottom. I knew she was nervous, but I didn't call her on it. After all, if she hadn't come with me to stay the night, I'd be in this big old house all by myself.

"Okay," I told her. "You wait there, and I'll be right back."

This staircase was even narrower than the main one, and every step creaked, making my stomach flip-flop all the way up. It's sort of eerie creeping around someone else's house, not knowing what you might find. The stairs led to the attic, and there wasn't any door at the top, so I suddenly found myself in Caroline's bedroom. It wasn't anything special; a white room with small windows, a lamp, and a bed. But the wild thing was, there were books piled everywhere. And I mean everywhere. She had a couple of low bookcases on one side of the room, but because of the sloped ceilings most of the books were stacked against the walls.

I leaned down to get a closer look. There was everything from leather-bound classics with gold lettering to paperback romances—a couple of which I'd even read. A tower of thick, brightly colored fantasy novels sat next to the headboard, and travel guides teetered in the corner by a space heater. So this is where Tracie and I got our love for books. I'd finally found a connection to Caroline! Like that handwriting thing I'd read about, it had transcended her absence.

A black pillow on the bed licked its paw and I realized it was the cat. "Oh, look." I stuck out my hand. "Hello, sweet kitty. Hello there."

It raised its head and looked warily at me, but didn't make a move. I sat on the edge of the bed and the cat immediately began to purr, so I scratched under its chin. "Nice kitty."

For about a tenth of a second, anyway. Then he rolled over and attacked my forearm with his claws and his teeth.

"Ouch, ouch, ouch! Let go, you stupid cat!" I had to literally shake him off to get free. I sucked the scratch on my thumb as I ran downstairs to Jessica. "That cat is crazy!" I told her.

Two hours later, Caroline still wasn't back and we'd already explored the entire house from the attic bedroom to the spidery basement. Our stomachs were rumbling and grumbling, so we decided to raid the fridge.

"How old do you think this chicken is?" Jess asked, sniffing it.

"How am I supposed to know?"

"Smell it, and tell me if you think it's good or not."

"Pass," I said. "I don't even eat meat, remember?"

"Oh, yeah."

Based on the contents of the fridge, I decided not to take my chances on anything. There was half a bottle of wine, a pitcher of water, a moldy cucumber, and leftovers from every restaurant in town. But nothing either of us was willing to try eating.

"Maybe there's something in the cupboards," Jessica suggested.

As I touched the pantry door the phone rang. "Do we answer it?" I asked.

"She probably has voicemail."

"But maybe it's her calling us," I said.

"Wouldn't she try your cell?"

"Maybe." I ran upstairs and fished it out of my bag, but the battery was dead. Story of my life. By the time I got back downstairs, the landline was ringing again.

"Maybe you should answer it," Jess said.

I picked up the receiver. "Hello? I mean, Walker residence."

"Susan? It's Caroline."

"Caroline who?"

"Touché," she said. "I'm really sorry this has taken so long. Are you guys all right?"

I sighed. "Umm…well…"

"Great. See you in a while."

The phone clicked in my ear. She hung up just in time

too, because I was about to tell her what I thought of her. Having me over was her stupid idea in the first place. I was beginning to see what I'd been missing all these years.

Nothing.

Chapter 27

In the living room, I pointed at a framed photo on the mantelpiece. "I wonder if that was her husband."

"Maybe," Jess said. "They look happy."

In the picture Caroline stood, smiling next to a tall man with reddish-brown hair. He didn't look old or anything, though. The way I'd imagined it, she'd married some ancient guy, and he kicked the bucket, and she got his dough, but now I wasn't so sure. After I'd seen this house the other day, I'd asked my dad if my grandparents were wealthy and he said it was none of my business where Caroline got her money. *Sheesh*.

"Do you think it's okay if we have a fire?" Jessica asked. "I'm freezing."

"There isn't any wood."

"I'm pretty sure it's electric."

On closer inspection, I saw she was right. We crawled around the fireplace trying to figure out how to turn it on, but after ten minutes, we gave up. "Maybe it's a hidden switch behind one of these old paintings," I said.

Jessica laughed. "I think pictures usually hide wall safes, not fireplace switches."

"Oooh," I said. "Do you think there is one? She must keep her diamonds somewhere." I shifted a painting to one side. No safe, just discolored wallpaper. "Wow. The paintings must've come with the house. That's sort of creepy. Maybe that bed really has been here since the beginning of time."

"Yeah, and think of all the people who've died in this house," Jessica said.

"Maybe even in that bed," I added.

Shivers crawled up my spine. I wasn't really scared or anything, but the cloudy day had dissolved into darkness, and I looked around the gloomy living room wondering about ghosts. I flipped a light switch by the door and the fireplace roared to life, making us both jump and then laugh.

"Boy, are we stupid," I said.

We settled down in front of the fire with a fancy scrapbook I'd found on a bookshelf. "Look at this." I held it open to a picture of a baby that could only be described as gorgeous.

"Too sweet to be you," Jessica said. "That must be Tracie."

"Susan, six months," I read, gloating. "I was a beautiful baby, wasn't I? I wonder how come Caroline got all these photos and Dad got zilch?"

"He got the real thing," Caroline said from behind me.

Both Jessica and I jumped about a mile. Man, now I knew where Tracie got her sneakiness from. I hadn't even heard Caroline come in.

"Yeah, well…" I said.

We both knew she could've had Tracie and me if she'd wanted us. At least for some of the time anyway. Caroline flopped down on the couch, kicking off her shoes. Jessica straightened up the pile of loose photos and albums we'd been digging through.

"When I said make yourselves at home," Caroline said, "it didn't occur to me you'd go searching through my personal things."

"We had a lot of time to kill," I told her.

"Touché."

Touché? I wish she'd quit saying that. She'd stolen that from Dad. Or had she? Maybe, just maybe, he'd gotten it from her? That might have been possible. Oooh, yuck. Maybe it was one of those "couple" things. Whatever. I didn't really like her using it. But what could I do about it? A big fat zero. That's what.

Caroline leaned her head back against the couch and shut her eyes. "Sorry it took me so long."

"That's okay," I said, because that's what polite people say, and Caroline and I were still in that civil stage.

"Are you two hungry?"

"No," I said. "Jessica had a candy bar in her bag and we split it." So much for civil.

"Well, I'm starved," Caroline said, my sarcasm totally blowing right over her blond head.

"So are we," I said. "I was joking."

"Everyone good with Japanese food?" she asked.

I made a face. "As long as it's not sushi."

She laughed. "I know how you feel about raw fish, Susan. Not that all sushi's raw fish, but don't worry, we'll get noodles, tempura, and rice."

Hopefully tempura wasn't squid or something gross. "Okay with you, Jess?" I asked, kind of hoping she'd say no.

"Yeah, fine. Sounds good." But her voice was high and squeaky like she was trying to be polite. Of course, Caroline didn't notice.

I wasn't sure if I'd like noodles, tempura, and rice either because when do I ever get to go out to eat? And when we do, it's never fancy. And even though Dad's grandparents came from Japan, he'd never been into his heritage or anything. To us, ethnic food was poutine.

The noodles turned out to be kind of like Top Ramen,

except better, and tempura was pieces of vegetables deep fried in batter and served with rice and soy sauce. I thought it tasted pretty good, but I could tell Jessica was struggling because she hates veggies. When Caroline went to get more wine I let her dump all the things she didn't like onto my plate. What were friends for, anyway?

Caroline brought the dessert out to the living room. She set delicate china bowls of mint ice cream in front of us. I took a big bite and gagged on the taste. "What flavor is this?"

"Green tea," Caroline said.

I made a "gross!" face at Jessica when Caroline wasn't looking, and then I sat there smashing it with the back of my spoon, encouraging it to melt.

"Did you make that scrapbook?" I asked Caroline.

"Yep."

"When we were little?"

"Nope. Last year."

So Uncle Bill was right…. She had been thinking about us sometimes. "You did a really good job."

"Thanks."

"I always wanted to try scrapbooking," I said. "But all the supplies are kinda expensive."

"I have a lot leftover," Caroline said. "You and Jess could have them."

"Really? Thanks." I hoped she couldn't hear how disappointed I was that she didn't want to show me how herself.

"Or we could do it together," Caroline said. She wasn't looking at me, and her voice sounded hopeful.

I smiled. "Yeah. Okay. If you want." I stirred my puddle of ice cream, and asked after a while: "So why *do* you have all the baby pictures?"

"It was your father's idea of a joke," she said.

"What do you mean?"

Caroline was silent for a minute, the plastic smile plastered on her face. Her teeth were so perfect they didn't look real. "Maybe we should drop it."

"No," I said. "I don't want to drop it." I saw Jessica get up and kind of motion to the washroom as she made her way out of the living room fast. "What kind of a joke?"

Caroline licked her spoon. "Why don't you ask him?"

"I'm asking you."

She sighed. "Fine. He sent them to me because he wanted your lives to start with the day I left, and he didn't want any record of what came before that."

I studied my distorted face in the back of my spoon. "You're right. That's not much of a joke."

Chapter 28

I lay in the huge, soft bed, gazing at a spot on the ceiling near the window. There was something weird about it, like bits of it were glowing in the dark. I squinted harder and then turned my head the other way. Some kind of iridescent squiggles. Weird.

Jess and I had only been in bed about ten minutes, but she was already out cold. Her breathing was so quiet I half wondered if she was still alive. I turned over, trying to get comfortable. It seemed strange not to have springs poking me every time I moved around. I sunk into the fluffiness and wondered if I'd be able to sleep.

Once, at the mall, Leigh and I had tried out all the beds

in the bedding department while Amanda stood off to the side pretending not to know us. We weren't doing anything. We were just lying around, but we still got kicked out. This bed reminded me of one of those mattresses, only even comfier.

I tilted my head to the right and squinted at the spot on the ceiling some more. It almost looked like letters. Finally I couldn't stand it, and I got up and stood underneath it. Now that the lights had been out for a while, it seemed to be fading, but finally I worked it out.

Caroline Elizabeth McIntyre.

She'd written her name up there in some sort of glow-paint. When? It seemed like kind of a weird thing to do as an adult. And it was her maiden name too. Was this her room when she was a kid? I wracked my brain but couldn't remember her mentioning it.

Shivers ran up my arms, but not because I'd finally seen a ghost or had an eerie feeling. It was freezing in here. I dove back into bed and stuck my head under the covers. I didn't think I'd ever fall asleep, but the warmer I got, the drowsier I felt. The next thing I knew, I had to pee really badly, and the clock said six-thirty a.m.

It was still pitch-black outside, but Caroline had left the washroom light on for us, and once I made it out into the hallway I could see a little better. I managed to make it to the bathroom and back without killing myself—although I did hit my hand on the metal radiator, which made a loud pinging noise. I fully expected my knuckle to be bruised in a few hours.

Once I was awake there was no way I could get back to sleep. After a while I decided to go downstairs and look for some coffee. There wasn't any food in the house, but I had noticed an espresso machine.

I put my clothes on because I didn't want Caroline to see my ratty old pajamas. At home I slept in shorty-shorts, but when you went to someone else's house you kind of had to wear something that covered more. The old pair of flannel jammies that AJ had given me two years ago were obviously too small but were my only option.

There weren't any lights on the stairs, and every step creaked underfoot kind of creeping me out. No one was up except Caroline's killer cat, who looked up from his dish mid-bite to glare at me.

"I don't trust you either," I told him.

Most of the cabinets had glass fronts, so it didn't take me long to figure out that the espresso machine was for show, and there wasn't any coffee anywhere. I did find about a dozen tins of David's Tea in all different flavors, though. While I was contemplating whether or not to try some, Caroline came in.

"Good morning," she said.

"Oh, hey."

"Sleep well?"

"Yeah. Fine. Thanks."

I stared at her. It was six-forty in the morning and she was already in full makeup. Maybe she'd had it tattooed on or something. I recognized the blue velvet designer sweats and revoltingly expensive tennis shoes from our forage into her closet, but I didn't say anything.

"Hungry?" she asked.

"Not really," I said. "I was looking for some coffee."

"It's in the freezer. But let's go out for some."

"Uh…okay." I wondered if she was one of those women who hung out in cafés drinking lattes and talking on their cell phones with an earpiece in. I was pretty sure she was.

"What about Jessica?" she asked.

"Still in bed. I'll go see if she wants to come along. And I have to get my coat."

"Right," Caroline said. "We'll bring her something if she'd rather sleep in."

I ran upstairs and touched Jess's shoulder. She sat straight up. "*What?*"

"Sorry," I said.

"Where am I?"

"It's me, Suze," I told her. "We're at Caroline's, remember?"

She flopped back on the bed. "Be still my beating heart," she said. "You did startle and afright me."

I rolled my eyes. "Sorry," I repeated.

"What time is it?"

"Six forty-five."

She moaned. "In the morning?"

"Yeah, listen," I said. "Go back to sleep. Caroline and I are going out for coffee, and we'll bring you a hot chocolate."

"Around nine o'clock," she mumbled.

"Okay."

I looked halfheartedly for my shoes, but it was still too dark to see without turning on a light, and I didn't want to bug Jess again. My slippers would have to do. They looked like ballet flats anyway. I snagged my coat out of the wardrobe and ran downstairs to Caroline. She was standing by the door, texting someone. For a brief second I wondered if maybe I could get on her phone plan. She probably had unlimited minutes. That would be so cool. But then I dropped the idea. I wasn't sure what I wanted from Caroline, and until I figured it out, I wasn't asking for anything.

"Ready?"

"Yep."

I followed her out the kitchen door. My breath froze in my throat, but Caroline didn't seem to notice the cold. She wasn't even wearing a coat, and I wondered for about the millionth time if she was totally crazy. And then she affirmed my suspicions by getting in the car.

Oak Bay is coffee central. I would've bet good money (if I'd had any) that there were at least three coffee shops within a five-block radius of Caroline's house. But she started the engine, and I climbed in. The place we drove to was kind of far away, so I figured it must be the best one or something.

After ten minutes of looking for a parking spot, Caroline said, "I forgot that everyone who lives around here has to park on the street and they're all probably still in bed. We'll never find a place." She headed back toward her house. "We'll just leave the car at home and walk to my neighborhood coffee shop," she told me.

"Okay."

When we pulled into the driveway, it was getting light, the sky a dull gray with the promise of more rain. I started to get out, but Caroline put her hand on my arm. "Wait, Susan. There's something important I have to tell you."

I froze in my seat. *Oh, my God, she is dying. That's why she's back. I should've known it was something like that.*

"I wasn't at work yesterday afternoon," she said. "At least, not the whole time."

Okay. She isn't dying. I let go of the breath I'd been holding.

"I…well," she said. "I want you to know this isn't your fault. It's totally me, okay?" I had no idea what she was talking about, but I nodded anyway. She nodded back, like we'd agreed on something. "I actually went to an emergency session with my therapist because right before you and Jess showed up, I had a panic attack."

"You have a therapist?"

"Yes. A new one. A referral from my doctor in Vancouver. She's very good."

I had no idea what to say to all this.

"Anyway," Caroline said. "I'm not explaining this very well because I'm nervous. But right before you showed up, I panicked, wondering if having you over was such a good idea. And also what we'd do together for so long."

I smiled at her. "If it makes you feel any better," I said. "I thought the same thing."

She smiled back. "Yeah. It does make me feel better. But I still wanted to apologize for taking off like that. It's something I'm working on. Can you forgive me?"

I nodded again. "Sure. No problem."

"Good. Thanks, Susan." We sat there for a beat, neither of us saying anything, and then Caroline said, "Okay…how about that coffee?"

"Sounds good."

We got out of the car and started walking. About four blocks from her house, we stopped outside a corner café. Caroline said, "I almost never come here because the workers are always high, and it takes them years to make a coffee." I started laughing, and she smirked and did the one-eyebrow thing. "It's true."

Caroline played it safe and ordered a plain coffee, black and oily, which she served herself from a pump pot. Then we stood around waiting forever, while they made my double latte with caramel and extra whipped cream, something I can never afford when I'm paying. I also got two blueberry muffins. One for me, one for Jessica. I skipped the hot chocolate because I knew it'd be cold by the time she woke up.

After the guy with half-closed, red-rimmed eyes handed me my drink, we looked around for a seat, but the tables were either occupied or covered in dirty dishes, and Caroline asked me if I wanted to go for a walk, instead. I said yes, in spite of my slippers, and stuck a muffin in each coat pocket, which made them bulge, like when I stuff my winter gloves in them.

The way I figured it, if we were walking, maybe the talking wouldn't be so awkward. At first all we did was stroll along, not speaking, sipping our drinks, me trying to avoid puddles. There were about ten thousand things I wanted to ask Caroline, and they hung over us like the encroaching fog. I didn't know anything about her, really. I didn't even know what she did for a living except that it was something at a bank. And there was that Walker guy. What had happened to her husband? I knew he had died, but how? Why did she move back to Victoria? Was she rich, or did she pretend to be rich? And what about that house?

That one I could ask her.

"I was wondering about the house," I said.

She sipped her drink and I noticed her lipstick didn't come off on the cup like mine always does. *I'll have to get some of that, whatever it is. Of course, hers probably didn't come from the dollar store.*

"What about it?" she asked.

"Well, I…is that *your* house? I mean, do you own it?"

She glanced over at me and I could tell I'd surprised her. "Of course. Why do you ask?"

"I don't know. I thought maybe you were renting it or something."

She did that half-smile-scrunchy-forehead puzzled thing. "Susan, don't you remember the house?"

Now I was the one who was confused. "Me? Why should I?"

"We lived there when you were little," she told me.

"What? We did? Are you serious?" This was news to me. Was my memory really that bad? We'd stopped on a corner to wait for the crosswalk to change, and a couple of people pushed around us, jaywalking.

"It was my parents' house," she explained, looking straight ahead. "I grew up there."

Aha…. That explained her name written on the ceiling in glow-in-the-dark paint. And also Tracie had said she remembered a house and was surprised I didn't. Now that finally made sense. The light changed, and we walked on. "When did we live there?" I asked.

"After your grandparents died the house came to me, and we all moved in," she said. "You'd just turned two."

Should I admit I didn't even know how they'd died? If I ever wanted to find out, I'd have to. "How did they…what happened to them?" I asked.

We'd walked right into a big line of people, who were waiting outside a diner, and it took a minute to get through them and meet up on the other side. "Their car was hit by a drunk driver," Caroline said when I caught up to her.

"Oh."

A warm flush of anger rushed through me, starting at the roots of my trashed hair and pouring into my heart and brain. For a minute I thought I was mad at the drunk driver. And then maybe at Caroline for not telling me sooner, but then, even with my blood boiling I knew that wasn't rational, and my anger was actually directed at Dad. I didn't know anything about anything, and it was all his fault.

Caroline might have been a miserable parent, she might have abandoned us and left us to fend for ourselves, and she might have ditched our father, but he should've told us stuff. After all, she was our mother. We had a right to know. Maybe if he'd explained things, important things, then Tracie wouldn't be so mad at Caroline. And if Tracie wasn't so angry, I wouldn't have to choose between everyone I loved and possibly having a mom too.

Chapter 29

Things were pretty tense in the apartment after I spent the night at Caroline's. Dad kept trying to buddy up to me, watching sports at home all evening, instead of at Uncle Bill's—even though he had a big-screen TV, and we didn't. Tracie, of course, still wasn't speaking to me. I tried not to let it bother me, but it did. I missed her.

I couldn't worry about it for long, though because the presentation had taken over my life. It was now Monday and we didn't have much time left to perfect it. Amanda and I had just run through it again for Baker, which is why I was still at school half an hour after the last bell rang.

Again.

Voluntarily.

We had to stop meeting this way.

Baker brushed his hands together, and at first I thought he was applauding us. I was about to take a big bow, but then I saw it was just that gesture people make when something is finished, and I straightened up fast.

"Well, girls, I need to wrap this up," he said. "But I think you have a very solid presentation and you'll be great at the meeting tomorrow night."

"So we're gonna get an A?" I asked, grinning up at him.

"Not if you use words like *gonna*," he said, smiling back. I laughed. I knew he was joking around. Half-joking, anyway. He walked us to the door of the classroom. "Girls," he said, stopping us, "I just want you to prepare yourselves."

"That's what we've been doing," I said.

He shifted on his feet like something was wrong, and he didn't want to say it. "What I mean is…the thing is, you've done a very thorough job, but I don't want you two to get your hopes up. It's probably not going to go your way."

"That's what my mom says, too," Amanda said.

"You mean they're really going to get rid of the jan— custodians?" I asked.

He nodded. "Yeah, I think they will. It's all about the bottom line."

Well that just sucked. Not only did we do all this work, but we still had to present it, even though we knew we'd lose and the custodians would get fired. We *had* to convince them. But how?

"We need something else," I said to Amanda as we walked down the hall to our lockers. "Something good... proof that getting rid of the union custodians and replacing them with subcontractors is a really bad idea."

"We'll just have to present what we have and hope for the best," she said.

"I want to win this fight," I insisted. "Don't you?"

Amanda shrugged. "Yeah, but face it, Suze. We're probably not going to. If we could've gotten an adult to take our side or something, maybe. But I don't see what else we can do."

An adult? *An adult...think, Suze. Think. Dad? No. AJ? She's pretty forceful.* And then I remembered Trina Blevins. Of course! AJ's neighbor. She was the only one who could help us. We had to have her.

I checked my pockets for change. Nothing. "Can I borrow a couple of bucks?" I asked Amanda.

"You still owe me five from last week."

"I know, but this is important. It's for bus fare," I told her. "I'm going to head over to AJ's and Uncle Bill's and see if I can talk Mrs. Blevins into helping us after all."

"Good luck with that," she said, clearly not convinced I could do it. She pulled out her wallet, anyway and gave me exact change for the bus.

"Thanks," I said. "I'll work it off cleaning your room."

"Don't worry about it," she said. "It's all for the cause, right?"

"Yep." I gave her a hug and hurried off toward the bus stop.

"Call me," she said.

"As soon as I know something."

I was going to get that woman to talk if it was the last thing I did.

"AJ, you've got to help me," I pleaded over a cup of hot chocolate and a cinnamon roll.

"I told you. Trina doesn't want to risk losing her job," she said. "And quit whining, or I'll give you something to whine about. No one's cleaned your uncle's washroom in a while."

I backed off right away because I'd seen it, and there was a reason he and AJ didn't share. I regrouped by downing a slug of hot chocolate and letting it warm me from the inside.

"Are you sure you won't help?" I said, not a trace of whine in my voice. "Not even to save the jobs of all those custodians?"

AJ got up, taking my plate out from under the last piece of cinnamon roll, which I snagged and stuffed in my mouth.

"If we could only assure her it was confidential," she said, more to herself than me. I could feel her starting to give in.

I licked the sticky cinnamon goodness off my fingers. "I have an idea," I said. I ripped a piece of notebook paper out of my binder and scribbled while AJ crowded my elbow to see what I was writing.

"I'll get you an envelope," she said.

"Two. One for the return."

"Good idea."

As soon as I was done, I hurried across the street to Mrs. Blevins' mailbox. Looking around to make sure no nosy neighbors were watching, I peeked inside. Good. She hadn't picked up her mail yet. I laid my envelope on top of the pile already in there and said a little prayer.

Four hours later the phone rang once, giving us the signal. I raced out to AJ's mailbox—stealthily, like a spy. Bingo! There it was. *The envelope.*

"Got it!" I said, once I was back inside. I pulled out six pages of anonymous typed script, and AJ and I huddled on the couch, poring over the "insider info." We could swear in court that we didn't know where it had come from too. We hadn't seen a thing. Not that we'd be going to court, but I'm just saying.

"The real question is," AJ asked, "how do we use this?"

I loved the *we*. She was going to help me come up with something great. I looked around the living room. "Do you have a sheer curtain?"

"Upstairs," she said. "In my study."

"Can you get it? We need it."

"What for?"

"Just trust me. I'll meet you back here in a second."

Downstairs, Uncle Bill was watching the hockey game with my dad. "AJ needs you," I said.

"At the end of the period," Uncle Bill said.

"Not you. Dad."

My father peeled his eyes away from the screen. "Now?"

"You have to run the video camera." His gaze wandered back to the game. "It's for school." I said.

He sighed. "Oh, okay."

Upstairs, the three of us hung the curtain in the middle of the dining room, using some plant hooks already on the ceiling. Then we put a chair and a lamp behind it, and sat AJ in the seat.

"Let's make a movie," I said. "And kick some school-board ass!"

"School board-butt," AJ and Dad said together.

"That too."

Chapter 30

I'd decided to take Caroline up on her offer to see her hairdresser. I'd waited too long, though. Her stylist was all booked up. Someone she worked with had a daughter who'd just graduated from beauty school, and she could fit me in on Tuesday afternoon in plenty of time before the meeting. It was a half-day at school and Caroline took some personal time and picked me up at noon.

"I hope this is okay," Caroline said when we walked into the salon.

She didn't look convinced, and I can't say I blamed her. The place was small and crowded, bright turquoise, didn't have a receptionist, and the magazines looked about to fall apart.

The local pop station blared from speakers in the corners, and I could hear a TV playing in a back room loud enough that I could make out the weather report for tonight—rain as usual. We waited for about ten minutes without anyone even noticing us, and then a bubble gum-chewing girl with fire-engine red hair and three eyebrow piercings came out to answer the phone and saw us sitting there.

She waved stubby purple fingernails at us, and then put the call on hold. "Nia!" she yelled. "Your one o'clock is here."

I'd barely sat down in the salon chair when Nia threw a purple cape over me and secured it in a chokehold around my neck. I watched her tall, skinny body in the mirror as she fingered the rough orange chunks of my hair.

She raised her blackened eyebrows at me. "Been playing with the bleach, have we?" she asked, smiling.

"My friend Leigh did it," I said. "We were trying to dye it electric blue."

"Blue?" Caroline asked.

"There's this cool author," I told her, "who writes vampire books, and he has black hair with blue streaks. It looks awesome. And since my hair was already black, we thought it would be easy to do, but the bleach part that you have to do first didn't really work out."

"Too right," Nia said. "But it sounds fab. So is that what's on for today?"

I brightened up. I hadn't considered the idea of having blue stripes done by a professional. "Okay," I said at the same time that Caroline said, "Definitely not."

"Susan," she said. "You've worked really hard on this presentation. Don't you want to make a good impression on the school board?"

She had a point. "I guess."

"So?" Nia asked. "What'll it be?"

"She'd like a trim and for you to dye it all one color," Caroline answered as if I wasn't even there. "Can you do that?"

Nia picked at the orange chunks again, rubbing them between her fingers. "Probably. The grow-out is healthy but the bleached stuff, which frankly there's a lot of, is pretty brittle."

The two of them discussed deep conditioners while Nia washed my hair. I concentrated on keeping my eyes shut tight so the water wouldn't run into them. I'd never had anyone except Tracie shampoo my hair before. Either she or AJ usually gave me my haircuts. It felt amazing, like a million fingers rubbing and massaging my scalp. I never wanted it to stop, but eventually, Nia sat me up and towel-dried my hair, squeezing my head like she was trying to squash a grape. Then she rubbed something citrusy and creamy into my hair, which felt almost as good as the shampooing. After that, she put a plastic bag over my head and stuck me under the dryer.

I messed around on my phone for a while, sending self-ies to Jessica and Amanda, telling them about my beauty treatment. Caroline had topped off my phone because she wanted to be able to reach me without calling the landline and making it worse for me at home with Tracie and Dad.

After twenty minutes, Nia rinsed my hair and then put me back in her chair. She pumped it up with a foot lever, and I rose in the air. I watched in the mirror as she took a smelly bowl of pasty goo and began painting the orange parts of my hair with it, and then wrapping those bits up in foil.

"Will it match the rest of her hair?" Caroline asked.

"Well," she said. "I hope so. But her hair's basically trashed. Corrective color can be a bitch."

"Can't you just dye it black?" I asked. "So it's all the same?"

"We could've," she said. "But it's kinda late now because I already started this. Besides, not very many people actually have truly black hair. Yours has a bit of red and brown in it, which makes it tricky."

"I don't care if it looks real," I told her.

"Well, like I said, I've already started this. Let's see what we get first, and we'll go from there."

She put a plastic cap over my head and told me she'd be back in a while. She got me a can of pop out of the machine and brought Caroline a glass of white wine out of a box, which Caroline thanked her for but set on the counter without tasting. Then Nia disappeared, leaving us alone.

"Thanks for bringing me here, Caroline."

"I hope we're not sorry."

"It seems like she knows what she's doing."

"Maybe. At least she started with the deep conditioner, although I'm not sure she would have if I hadn't mentioned it."

I reached for my phone, thinking Caroline would probably do the same, but she stopped me with her words. "You know, Susan," she said. "You don't have to call me Caroline. You could call me Mom."

I choked on my pop, and she got up and thwacked me on the back until I stopped sputtering. "Or not," she said, half-smiling.

"Ummm…I don't know. I mean…I guess. You still seem kind of like a stranger, though." I didn't mean to hurt her, but I could tell by the way she flinched that I had. "I feel like I don't know all that much about you."

"What do you want to know?" she asked.

Why did you leave?

How come you never called?

Did you miss me?

Do you love us?

"I don't know what happened," I said.

"When?"

"When you left. One minute you were there, the next you were gone, and no one ever talked about you again."

She thumbed through a beat-up fashion magazine for a minute, and then she met my eyes in the mirror. "I didn't mean to go away for forever." She dropped her gaze back to the page. "After your grandparents died, well…I was only twenty-nine, and I know that seems really old to you, but someday you'll realize how young it actually is. No one I knew had ever died. And to lose them both like that. I could barely get up in the morning."

I studied my fingernails, so I didn't have to look at her.

"I didn't even know how to be me," she said after a while. "Let alone a wife and mother. I felt so alone."

"So you just left?" I asked. It came out way more bitter than I meant it to, but I didn't stop there. "We kind of felt the same way, you know. When you left? Like totally abandoned?"

"Susa—"

"Okay," Nia said, interrupting. "Let's see how that hair looks now."

God, she was chirpy.

Caroline and I sat there, neither of us saying a word, but Nia didn't seem to notice the tension. She just unwrapped one of the foils, and then folded it back up and checked another. "Well, I don't like how that looks, but let's give it a few more minutes." She snapped the plastic cap back into place.

As soon as we were alone again, Caroline said, "You don't understand."

"No, I don't."

"Listen, Susan, I'm trying to explain." She blew out air between her teeth, frustrated. Or maybe annoyed. "I just *had* to get away," she said. "So I rented out my house and your dad took you two to live with Jenny and Bill."

"And?" I demanded when she didn't go on.

"I moved to Vancouver. Just for a little while, but then, I don't know. I liked living alone. I told myself it was because it was the first time I'd ever had my own apartment, but actually, it was because I didn't have any responsibilities."

"Like...oh, I don't know...two little kids who were counting on you?"

She shrugged. "And your father."

"You could've lived in your house here," I said, "and still seen us on weekends or something."

"I know, I know, but—"

Nia popped back in. "Oooookay," she said. "It's got to be done by now, or we're in big trouble."

"What?" I asked. "Are you serious?"

She laughed. "Just kidding. It'll be fine. I haven't lost anyone yet."

I wasn't reassured.

"Can we just have a minute here?" Caroline asked her.

"Well…"

I was actually thinking maybe I didn't care what Caroline had to say if it meant my hair would be ruined, but she was nothing if not persistent. "Just one minute. Please?" she asked again.

"Yeah, okay," Nia agreed. "But I don't want to leave the color on much longer."

"I understand." As soon as Nia left, she turned to me. "It took me a year to pull myself together. I didn't even have a job because I couldn't face looking for one. I thought about coming back, but after all that time, I was embarrassed."

"About what?" I asked.

"Leaving you. It seemed so selfish."

"It was," I told her, and she flinched again. "Do you have any idea how much it sucks to get a check—but nothing else—every month from your mother?"

"Sus—"

I spun the salon chair around so I faced her. "It would've been better if you hadn't even sent the checks," I said. "Then we wouldn't have had any hope that you actually cared about us."

"I did care, though," she said. "I do care. I just—"

"It's not like the checks make that much difference anyway," I said.

Caroline drew back as if I'd slapped her. "What do you mean?"

"Nothing."

"Susan?"

"Fine. Look at you," I said, "with all your dripping diamonds, a fancy house and car. And the three of us live in a crappy apartment and buy our clothes at thrift stores. I always figured you just didn't have any money, so I didn't worry about it. But obviously it's just that you never even thought about us."

Caroline took in several deep breaths. "I don't think you know anything about the arrangement I have with your father," she said.

"I bet I know more than you," I said, challenging her. "How much do you pay in support every month?"

She swallowed hard.

I shook my head. "You don't have a clue."

But I knew exactly how much she paid, and it didn't even cover our cheap rent. The truth was, she still sent what she and Dad had agreed on ten years ago. They'd settled it between them, out of court. AJ and Bill had tried talking him into asking for more over the years, but he wouldn't do it.

"Susan, listen to me," Caroline said. "If your dad needed more support, he should've told me."

"Like that's going to happen," I said.

"Okay," Nia said, striding in and taking my arm. "We have to get this stuff off right now." She sat me down at one of the shampooing sinks.

Caroline followed us. "My accountant takes care of it," she told me, "which is not an excuse, but I will make sure I review it first thing tomorrow. I promise."

Nia turned on the water and started yanking the foils out of my hair. Warm spray ran down the sides of my face, dripping under my collar.

"Whatever," I told Caroline, raising my voice over the noise of the water.

Nia's eyes stayed on my hair, and her hands worked inexpertly, tugging hard. Finally she got the last foil out and ran the water through my hair while she massaged my scalp. Her forehead was all scrunched up with worry, and I started to feel sick to my stomach. I wasn't sure if it was Nia or the conversation with Caroline, though.

She stood me up and led me back to the chair.

"Susan," Caroline said.

"Just forget it," I said. "I don't want to talk about it anymore."

"You're not being very fair," Caroline said. "I said I'll send more child support. What else do you want from me?"

I'd been asking myself that question ever since Halloween, and I still didn't know. When I didn't answer right away, I saw Caroline's body language change. She pushed back her shoulders, her eyes went cold, and we didn't speak for the rest of the appointment, except to answer Nia's questions about my hair.

When Caroline dropped me off at home, I got the distinct feeling I might never see her again. And I didn't even care. At least, that's what I told myself.

Chapter 31

Jessica hoisted herself up onto the washroom counter and watched me put on my makeup. Her mom still wouldn't let her wear anything except lip gloss, unless she was in a play. Caroline and I had barely spoken after the shampoo-bowl discussion, but she'd still paid to have my eyebrows waxed and the skin around them was pink and sore, so I dabbed on a bit of concealer.

"I can't believe how good your hair looks," Jessica said.

I laughed. "Gee, thanks."

"No, I mean, it's so natural."

"I know," I said. "The hairstylist had trouble with it, though. After she fixed the bleached parts, they were sort of a weird brownish color. She ended up putting a temporary wash over the whole thing to even it out."

Nia hadn't wanted to do anything more to it after the first round of color because she thought my hair was too damaged for more chemicals, but Caroline had insisted. Since she was paying the bill, Nia had done it in the end.

My hair rocked, but the sick feeling in my stomach would not go away. The one where you did something mean, or you said something you wish you could take back. Maybe Caroline had been poor until recently. Maybe she'd been paying what she could afford. She was right, I didn't really know.

I doubted she'd show up tonight. She hadn't mentioned it when she dropped me off. But I decided I'd call her tomorrow and try to talk it out a bit more. She wasn't the best mother in the world, but so far, I hadn't been a world-class daughter either. We were still feeling our way, I guess.

So much for my big plan to get my whole family in one room and make them proud of me. Right now, I'd be lucky to get through the presentation, let alone save the janitors or convince my family to stop acting like idiots toward each other.

"Are you going to wear your hair down tonight?" Jessica asked.

"Yep. But I'm going to use Tracie's flat iron." I'd found it hidden under her bed when I was looking for my good shoes. She'd stuck it there to keep me away from it because she said my hair was fried enough already, but I had it heating up on the counter right now. With any luck, I'd be done, and it would cool down and be back in place before she got home.

I put the final touches on my eye shadow and went to work on my hair. Jess and I were talking about our Christmas lists—both what we wanted and what we planned to buy—when I noticed a funny smell.

In the mirror, I saw a little puff of smoke above my head and I jerked my hand away. We both stared wordlessly at a huge chunk of hair still clamped in the iron, even though I was now holding it away from my head.

And then I said, "Oh, my God. Jess!"

She sat there, frozen, her eyes huge.

"How bad is it?" I asked, spinning around so she could see the back. I was now holding the long hank of hair in my hand, its ends singed, so I had a pretty good idea already. "What happened?"

"I think maybe that was the chunk that was bleached before," Jessica said, fingering the back of my head. "All the hair around it looks okay, but you've got this little patch where it's about two inches long, and all frizzy."

I grabbed a brush and started pulling it through my hair. "Do you think I can cover it up?"

"Umm…wait," she said, grabbing my arm. "Stop brushing!"

Another chunk of hair had broken off and was caught

in the brush. Now I had a bald spot on the side of my head where one of the bleach streaks had been.

"What am I going to do?"

"Well…"

I stared at my hair in the mirror. Or what used to be my hair. I looked like a total dork. It was way worse than when Leigh bleached it. "Maybe I can slick it back into a ponytail with some gel."

"Either that or a hat," Jessica said.

"Against school rules." I slopped some gel over my hands and ran them through my hair, pulling it up. I couldn't make it smooth because I was too scared to brush it, but it was an improvement. "This so sucks," I said. "But if I can just get it to lie down for tonight, I'll have Caroline take me to her good hairdresser tomorrow, and she can fix it."

"Yeah," Jessica said. She didn't sound convinced.

I couldn't worry about it now. "Maybe it will look better when it dries," I said. "I should get dressed."

She followed me to my room. "What are you wearing?"

"Caroline got me this suit," I said, pointing at a navy skirt and jacket hanging on the door of my wardrobe. "But seriously? I am so *not* wearing that."

"It's nice," she said, touching the sleeve.

"I know, but it's for a grown-up. I'd feel stupid. Amanda won't be wearing a suit."

"Yeah, doubtful."

"I'm just going in my standard outfit: black sweater, black skirt, black tights."

"That's probably better."

I'd never gotten around to sewing on the button that had popped off my good sweater, so I had to go with second-best. After I changed, I checked myself out in the wardrobe's mirror. The gel hadn't held very well, and the bits where my hair had broken off stuck out funny and stiff.

"What I need is one of Tracie's headbands," I said. "That would cover the bald spot on the side."

We hurried back to the washroom and I rummaged through Tracie's drawer. Something poked me in the hand. Dad's manicure scissors. "Hey," I said.

Jessica could read my mind.

"I don't think you should."

But I was in no mood for reason. "Just the bits that are still sticking out."

"Suze," she warned. "What about when you take the ponytail down?"

But it was too late. I was already snipping away. "I don't care about tomorrow." I said. "I'm just worried about right now." My hair laid a little flatter with every clip. After a few more snips, I studied it. "I don't like the gel look," I said. "I'm going to wash it out really fast." I stripped down and jumped in the shower as quickly as I could, trying to keep my face out of the water so I didn't have to re-do my makeup. Two minutes later I was out and getting dressed. I swiped the towel fiercely over my hair to dry it as much as I could.

"Suze, stop!" Jessica yelled, grabbing my arm. "Another chunk just broke off."

I examined the towel, which was now covered with long strands of hair. Above my right ear was a bald patch to match the other side.

The front door slammed.

"*Aggh!*" I said. "It just keeps getting worse."

"Your hair?"

"My life."

"What do you mean?"

"Tracie's home."

Chapter 32

I slammed the washroom door and locked us in. "She can't see my hair."

"Maybe she can fix it. Didn't you say she's going to be a hairdresser?"

"Yeah, but she's not even talking to me. There's no way she'd touch it."

How could I ask Tracie for help now? For one thing, she might realize I didn't ruin it myself. That would mean a lot of questions on her part and a lot more trouble on mine. On the other hand, what was I going to do if she didn't help me?

"Do you think you could lie and say you colored it?" I begged Jessica.

"What? Why?"

"Because Tracie might help me if she thinks we screwed it up, but she won't if she knows I went with Caroline."

"Oh."

"So, will you?"

"Well, it's not that I don't want to," Jess said. "It's just that I'm not a very good liar."

"You're an *actress*."

"That's different. Besides, what will I say if she asks me what I did to it exactly?"

"You could confuse her with your Shakespeare talk."

Tracie tried the washroom door. "Suze? Are you in there?"

"Yeah. I'll be out in a minute."

"I need to pee."

"Just a sec." I looked around for something to cover my hair. Jessica handed me the towel off the floor. "Good thinking." I scooped up all the bits of loose hair and stuffed them in the garbage can and covered them with scrunched up toilet paper.

"Now!" Tracie yelled.

I wrapped the towel around my head and opened the door. Tracie pushed past me and I thought I was home safe, but why would my luck change now?

"Hey! That's my towel," she said.

I tried to duck out of the way, but Tracie was way too fast for me. It was all those years of skating. She got a hold of a corner and pulled it off my head. Loose hair fell out of the towel onto the floor. God knows what my head looked like.

We all stood there, frozen in time. "What happened to your hair?" Tracie finally asked.

That's when I lost it. I burst into tears and ran off howling to our room. Jessica and Tracie followed on my tail. I threw myself down on the bed sobbing. I could hear Jessica explaining that we'd dyed it. She didn't say anything about Caroline or the salon trip, but I knew Tracie would probably ask to see the box from the hair color and the truth would all come out. Then she'd stomp off and leave me like the badly pruned bonsai tree that I was. She'd probably have a good laugh, too.

"Sit up, Suze," Tracie ordered. I sat up. "Let me look at it." She fingered what was left of my hair. "It's pretty bad," she said, as I snuffled, and she turned my head to one side. "All I can do is shave it off with Dad's clippers."

"Shave it?" Jessica and I yelled together.

"Well, cut it really short. Like a pixie cut. It's the only way I can make it even. Plus you're going to want to grow it all out, so you might as well get rid of as much of this bad dye job as you can."

"I don't know," I said. "That sounds so drastic. Don't you have any wigs, Jessica?"

"All of mine are costume ones," she said. "They wouldn't pass for real hair."

"That's fine," I said. "I don't care."

"Come on," Tracie said. "It won't be so bad."

"Why don't you just take my head off and be done with it?" I whimpered.

"There are some really beautiful models with really short hair," Tracie said.

"If only I were beautiful, that might be reassuring."

"I'll meet you in the kitchen," she told us.

Was she trying to pay me back for being such a sucky sister, or was that really all she could do? I touched my head with my hand. Across the room I saw Tracie's alarm clock. Oh, my God. AJ was supposed to be here in ten minutes.

"Okay. Okay. Shave it," I said, running after her. "But do it quick, before I can think too much about it."

In the kitchen, Jessica and I laid newspaper down on the floor. Tracie came in and sat me in a chair with a towel around my shoulders.

"See," she said, holding up the clippers. "I put the one inch guide on it so it won't make you bald or anything."

"Whatever," I said. "Just...hurry."

When she flipped the switch the clippers buzzed angrily in my ear. Before she made even one inroad into my hair, something broke inside me. I couldn't let Jessica take the blame for this. I couldn't lie to Tracie. I had to own up.

"Wait."

She turned off the clippers. "What now?"

"Before you help me," I said. "I owe you the truth."

"Which is?" Tracie had her hands on her hips, her eyebrows raised.

And so I told her about Caroline and the salon. And she took it remarkably well. At least I think she did. She didn't actually say anything at all. She waited until I'd finished, flipped the switch, and shaved my head.

While she was working, Caroline showed up. I didn't hear her over the loud buzz, but Jessica must've let her in, because when I looked up she was standing in the archway to the kitchen. And boy, did she look mad.

"Susan? What happened to your hair?"

"What are you doing here?" I asked, over the angry hum.

"I came to give you a ride."

"AJ's picking me up."

Tracie flipped off the clippers and began to brush loose bits of hair off of me.

"Did you do that to her?" Caroline demanded, turning on Tracie. I wondered if she even realized that was her other daughter standing there. As far as I knew, they hadn't seen each other since that one Christmas Eve. When Tracie didn't answer her, she switched back to me. "I just spent a small fortune getting that miserable hair fixed."

"I know, but it all broke off when I tried to brush it." How could she care about her money so much when my hair had looked so bad? For about the millionth time since Caroline had come back into my life, tears sprang to my eyes.

"And what are you wearing, Susan?" she asked.

"I decided to go with my regular clothes after all."

"What about the suit I bought you?"

"I told you I had something to wear."

"I was hoping you'd changed your mind."

"Well, I didn't."

I noticed Jessica had totally disappeared and Tracie slipped out of the kitchen fast, leaving me alone, facing the enemy. I shook my bangs into my face for protection but nothing happened. What was left of them lay in piles on the floor.

"I can do what I want," I said, sounding like a two-year-old.

"Susan, tell me you don't want the suit. Say you don't want your hair done. But don't let me waste my time and money on you."

"I *did* want my hair done. You're not listening to me. It *broke* off when I brushed it." I didn't mention the flat iron since I was pretty sure that was part of the problem. "Besides, you've wasted a big ten minutes on me," I mumbled under my breath.

"What?"

"Nothing."

"What did you say?"

"Look, you may think you're my mother, but Tracie's right. You've never acted like one before, so you can't just waltz in here demanding all sorts of things."

"Demanding? All I've done is give you things since I moved to Victoria."

She didn't get it, and I didn't think she ever would. At that moment I could see exactly where Tracie was coming from. How could a woman who let her daughters get away from her for ten years suddenly become a mother? She couldn't.

"You asked me what I wanted before," I said, softly. "And I didn't answer because I'm not exactly sure. But I do know I can't do this instant mother-daughter stuff."

"So...what?" she asked, her body visibly tensing. "You don't want to see me anymore?"

"No. I do. I want to see you. But maybe we can be friends for a while first?"

"Friends?"

"This relationship thing isn't working that well," I explained. My stomach was really churning now, but I kept going. "It's just...it's a lot to take in, having you here suddenly. Maybe we could get to know each other a little bit more before I have to start thinking of you as my mom or something."

Caroline stood there looking at me like I was speaking a foreign language. It was as if she didn't really understand what I was saying. It's not like I was being really clear or any-thing. But I wasn't totally ready to give up on her either.

"Like with the suit…"

"What about it?"

"Oh, I don't know. Never mind."

She sighed. "I just wanted to buy you something nice to wear."

"I know. And it's really nice if you work in a bank. I mean, it's from Anne Taylor. I'm thirteen, not twenty-five. I don't have a job." She stared at me and then we both laughed a little. "Also," I said, getting serious again, "I'm not some doll for you to dress up. You missed that part of my life."

She nodded. "I know. I'm painfully aware of that."

We stood there in silence.

"The thing is," I said after a while, "it's like…on the one hand, you want me to be your daughter, but you also treat me like a grown-up, which I'm not."

"I thought that's what teenagers wanted," Caroline said.

"We do. Sort of. I mean, yeah, but I'm not interested in grown-up stuff, or their clothes. Like…when we get together, we always do what you want to do. You don't even ask me. I mean…fancy restaurants with confusing valets and too many forks? And sushi? Kinda not my scene. Can't we just have something easy like a pizza and a DVD at your house some time?"

Caroline nodded. "Yes, I see what you mean."

"And you sent me a bottle of Prosecco."

"What?" she asked. "When?"

"In that gift basket."

"Really?"

"Yep. And I get that it was probably a mistake, but sending me a gift basket is totally something you'd do for a client, not a kid. It was delicious, but kind of weird."

"Sorry. I wasn't thinking, I guess." She paused, like she was reviewing what she'd learned, and then said, "Okay… so…no suits, pizza instead of sushi, definitely nix the gift baskets, especially ones with wine. Anything else?"

I shrugged. "Well, there is one more thing you need to know," I told her, taking advantage of the moment.

"Only one?" she asked, still smiling.

I laughed. "Well, one important thing."

"What's that?"

"Unless I'm in trouble, no one calls me Susan," I said. "I go by Suze now."

She nodded. "I'll try to remember that."

Tracie stuck her head into the kitchen. "Amanda's dad is at the door and he wants to talk to you, Suze. He says it's an emergency."

Chapter 33

Steve handed me Amanda's laptop and our folder of notes. "Can't she go to the hospital *after* our presentation?" I asked him.

He shook his head. "Suze, her hand is the size of a softball and it's already turning blue. She needs an X-ray."

"But you said it's just a finger, right? She could tape it up like she did last year during the baseball season. She's tough. I can't do this without her."

He grabbed me in a bear hug and ruffled what was left of my hair. "You'll be great," he said. "You can tell her all about it tomorrow."

"But—"

"I really gotta go. Leigh's in the car with Amanda, and you know how bossy she is. She gave me two minutes, and she's probably timing me. Good luck!"

I watched him run down the stairs, leaving me all alone.

"Well, that settles that," I said. "What should we watch on TV? Anyone up for a pizza?"

"Susan," Caroline said. "I mean, Suze, you don't have time for pizza. We need to leave."

"Are you crazy?" I asked her. "I'm not going without Amanda."

"Of course you are," she said.

"Suze," Jessica tried.

I held my hands up, palms out. "Don't waste your breath," I told anyone and everyone. I collapsed on the couch and flipped on the TV. Too early for my game show. I'd have to watch a sitcom. Which one? Didn't matter.

"Listen," Caroline said. I ignored her. Jessica plopped down next to me on the couch. Caroline tried again. "Get your coat."

"I told you all, I'm not going without her." I flipped channels. There wasn't anything good on. What a drag. I pulled the fuzzy yellow blanket over me and settled in for a long, boring night.

I guess they could tell I meant business because Tracie disappeared into our room, and after a minute, Caroline retreated to the kitchen and I could smell coffee. How weird.

She was apparently making herself at home. I wondered if she'd bake a cake next. Probably not. She was much more likely to have one delivered from some upscale bakery.

The TV flickered blue-and-green in the dark room, lighting up Jess's face, ghostlike. The shrill of the phone pierced the thick silence between us. I reached across her and grabbed the receiver. "Hello?"

"Suze? What are you doing home?" Amanda asked.

"Why do you always call and ask me why I'm here?"

"I wanted to leave you a message saying I hoped it went well. Why aren't you at the meeting?"

"Yeah…that…I'm not going."

"What do you—" Her cell phone cut out for a second.

"What?" I asked.

"What do you mean you're not going?"

"I'm not doing it alone, that's all."

"But you have to. You'll be fine."

"I can't do it without you."

"You *have* to," she repeated. "What about Honors English?"

"I don't care."

"Yes, you do."

"No, I don't. I wish everyone would quit telling me what I think."

"You don't want to go back to regular English," she said. "I know you don't."

"Yeah, well, you should've thought of that before you went running around like an idiot breaking your finger."

"I didn't do it on purpose, you know? Leigh and I were playing catch and I slipped in the mud."

There was no way girly-girl Leigh was playing catch. Amanda had been doing something stupid again and didn't want to admit it. "Whatever."

"If you don't care about yourself," she said, "what about the custodians?"

"Not my problem."

"What about Yoda?"

Well, that wasn't playing fair at all. I was really disappointed in Amanda. How could she throw Yoda into it? "He's ready to retire anyway," I mumbled.

"Fine. Be that way. Just think about yourself and your own pathetic little life."

Dead silence on her end. She'd obviously hung up so I did the same thing. "Suze," Jessica said, in a low voice.

"Yeah?"

"What about your insider info?"

"Who cares about that?"

The front door flew open.

"*Susan Jennifer Tamaki!* Where the heck are you?" AJ stormed into the living room huffing and puffing. "I've been sitting in the parking lot for ten minutes and your phone's been busy and you're not answering your cell. I better have climbed these stairs for a very good reason. Like you better be dead."

"I'm not going." It came out more squeaky than I'd intended.

"Like hell you're not. Get up."

"Amanda broke her finger," I said. "And I'm not doing it alone."

"Get your stuff and let's go."

I didn't move. Jessica squirmed on the couch next to me.

"I'm driving her," said a soft, clear voice from the kitchen doorway.

AJ swung around and faced Caroline. They took each other in slowly, checking out the damage of ten years on their bodies. AJ nodded curtly. "Caroline."

"Jenny."

Silence.

"I'll give Susan a ride," Caroline said. "We were just leaving."

"As long as she gets her butt over there, I don't give a damn how she does it," AJ conceded. As she lumbered out of the room, she yelled back at me. "I'll see you at the high school in ten minutes. Or else."

The door slammed behind her and I turned my attention back to the TV. "I'm still not going."

"Well, don't you think you should at least call your dad at work?" Jessica asked.

"Why?"

"Wasn't he going to pick up Yoda and take him to the meeting?"

Oh. Dad. Hmmm. Yeah…. "What time is it?"

"Ten to seven," she said.

"Really? He's probably already there."

I knew what she was trying to do. She wanted me to jump into Caroline's car and whiz over to the school and give my presentation. Well, nothing doing. Dad would figure it out for himself when I didn't show. What did he care anyway? I doubt he would've even taken the time off from work if he hadn't heard Caroline was going to be there. Not that he wanted to see her. He just didn't want to be the slacker parent.

That thought stirred something in my brain. Hadn't my plan been to get my entire family in the same room? Wasn't that one of the reasons I'd agreed to do it? Aside from the whole SuperUnderdog thing, making everyone proud of me might pull my family together. I wasn't stupid enough to think we'd be a "happy little family" after the meeting, but maybe if I did it, we'd all go out for ice cream afterward like Amanda's family always does. For good ice cream, though, not that gross green tea stuff.

I got up and went to our bedroom, throwing the door open with a bang. Tracie jumped, startled. She was sitting at her desk, her textbooks piled in front of her, but none of them were open.

I put my hands on my hips and gave her my best AJ laser-look. "If I do this thing tonight, are you coming along to cheer me on?" I asked.

"What? Yeah. Of course. Are you going to do it after all?"

I stood there, not answering, still trying to work it all out in my mind. Caroline was going to drive me, which meant she'd be in the audience. And AJ and Uncle Bill were probably already there with my dad.

I nodded, more to myself than in response to Tracie's question. And then I drew in a deep breath, steeling myself… calling up my Super Powers to get me through this. Because what I realized was Yoda wasn't the only underdog around here. Tonight, doing this presentation all by myself, for what was probably already a lost cause, made me the biggest underdog in the room.

"Well, get up and let's go," I told Tracie. "Or we're gonna be late."

I found Caroline and Jess sitting in the living room, whispering. No doubt about how to talk me into going to the meeting.

I grabbed my coat off the back of the chair. "What are you guys waiting for? Christmas?" I asked. "Let's get this show on the road."

Chapter 34

Jessica and I stood in the doorway of the high-school auditorium.

"Where is everyone?" I whispered to her. She shrugged.

I guess I'd expected it to be full, so I was pretty surprised to see only a handful of adults in the first few rows. Surprised, but not disappointed. About halfway back sat the entire Honors English class, most of them texting on their phones. Baker gave them extra credit for coming. I wondered if I'd get extra credit too. Ha. I'd be lucky to get a passing grade.

On the stage was a long table with seven or eight people seated behind it. On one side were Farbinger, Baker, and two empty chairs. I began the long walk down the aisle, knowing one of those empty seats was for me but wishing it wasn't.

Caroline was parking the car.

Tracie had walked.

Sometimes she's just dumb.

Baker saw us come in and waved me up onto the stage. Some of the parents turned to look, and I clutched Amanda's computer to my chest so tight I'm surprised I didn't crack the case. As I passed the front row, AJ reached out and squeezed my wrist presumably for good luck. Either that, or as a threat.

The stairs were on one side and Baker was on the other, so I had to walk all the way across the stage behind the meeting to get to him. How totally embarrassing. I bet the whole Honors Class was whispering about my hair. Or lack thereof.

"I'd just about given up on you," Baker said in a low voice as I sat down. I could tell he was trying not to show me how shocked he was by my new look. "Where's Amanda?"

"She broke her finger playing catch."

"Oh, okay," he said. "Well, you're up next."

Great. Just great.

Amanda had shown me how to hook up the computer to the projector in Baker's room, it was just a plug-in thing, so not a big deal. It was choosing the projector from the menu that worried me. What if I couldn't figure that part out? I sat there sweating, my face burning, my scalp naked. And then Baker stood at the microphone, introducing me. Everyone clapped politely as I walked to the podium. What was I going to say? Here I was, standing in front of the whole world with a bald head, a laptop that wasn't mine, and twice as much stuff to present as I'd practiced saying.

I was steaming under my sweater and my tights made my legs prickle. Pretty soon I'd be a pile of clothing on the stage floor just like the Wicked Witch. Before I could melt into oblivion, which by now was my only goal, I'd finished plugging the cable in and miracle of miracles, I thought the projector was going to work, but then I looked behind me at the screen, and it was black.

I really needed the Good Witch now. Or maybe my fairy godmother. Or that sorceress who made everyone go to sleep in *Sleeping Beauty*. That would be great.

Something!

I tried pushing a few buttons on the keyboard, but nothing happened. Everyone was waiting. I couldn't stall forever. I'd have to do the talk without the visuals. I stepped up to the microphone. My mind whizzed around like a trapped fly. *English. Baker. French. Exams. Cheating. Studying. AJ. Caroline. Tracie. Amanda. Dad. Jessica. Fried hair. No hair.* Pretty much everything filled my brain except our project.

I needed to concentrate. I needed to talk about janitors. *No. Not janitors. Don't call them janitors.* Panic rose in me as I looked out over the sea of faces in the auditorium. Well, mostly it was a room full of empty seats, but there were still plenty of people to freak me out. I could hear a voice speaking, but I didn't know who it was.

"Custodians are an integral part of the school system."

Hey! It was me talking. And the speech part was going okay. In fact, I was starting to relax a little. And then I got to where we showed our first graph, but of course, the screen was blank. I tried to keep going, but it was totally stupid without it. I had to get the computer working, so I tried again, pushing a few keys here and there. Nothing happened. I looked out at the audience, hoping a tech geek would jump up and offer to help. No one did. I pushed another button. Forget the graph. I'd have to plough through anyway.

"In this figure…" I said. "Well, if you could see the figure, you would see we did a poll at the grade school."

This was not working out. Hot tears welled up in my eyes. What was I going to do? Not only was I flunking English, but I was making a fool of myself too. Plus, I'm sure my family was so proud. Not.

"I…ummm…I'm really sorry," I said, turning to the school board. "My English partner, Amanda Whitmore…she broke her finger a few hours ago and she couldn't be here. This is her computer and I don't know how to make it work."

I knew my face was bright red and no bangs protected me from the crowd. I stood there bare-faced, hairless, lights shining in my eyes…nowhere to hide.

A man at the school board table stood up. "Let me see if I can help," he said. He pushed a couple of buttons and behind me, the screen lit up with our graph. My knight in shining armor! An old knight, but still.

"Thanks," I said, letting out a shuddery breath.

"My pleasure."

Miraculously, even with the bad start, it all came flooding back to me. I got out all the info about the polls we took without too much trouble. That was my section, so I knew it pretty well. I couldn't help glancing back at Farbinger when I mentioned how I'd tested the custodians to see if they noticed kids in the halls who shouldn't be there, and he narrowed his beady little eyes at me, which almost made me laugh. When I got to the finances I was a little bit worried. I hoped I had the latest numbers. I took a deep breath and plunged in. I doubted anyone was going to check our info anyway.

"Although it may seem as if the school district would save money," I read from Amanda's cards, "it is not likely the projected numbers are correct. For one thing, eight of the custodians who would be replaced are actually eligible for retirement, which means they will continue to cost the district money but they won't be working.

"Also, the proposed company the board would subcontract with would provide cleaning people, but not trained workers capable of maintaining the older buildings. They would be unfamiliar with past repairs and procedures."

I put up a few more figures on the screen and then rattled off some numbers Amanda had calculated herself. I hoped they were remotely close. The slideshow followed, and as far as Baker knew, that was the end of the presentation. But I had one more thing up my sleeve.

I took a deep breath and let it out slowly.

"I want to wrap up this presentation with a video I made."

I slipped the thumb drive into the USB slot and clicked the file open. On the screen, the video started with a scene of me standing in front of the curtain in AJ's living room. The camera zoomed in on my face. "What you are about to see are true facts," I said. "The person providing this information must remain anonymous to protect her job, family, and future."

I was exaggerating a little about the family part. It's not like the school district would knock off any of Trina's kids. At least, I didn't think they would. The camera panned back again showing someone (it was actually AJ) silhouetted behind the sheer drape.

"What can you tell me about the custodian situation in your school district?" I asked the shadowy figure.

"Overall, since the replacement of custodians by the subcontracted janitors, the schools are becoming visibly worn down." AJ read from Mrs. Blevins' notes. "The halls have not been painted in three years. That was something they did every summer in the past. Lockers are jamming, and no one can get them open, which is causing a shortage of locker space. And rain gutters are literally falling off the buildings."

"Were the custodians replaced by the same number of janitors?"

"No. Not even close," AJ continued. "On average we now have one of the subcontracted janitors for every four former custodians."

"One janitor is doing the job of four custodians?"

"Yes, and no. That's the problem. There's only one janitor, and not only is he not physically capable of doing the job of four, he also isn't trained at all in maintenance."

"So, you're saying no one does the maintenance anymore?"

"Exactly."

I watched myself up on the big screen. I looked pretty good. Of course, that was before I was a pixie. "If no one's doing maintenance, what happens when there are serious problems?"

"Well, for the big stuff, they hire professionals. The real issues are what would normally be considered small problems. For example, last autumn no one knew how to turn the boiler on, so we didn't have any heat. They had to send all the students and staff home until they could hire a furnace service to come and turn it on."

"What about the school grounds?" I asked her.

AJ and I had written the script based on the notes we'd

"found" in the mailbox so I was sort of leading her on, like a big time TV reporter. It was cool.

"Parents and volunteers are taking care of the school grounds now. If they don't, then the grass and weeds get out of control."

I asked a few more pertinent questions, which my "source" answered. I was aware every now and then of some murmuring in the audience when she said stuff that was so ridiculous it was sad. It was very exciting for me. When the video was over I stepped up to the microphone for my final point.

"According to *Webster's New World College Dictionary*, a custodian is a person with the responsibility for the care and maintenance of a building. Responsibility. Care. Maintenance. That's what our custodians provide the Maywood School District."

The applause was deafening. Well, it was in my head. In reality it was pretty solid. Okay, a little scattered. But people definitely clapped. At least they were awake. I slid into my seat next to Baker, exhausted and exhilarated at the same time.

SuperUnderdog to the rescue!

Chapter 35

I sat there in English class, my bangs draped over my face, covering me, protecting me. Sleeping. Dreaming.

"Suze," Baker said in my ear.

I snapped to attention.

I was still on the stage. The school board was discussing something, but I had no idea what. Once I had sat down next to Baker, all the exhaustion of my day had wrapped itself around me like a blanket. The stage lights felt warm and soothing, instead of cold and harsh, and I guess I'd zoned out. "What?" I said. "I'm awake."

"They're going to decide," Baker said.

My knight was in charge. "How do you vote?" he asked each member.

"After careful consideration of the facts," said a woman in a green suit. "I vote in favor of replacing the custodians with subcontractors."

After careful consideration? Was she paying attention to anything I'd said? What about Amanda's numbers? My knight asked the next man in the navy pinstripe suit. And then the woman with long red hair. And every one of them voted to get rid of the custodians.

"Well then," the man—no longer my knight—said. "We've reached an agreement."

"Wait!" I yelled jumping up from my seat. "Are you all crazy? Weren't you listening?"

"Young lady," he said. "I'll have to ask you to sit down."

Baker put a hand on my shoulder. "Suze."

"No. I won't sit down," I said. "This is insane. Didn't you hear what my source told you? Don't you realize everything she said is true? I didn't make up any of this stuff."

"Young lady—"

"Sit down," Farbinger hissed at me.

"Suze," Baker said again.

"I won't sit down!" I shouted. "You people are incredible. No one was paying attention to what I said. No one cares about anything. You're all a bunch of self-serving, special-interest…" I searched for the word…. What had Trina called them? *Politicians.* That's right. She'd said the school board was a jumping-off position for a career in politics. "You're all just a bunch of politicians, and you only care about your-selves and your careers."

Farbinger jumped out of his seat. "Miss Tamaki! That is enough!"

I gave the stairs a miss and leapt off the edge off the stage, running up the aisle. The fact I'd lost, that the custodi-ans had lost, made me so mad I wanted to break something. My insider information should've convinced them! Didn't they see what they were proposing was preposterous? I couldn't get past knowing that I'd let Yoda down either.

If only Amanda had been here. I know she could've con-vinced them to do the right thing. In the lobby I wiped my streaming eyes. This was too stupid to be true. In a matter of seconds, Jessica was there with her arms around me, and I clung to her, dripping hot tears all over her shirt.

I felt a warm, meaty hand plant itself on my shoul-der. "Suze?" AJ stood over me. She handed me a tissue, and I mopped my face. She was about to say something when Caroline walked into the lobby. The two women, who both wanted to lay claim to me, stared at each other, and I buried my head in Jessica' shoulder. This wasn't exactly what I'd had in mind when I planned to make my family proud of me. After a minute, when no one said anything, I raised my eyes. They'd disappeared.

"Where'd they go?" I asked.

"Back inside," Jessica said. "I waved them away."

"Thanks."

"Suze?"

"Mmmhmm?"

"You left Amanda's computer in there."

"Will you get it for me?" I asked her.

"Sure. No prob. We'll have to wait until they finish, though."

We sat down on a scarred wooden bench to wait. Jessica held my hand tightly, and her solid rhythmic breathing comforted me. I could hear the traitor guy's voice from inside droning on and on. *Turncoat.*

The longer I sat there, the more embarrassed and ashamed I began to feel. How could I have acted like such a baby? And now Farbinger would never let me stay in Honors English. The custodians had lost, I'd have to go back to Lame-o English, and I'd made a fool of myself in front of all the smarties in school. Not to mention my family. So much for my Super Powers. I knew I should've stayed home and watched TV tonight.

The wave of self-pity gave way to more anger. Furiously I swiped at the tears, stood up, and walked back into the auditorium.

Jessica ran after me. "Where are you going?" she hissed.

I ignored her and she stopped following when everyone turned to look at us. My gait down the aisle was unsteady. My thoughts wavery and unclear. When I got to the stage I could feel all the parents and the Honors English Class staring at my back, but I didn't care. I waited for a pause in the school board discussion. Benedict Arnold noticed me.

"Yes?" he asked.

"I'd like to apologize," I said, climbing the stairs. "For acting like a baby." I walked up to the table and looked around slowly at each person, meeting each pair of eyes, one by one. "I'm sorry for my outburst. It was wrong and rude."

"Understandable."

"Of course."

"Thank you for apologizing," they muttered.

I went to the podium and unhooked Amanda's computer from the projector. As I walked back across the stage to the stairs I stopped directly behind the table and waited for them all to look up at me. "I am right, though," I said, "and you all know it. Personally, I don't see how you sleep at night."

And then I was out of there as fast as I could possibly move without running.

Chapter 36

Dad had to give Jessica and Yoda a ride home after the school board meeting, and all the way Yoda talked to my dad about baseball as if nothing had happened. Tracie, Jess, and I sat in complete silence in the backseat. My heart ached from failure, and listening to Yoda yammer on about his favorite team wasn't helping. He'd have plenty of time to watch baseball next summer once the custodians' contracts expired.

I went straight to our room when we got home, but Tracie didn't follow me. She still hadn't said two words. I don't know why she even went tonight if she was so mad about Caroline that she couldn't give me a hug and tell me she was sorry I'd lost the fight. Some sister she turned out to be.

What seemed like hours later I was lying there, unable to sleep, waiting for Tracie to come to bed. It was now or never, I had to tell her everything tonight while I was still in a reckless mood. And the most important part was what Caroline had told me that weekend I'd stayed with her and we'd gone for our walk. Not about our grandparents dying, but about her husband.

Caroline and I were walking around Oak Bay drinking our coffees, when I got a rock in my slipper. "Stop for a minute," I'd said to her. I set my drink down on a bus bench and stood on one leg, so I could fish out the pebble.

"Susan?" Caroline said. "Why are you wearing slippers?"

"It was dark in the bedroom, and I couldn't find my shoes. I didn't know we were going for a walk. Okay, got it." I grabbed my drink, and we started moving again.

"Are you all right?" she asked. "Do you want to head home?"

"I'm good. As long as I avoid the puddles."

Caroline smiled, shaking her head. But it was kind of a nice smile, like she thought maybe I was a little bit like her or something. We turned off the main street and walked through a neighborhood of houses a lot like Caroline's. Lights were popping on as we walked by; people getting up to face the day.

"What else do you want to know about me?" she asked after a while.

I'd finished my drink, but there weren't any public garbage cans, so I carried the cup, squishing it with nervous hands. "Well…why did you come back? To Victoria? Now, I mean?" I had Uncle Bill's version, but I wanted to hear hers.

She cleared her throat. "You know I was married, right?"

"I guess."

"Well, I was. For five years, three months, and eleven days."

We walked without looking at each other.

"Ray, my husband, was…I can't even explain it. It was like we were one person, almost, but we still had our own interests and friends and all that. It was exactly what I hope you have someday."

I liked the idea of her thinking about my future. I smiled at her, and she tried to smile back. Her eyes looked a little watery. We were only a block away from her house now, and she slowed her pace. "Ray tried to get me to contact you girls, but I was afraid. He told me practically every day that life is short, and I should just go see you."

We climbed the steps to her front porch, but neither of us wanted to go inside, in case Jessica was up. We couldn't lose the moment. We both sat on the top stair as if we'd talked about it and agreed.

"What happened?" I asked.

"Last winter, on February eleventh, Ray had a heart attack at the gym. He died at the scene."

Oh, God. How horrible. Why did I ask? That little tingly feeling across the bridge of my nose made me think I might cry for this man I'd never met. "Caroline," I said. "I'm so sorry."

What else could I say? She looked like her face was going to dissolve into a pool of sadness. After a minute, she sucked in a deep breath through her nose and let it out with a shudder. Then she sort of shook herself, like a wet dog shakes off rain, and forced herself to smile.

"I realized that Ray was right," she said. "I needed to see you girls. It took me a while to work up the courage, but I promised him…I still talk to him…I'd do it before the end of the year."

I laid my hand on her knee. I was afraid she'd think it was stupid, but she put hers over mine. "Maybe your uncle Bill told you," she said, "but I ran into him not long after Ray died…. It seemed like an omen. A good one, I mean. Like a sign."

"Yeah. He mentioned it. Not about your husband, but lunch."

"Bill's been great. It's funny, but we weren't that close before…back when we were younger. I mean I always liked him, but we didn't know each other that well. I'm here mostly because he assured me I could do it, though."

After Caroline had told me that, we sort of hugged. But then her phone rang, and I went inside to find Jess, and that was it. We hadn't talked about it again.

I was still thinking about it, replaying that conversation in my head when Tracie finally came in for bed. She got undressed in the dark and I waited silently, pretending to be asleep. Once she'd crawled under the covers, I took the plunge.

"Trace?"

Nothing.

"I know you're awake."

More nothing.

"If you're not going to talk to me, will you at least listen?"

A bigger, fatter nothing.

"Fine. Be that way." Unless she wanted to get out of bed, she was a captive audience, so I'd say what I had wanted to tell her for a while now. "About Caroline…"

A heavy sigh from across the room.

"Just listen for once," I told her. "About Caroline…I know you have your reasons for not wanting to talk to her, but I've kind of been getting to know her, and I think it's worth it. At least for me."

When she didn't throw anything, I kept going. I told her about our first dinner and how Caroline didn't show up, but she sent me the gift basket. When I mentioned the wine, Tracie snorted. I wasn't sure if it was laughter or disgust, but I kept going. I'm pretty sure she had to cover her head so I wouldn't hear her giggle when I told her about the cat and falling into the rhododendron.

I wanted Tracie to understand that Caroline regretted abandoning us, but I knew better than to say it. Also, it wasn't like Caroline had actually told me she did, but I sort of knew. I didn't want to put words in her mouth, though, so I stuck to the things I was certain about.

"You're probably wondering why she came back all of a sudden," I said. "And I was wondering that too. It was because of her husband. He died last year."

Tracie didn't answer, so I jumped into the silence and told her about the walk with Caroline and Ray's heart attack three days before Valentine's, which made it extra sad to me somehow. Tracie didn't stop me, and I went on, telling her about Caroline running into Uncle Bill and thinking it must be a sign. "Her husband was only forty-nine," I told Tracie. "He'd tried to get her to contact us…and after he died, she promised him, his memory, I guess, that she would. She'd always wanted to, but she was scared, Tracie, that's all. She figured we must hate her."

Tracie shifted in her bed. "She's smarter than she looks, then," she said. She flung off the covers, and for the tiniest moment I figured I'd won her over in spite of saying that about Caroline, but as usual, I was wrong. Instead of the hug I'd been hoping for, she stormed out, banging the door behind her.

I jumped out of bed and ran after her, grabbing her arm just as she got past the kitchen and into the living room. "What's your problem?" I asked.

"Just leave me alone!"

"Tracie, this is so stupid. Will you please talk to me?"

"Suze? I'm going to punch you if you don't shut up."

Dad came out of his bedroom, fumbling with his glasses, his hair tousled from sleep. "Hey. It's after midnight. What's going on out here?"

Tracy yanked her arm out of my grip. "Do you think some little sob story like that is going to change my mind?"

"I wasn't trying to change your mind." Okay, maybe I was, but I didn't have to admit it now that it hadn't worked. "I just wanted you to know why I'm gonna give Caroline a chance."

"Fine. Go ahead. But leave me out of it!" She flounced over to the couch and threw herself down.

"Everyone just chill," Dad said. "Who wants hot chocolate?" He still thought all our fights could be smoothed over with something sweet.

"You know what, Trace?" I said. "I'm sick of this."

Dad took my arm. "Suze? Help me in the kitchen."

He sounded so much like AJ giving orders that I let him lead me away. He put the kettle on, while I tore open three packets of hot chocolate and dumped them into mugs. All that separates the kitchen from the living room is a counter with stools, and I glared at Tracie, who was sulking in front of the TV.

Dad poured the water into the cups as I stirred, and

then he plopped a marshmallow into each one. I took the chipped mug out to Tracie, keeping the nice blue one from my gift basket for myself.

"Here." I thumped it on the end table, making it slosh over the side. Tracie didn't even say thanks. I grabbed the remote and put the TV on mute.

"Tracie? What's the deal?" I asked her. "Was she really such a bad mother you'll never give her another chance, or what?"

"Suze—" Dad said.

Tracie threw off the yellow blanket and stood up. "No, Suze," she said in a deeply scary voice. "No. She wasn't a terrible mother. She was a great one."

"What?" I asked, totally thrown.

"Yeah," Tracie said, her voice still low and dangerous. "The best. You don't remember, but I do. For five years she was the best mom in the whole world. She walked me to school every day, pushing you in the stroller. She was there the second they let us out too. With a smile and a snack to take to the park on sunny days. And on the rainy ones, we went home and she gave us cookies and peppermint tea sweetened with honey. She made birthday cakes and Halloween costumes. We dyed Easter eggs and left out carrots and celery sticks for Santa's reindeer. She sat up all night when I had the flu, and she read me stories."

"Now I really don't get what your problem is."

"I know you don't. But I don't want to talk about it, okay?" Tracie's voice had been getting higher and higher the longer she talked, and when she stopped for breath, the tears building in her eyes spilled over.

"Oh, Trace—"

"Why can't you just leave me alone? Why are you making me say this? Fine! You want to know why I don't want to see her? It's because she was perfect, which means that *I'm* the reason she left!"

"What?"

"After Grandma and Grandpa McIntyre died, she was so sad. And I tried to be good. I tried to do everything right. I took care of you. I cleaned my room. I was quiet so she could sleep, but in the end she left anyway. Because she had to get away from me!"

"Wait a minute. Hold on—" Dad said, hurrying over to Tracie. "Honey, that is so not true."

"Then why *did* she leave?" Tracie's whole body shook with sobs, and my heart broke with every word she said. Dad took her in his arms and I stood there, alone, watching him hold my shattered sister. Tracie crumpled in his arms, and he lowered her to the sofa. He motioned me to join them and I sat on the other side of him, his arms around us both.

"If it was anyone's fault Caroline left," Dad said, "it was mine."

"What do you mean?" I asked.

He stared straight ahead, his arms tight around us. "When Caroline's parents died, she was devastated. But I was too stupid to understand what that meant. At first, when she couldn't get out of bed because she was so sad, I sent you girls to AJ and Bill's. But they weren't really set up for kids. AJ was still in grad school, and Bill worked two jobs. So then I tried to take care of you myself. And Caroline, too...."

He took a deep breath and let it out slowly. I could feel how shaky he was next to me.

"But with my job, it was too much. My parents offered to take you both, but they had already moved to the Okanagan and I couldn't stand the thought of you two being so far away. Months passed, and Caroline seemed to retreat more and more. We moved into her parents' house, which I thought might help, but instead, it made her worse.

"It got to the point where the place was a mess. I'd come home and she'd still be in bed, and Tracie'd be trying to take care of you, Suze. Cheerios for dinner, that sort of thing."

Tracie had stopped crying now and was leaning against Dad. "I remember that," she said.

"And one day I just lost it," he said. "I yelled at Caroline to get up. I said you girls needed her, it'd been almost a year since her parents died, and life had to go on, and it was time to snap out of it."

He paused so long, I finally asked, "What happened?"

He shook his head. "She got out of bed. She fixed

herself up, she took a shower, put on fresh clothes, got into a routine…and I wondered what had taken me so long to put my foot down…. A week later, she was gone."

The three of us sat there in silence. I thought about what Caroline had said about having panic attacks and seeing a pro about it. Was it okay to tell them? I was so tired of secrets. "She sees a therapist now," I said.

"Yeah, I know," Dad told us. "We've been meeting for coffee once a week and just talking about stuff. I want you both to understand she wasn't just sad back then. She was clinically depressed, but I didn't even know what that meant at the time."

"I don't think it was your fault she left," Tracie said.

"Well, I *know* it wasn't your fault. And I'm really sorry I didn't realize you thought it was," he said, pulling her even closer.

"I guess I'm the only blameless one here," I said, trying to make them laugh. And they sort of did.

"First time for everything," Dad and Tracie said together, and we all laughed for real.

"I still don't think I want to see her," Tracie said.

"Fair enough," Dad told her. "But I think it's time we all stop making Suze feel guilty for wanting to get to know her mother."

Tracie reached around Dad and ran her hand over my fuzzy new haircut. "Yeah. Okay. I'm sorry, Suze."

"Me too."

After that, we sat there watching the hockey highlights on mute, drinking our cold hot chocolate. When Tracie and I finally went to our room about two o'clock in the morning, we did something we hadn't done in years. We slept in the same bed, holding on to each other. I'd missed her.

Chapter 37

With only ten minutes to go before the weekend started, I thought I'd made it free and clear. No such luck.

"Please send Susan Tamaki to the office," Mrs. Cameron's all-too-familiar voice said over the intercom. She could save time by making a recording of that announcement and just play it into the microphone whenever she needed to.

The art teacher, Peterson, nodded at me to go. Great. I had to stop getting in trouble, or Jessica and I would never get our mural done. "Will you wash out my brushes?" I asked her.

"Sure," she said. "What'd you do this time?"

I grabbed my bag and coat. "I shoved Gabe into his

locker for making fun of my haircut. But I didn't shut the door or anything."

Jessica shook her head, laughing.

In the hallway, I heard someone whistling "Take Me Out to the Ball Game" and looked around. Sure enough, Yoda was coming down the hall with a toilet plunger.

"Hiya," I said.

"Hi Sooooz Tamaki. Class is not over."

"I know," I said. "I got called to the office."

Yoda shook his head, but he was smiling. "Again?"

I nodded, resigned. "Again."

"Santa will bring you coal," he said, laughing.

"Definitely," I told him.

He went into the boys' washroom, and the whistling started up again. A week had gone by and the school board hadn't backed down, not after my presentation, or my outburst, or the individual apologies Farbinger had made me write to the board. Not even the editorial in the newspaper had moved those cold-hearted politicians. Yoda would still lose his job at the end of the school year when his contract was up. There wasn't anything I could do about it, but at least SuperUnderdog had tried.

While I waited on the office bench, I narrowed it down to two suspects who probably reported me—Adam or Caleb. They'd be next to find themselves in a locker. Seconds before the final bell rang, Amanda came into the office and Mrs. Cameron looked up. "You two can go in now," she said.

"What's going on?" I whispered to Amanda.

"No clue."

I let her lead the way. "Come in, ladies," Farbinger said. "Come in and shut the door."

I gave Amanda a look, but she was watching Farbinger and missed it. Nothing good ever happens when he makes you shut the door. Not that anything good had ever happened to me in his office, anyway.

"Sit down, girls." We plopped onto the plastic chairs. "Miss Tamaki?" he asked. "Did you write all your letters of apology?"

"Yeah," I said. He knew I had, he was just being a pain. "Mr. Baker already looked them over and mailed them out for me."

"Right, right, just checking," he said. "I called you in today because Miriam Dearborn, the president of the Parent Advisory Council, dropped off a letter for you both. It's addressed to Miss Tamaki, but when she found out that you, Miss Whitmore, were originally part of the custodian project, she asked that I include you, too."

He handed me a thick cream-colored envelope with my

name written in purple ink, and I opened it, trying not to tear the beautiful paper. Inside was an equally thick piece of folded stationery. I pulled it out carefully. Amanda tried to read over my shoulder, but since it was addressed to me, I held it at an angle so she couldn't really see.

I scanned the note, smiling in disbelief.

"Well?" Farbinger asked.

"Should I read it aloud?"

"Go ahead."

I cleared my throat and read as clearly as I could, making it sound formal and important:

Dear Miss Tamaki,

I am sorry to have missed your presentation at the school board meeting, but I was ill. I heard it was both informative and somewhat explosive. While I was aware that the school board intended to discuss the matter of replacing the janitors, I had not realized they were planning to vote on it at the December meeting. Thanks in part to your presentation, and also to the article in the Victoria Times Colonist, many parents who were not aware of this possible change are now very unhappy. In the last week I have received many phone calls from upset parents, and, from what I understand, the same is true at most

of the elementary schools in the district. Therefore,
we have decided to make this the primary topic of
discussion at our district-wide meeting in January.
We would like to ask you to present your talk again
at that time.

Sincerely, Miriam Dearborn
PAC President, Maywood Senior High School

I grinned for maybe the first time ever in Farbinger's office.

"Wow!" Amanda said. "Cool."

Farbinger's face had gone an interesting shade of purple, but he managed to choke out a congratulations, along with a warning that he hoped I could behave myself if things didn't go well.

"No problem," I said. "Don't worry. Can we go now?"

He dismissed us and Amanda and I hurried to our lockers to get our stuff, hugging, laughing, and talking about ways to improve our presentation all the way back to her house, where we shared the great news with Heather. Steve came out of his office when he heard the excitement and gave us big hugs of congratulations.

On my way home, I sent Caroline a text, but instead of answering, she called me back. "Congratulations, Suze," she said.

"Thanks…Mom."

It was only the third time I'd said that, and it always stuck in my throat a little. I was hoping if I said it enough, I'd eventually lose count. It would be kind of weird to know when I called her Mom for the forty-sixth time, or the three-hundred-and-twelfth. She'd been pretty good about remembering to call me Suze, so I was trying to return the favor. Plus, it was kind of nice to have a mom.

"Everything still on for tomorrow?" she asked.

"Yep," I said. "See you at four o'clock."

"I'm looking forward to it."

And she kind of sounded like she was.

The line at Escape From New York Pizza snaked out onto the sidewalk, so Amanda, Leigh, and Jessica decided to wait outside while I went in to pick up our order. Most of the customers were there to get slices, but Caroline had ordered two whole pies for us. That's what they call pizzas in New York, I guess. *Pies.* Weird.

I wasn't sure if I could cut the line and go to the register or what, so I waited. On my left, two guys with tattoos running all the way up their arms tossed giant rounds of snowy-white pizza dough high into the air. I wondered if they ever dropped them. Ahead of me, a guy with dreadlocks and multiple piercings ordered two black olive slices, and the guy behind the counter scooped them up and slid them into the oven.

"What can I get you?" he asked me.

"I'm picking up an order to go," I said. "One mushroom, one cheese for Walker—or maybe Tamaki." I wasn't sure whose name Caroline had used.

He took two white boxes off the top of the oven and motioned me to the register. I got five root beers to go, because you have to have root beer with pizza, and was trying to balance them on the boxes when Leigh saw me through the window and rushed inside to help.

"Your mom just went around the block again about two minutes ago," she said. "She should be back any time."

We waited in the street, and the second Caroline came to a stop, we piled into the car. Traffic was totally stuck behind her, but no one honked because this neighborhood was always busy.

Back at her house, we spread out on the living room floor and dug in.

"Oh, my gosh," Amanda said. "You're right. This is the best pizza ever."

"I know," I said.

"That place looked kind of dingy," Leigh said, her mouth full, "but they really know how to make pizza."

"Jess was scared to go in there the first time I took her," I said.

She blushed. "I was not!"

"You so were. But we love you anyway."

"We used to go there when I was in high school," Caroline told us.

"Really?" we all asked.

"Don't look so surprised," she said. "I *was* young once. It's been there for over thirty years."

"No wonder," said Amanda, stuffing her face. "Mmmmm…so good!"

The pizzas were huge, but the five of us ate most of them anyway. Caroline didn't have a TV, so I wasn't sure what we'd do for the rest of the night, but I had seen a bunch of board games in the wardrobe. Maybe we'd be old fashioned and play Monopoly or something. Whatever we did, the night was already way better than the sushi sleepover.

I'd barely closed the washroom door behind me when it burst open, and Amanda and Leigh threw themselves inside.

"Hey," I said. "A little privacy, please?"

"Why?" Leigh said. "Are you going to stink up the place?"

"Shut up." I punched her shoulder. She grabbed my hand and we wrestled for a minute, laughing, until Amanda told us to break it up.

"We're here on a mission," she said.

"Leigh is not touching my hair," I told them.

"What hair?" she asked, and I punched her again.

"We have decided," Amanda told me, in that imperious voice she sometimes uses that makes her sound like a teacher, "that we love Jessica, and she is now going to be *your* best friend, which makes *her* one of us."

"Really?"

"Yeah," Leigh said. "She's way funny."

"So we're going to be the four musketeers," Amanda said.

"You in?" Leigh asked me.

"*Duh,*" I said. "She was my friend first. Of course, I'm in."

Leigh grabbed Amanda's arm, avoiding her broken finger, and my hand and pulled us out of the washroom. "I need to brush my teeth," I protested.

"In a minute," Leigh said. "Let's go tackle Jessica first and tickle her until she pees. It'll be the initiation." She dragged us through the hall and back to the living room.

"Hide, Jess!" I warned her. "Bury yourself in your sleeping bag!"

Unfortunately for Jessica, she only had time to look up at us, totally confused, before we all jumped on top of her.

Chapter 38

Leigh, Jess, and Amanda slumped against each other, half asleep in the backseat of Caroline's car the next afternoon, while she drove us home. My stomach still felt a bit queasy from all the doughnuts we'd eaten for breakfast. Or maybe it was the double mocha.

After we'd dropped them off and were in my apartment parking lot, Caroline said, "Do you want to go to Vancouver with me during your holiday break?"

"What? Really? Cool. I've never been there before. Except like twice, and both times were for Tracie's hockey tournaments, so they don't really count."

"We won't do anything hockey-related," she said.

"I promise. I do have to go for a morning meeting, but I thought we could take the ferry over the night before, and as soon as I'm finished, we can do some Christmas shopping."

"Okay!"

"Ask Tracie if she wants to come along too."

"I will." I would, but we both knew not to get our hopes up. Still…you never knew with Tracie. Eventually she might give in.

"See you, Mom," I said, getting out of the car. "And thanks for a great night."

She smiled. "You're welcome. It was fun to have you all there. But just so you know, sometimes we'll still have to eat sushi, too."

"Yeah, okay."

"Just not raw fish," we said together.

I took the stairs two at a time and unlocked the apartment door. When I dropped my bag in the hallway, I barely missed Sammy who shot inside after me, as usual. "I'm home!" I yelled.

Tracie answered from the bedroom. "Suze? Is that you? Don't come in here."

"Why not?" I moved closer to our door. "What are you doing in there?"

"Nothing. Don't come in."

"Okay, but you come out, because I have something to show you."

Tracie had stayed Friday night with her friend Emma, and then I'd been at Caroline's, so I hadn't shown her the letter from Miriam Dearborn yet. She opened the door a crack and stuck her head out. Her face was all red, and her hair was a mess.

"What exactly are you doing in there?" I asked, raising one eyebrow.

"Nothing. Just don't come in, okay?" She closed the door again.

"Do you have a boy in there?"

"What?" she yelled. "No! Of course not. I just need a few more minutes alone."

"Okay, but hurry up."

I went out to the kitchen to get some juice, but I kept wondering what she was up to. She'd said she was alone, but I wasn't so sure. Why was her face all flushed? And what about her hair? Maybe she was exercising. I'd just decided to go outside and see if I could catch a guy climbing out our window onto the landing when she came into the kitchen. "Okay, you can come in now."

I was still suspicious as I walked into our room, and I looked around for a booby trap just in case. Lately she'd been pretty nice to me, but I *had* just spent the night at Caroline's. I half expected a bucket of water to fall on my head from above. I seemed to be in the clear, though. Our bedroom was tiny, so it only took me about half a second to see what she'd actually been doing. And it was really, really nice.

"Oh, my God!" I said, stunned.

My bed had been made up with a gorgeous powder blue-and-white flowered comforter. It was folded back a little so I could see the matching sheets. There was a fluffy pillow with a sham, and two decorative pillows piled on top. It looked those people from HGTV had paid us a visit.

"Where did all this come from?" I asked.

"From me," Tracie said, grinning. "For ruining your other comforter. And look, you can take the cover off and wash it. Or change it for a different color if you don't like this one."

"Tracie. It's perfect! It's so…you didn't have to…I can't believe…" I couldn't even finish my sentence. I threw my arms around her. "Thank you so much!"

"But wait, there's more," she said. "Take your shoes off and lie down."

The first thing I noticed when I pulled the sheets back was the sag in the middle of my mattress was gone. And the lumpy spot up where my shoulder goes was smooth and flat. I climbed onto the bed and fell into a dream.

"It's a new mattress!" Tracie yelled, her excitement bubbling over. "It's just one of those ninety-nine-dollar specials, but it's got to be better than your old one."

"But how could you afford this?"

"I used my savings."

"But that's for university!"

She shrugged. "If our mother can afford a therapist and to live in Oak Bay, she can probably pay for university. I thought I'd let her buy my affection."

"You're so bad!" I said.

She laughed. "Yep."

"Caroline invited you to go to Vancouver with us for a couple of days…to Christmas shop."

She shrugged again. "You never know."

"Really?"

"I'll think about it, but I'm not saying yes."

We were making progress! I jumped out of bed and hugged Tracie again. "Thank you for this."

She hugged me back and ran her hand over my super short hair, petting me like a cat. "That feels so cool," she said. "Now, what did you want to show me?"

"Oh, right." I ran out to the hallway and got the letter out of my bag. In our room, I perched on my new bed while Tracie looked over the letter.

"You rock star, you," she said, hugging me.

"Yep. And don't you forget it." I flopped back onto my new mattress and she lay down next to me. "I bet people who don't have sisters have boring lives," I said.

"Oh, no, don't tell me you're becoming Sentimental

Suze," Tracie teased. I shoved her off the bed and she landed on the floor with a thump. "Hey!"

"How's that for sentimental?" I asked, hanging over the edge and looking down at her. "And don't you even think of trying to sleep with me tonight."

"Why would I want to sleep on your mattress when mine's so new it still has the wrapper on it?" she said. Tracie shoveled her ragged comforter out of the way and flopped back on a brand-new mattress of her own, the plastic crinkling under her. I threw one of my decorative pillows across the room, and she snagged it out of the air and tucked it under her head. I'd never get that pillow back again. Oh, well. Sometimes you gotta share the wealth.

Acknowledgments

Thank you so much to everyone at Second Story Press. Your enthusiasm and kindness is much appreciated, as is the charming cover.

Thank you to my mother who has been with me (and Suze) every step of the way. Also big helpings of thanks to Cheryl Tradewell and Mark Shaw for research assistance, and Alexa and Eileen, fellow Brouhahas. I must include Will Barry here, too (for no other reason than he's an awesome kid and a reader).

Michael Bourret, agent extraordinaire—merci beaucoup—I finally got some French in my book, just for you (and not just in the acknowledgments).

And as always, Victor Anthony...this is the first thing of mine you ever read and you believed in it way back then. You're my shining star.

About the Author

JOËLLE ANTHONY loves the rain, which is good because she was born and raised in Portland, Oregon and now lives in British Columbia, Canada. She's worked as an actress, a Minor League Baseball souvenir hawker, the Easter Bunny, and various other not-so-odd jobs. Now she mostly writes novels, but she still dabbles in sketch comedy, nonfiction articles, and teaching writing to both kids and adults. She recently wrote and starred in her first full-length play, along with her husband. Her other novels include *Restoring Harmony*, *The Right & the Real*, and *Speed of Life* (writing as J.M. Kelly). Visit her at www.joelleanthony.com.